THAT SUMMER NIGHT

(Callaways #6)

BARBARA FREETHY

THAT SUMMER NIGHT
© Copyright 2014 Barbara Freethy
ALL RIGHTS RESERVED

For information contact: barbara@barbarafreethy.com

Also Available
In The Callaway Series

PRAISE FOR THE NOVELS
OF BARBARA FREETHY

Chapter One

Shayla Callaway woke up in a sweat, her heart racing, her mind spinning with horrible and disturbing images. It took her a moment to remember that she wasn't in a remote village in northern Colombia, but in the San Francisco apartment she shared with another medical resident. She'd been home for five days, but she had yet to fully process what had happened.

A persistent ring broke through the haze of her nightmare. She hoped it wasn't the hospital, asking her to come in and cover a shift. She wasn't ready to go back to work yet. Her hands needed to stop shaking first. She had two weeks before her next rotation started, and she hoped by then she'd be ready to return to the career she'd been pursuing for the past ten years.

But there was no familiar hospital number flashing across her phone, just the word *blocked*. Adrenaline ran through her already hyperaware body. She drew in a breath and told herself there was nothing to be afraid of. Grabbing the phone, she uttered a breathless, "Hello?"

"Shayla?"

The male voice crackling on the other end of the line

belonged to Dr. Robert Becker, her friend, her mentor, and the brilliant doctor who had been missing since a trio of armed gunmen had broken into the Colombian clinic where they'd been working and killed three people, leaving a trail of injuries and trauma behind.

Robert had not been one of the dead or the injured; he'd been unaccounted for—until now.

Her hand tightened around the phone. "Robert? Are you all right? Where are you?"

"I'm in trouble, Shayla. I need your help."

"What can I do?"

"I need you to go to my office and get the gift you gave me for my last birthday. You remember what that was, don't you?"

Her brows knit together at the unexpected request. "You mean—"

"Don't say it out loud," Robert said quickly. "I don't know who's listening."

"What are you talking about?" she asked in confusion. "Who would be listening?"

"I can't explain right now. I need you to get the present and give it to my brother, Reid. Ask him to bring it to me on Sunday."

"Your brother? Isn't he in the Army somewhere?"

"He's out now. He's living in San Francisco, and he might just be my only hope of getting out of this alive."

A shiver ran down her spine at his ominous words. "Why don't I talk to the police, to my brother-in-law, Max? He can help you with whatever trouble you're in."

"This is bigger than the local cops. You need to find Reid and tell him to meet me. Please, Shayla, you're the only one I can trust."

"All right," she said, hearing the agitation in his voice. "Where do you want him to go?"

Robert hesitated. "I want you to tell him something, Shayla, and you have to say it exactly this way. Are you ready?"

"Go ahead."

"It is not the mountain we conquer but ourselves. Say it."

"It is not the mountain we conquer but ourselves. What does that mean?"

"My brother will know. Tell him Sunday afternoon, three o'clock."

"Sunday is three days from now."

"I'm not sure how long it will take me to get there or for you to convince my brother to help me." He paused. "Has anyone spoken to you since you got back, anyone from the State Department, the FBI or any other agency?"

"Yes, I've been interviewed by both agencies, and there have been a lot of questions about you. Your ex-wife also came by to see me. Lisa is extremely worried about you. I didn't know what to tell her."

"Don't tell her anything. You can't talk to anyone but Reid. Promise me."

"All right. I promise."

"I'll explain everything when this is over. I have to go, Shayla."

"Wait, where am I going to find your brother? Do you have his number?"

"No, but his best friend, Jared Stone, owns the Cadillac Lounge. He'll know where to find Reid. Don't tell anyone about this call but Reid. And don't remove the present from my office if anyone else is around. It needs to be done secretly. This is very important Shayla. Don't let me down."

"All right—"

The connection broke just as she got the last word out.

Her heart was still pounding against her chest as she set her phone down on the bed and glanced at the clock. It was almost eight a.m., and early morning light filtered into the room. At least, the sun was coming up. She didn't have to think about trying to force herself to go back to sleep for another few hours.

She walked across the room to the window and pulled the curtains open. The street of apartment buildings in the shadow of Twin Peaks was quiet, and the calm scene took down her anxiety level. Everything was fine in this part of the world. She didn't need to feel afraid.

As sweat dripped down the back of her neck, she turned her face toward the fan in the corner, lifting up her blond ponytail to let the air cool down her heated skin.

Normally, San Francisco in the summer was cool and foggy, but an unusual July heat wave had hit the day before, and the city would see temperatures into the hundreds by the afternoon, lasting into the upcoming weekend.

It was the same kind of weather she'd experienced in Colombia where she'd spent three months working in the region of El Catatumbo. In the language of the native people, the Bari, Catatumbo meant God of Thunder, and she'd quickly learned how appropriate that name was. Heat waves followed by massive electrical storms sent streaking bolts of lightning down from the sky that could devastate and destroy with spectacular and deadly beauty.

But then that was Colombia, a beautiful country but one of the most dangerous places in the world.

She'd gone there for two reasons, to provide medicine to the poor, to the people who were a three-day boat ride away from any kind of care, and to help collect data for a clinical drug trial Robert was running for Abbott Pharmaceuticals, a company on the edge of a breakthrough drug that would change the lives of millions of people suffering from Alzheimer's, including her grandmother.

It had started out as an adventure and an opportunity to take her medical skills into the field and to be a part of something amazing and wonderful, but it had ended in death and destruction. She'd barely escaped with her life.

She'd never been so close to death before, and she was having trouble dealing with not only the close call but also the guilt she felt for being one of the few to survive. But she had survived, she reminded herself. And she needed to keep moving forward, something that would be easier to do once Robert was safe.

She'd never heard his voice filled with so much fear. Robert was usually purposeful, analytical, and methodical—all the things a good scientist should be. But today he'd sounded desperate and out of control. What on earth was he involved in? It had to have something to do with what happened in Colombia, but she couldn't imagine what trouble could have followed him back to the U.S.— unless he wasn't back yet? Maybe he wanted his brother to meet him somewhere in South America.

The whole thing was crazy. She felt like she was in the middle of a spy movie. Robert's cryptic words about conquering mountains, his unwillingness to tell her anything over the phone for fear someone was listening in, and his questions about the FBI and the State Department were all very disturbing. She felt anxious and way out of her comfort zone. But what Robert had asked her to do was not that difficult, retrieve the present from his office and contact his brother. She could do that, and she *would* do that, because she owed Robert.

She'd met Robert during her first week of college. Having skipped two grades, she'd been an awkward sixteen-year-old her freshman year, able to compete academically but completely out of her depth when it came to social relationships. Eight years older than her, Robert had been a medical resident who'd come to speak to her class about a career in medicine.

After that lecture, he'd taken her under his wing, telling her he'd hit college when he was fifteen and knew exactly what it felt like to be isolated by a brilliant mind and social immaturity. Over the years they'd kept in touch as she made her way through medical school and Robert gained a reputation as a brilliant medical researcher. When she'd had a chance to take a twelve-week residency in Colombia that would include both clinical practice and medical research under Robert's lead, she had jumped at the chance, never imagining how it would all end.

Turning away from the fan, she walked into the bathroom and stripped off her damp tank top and pajama bottoms and stepped into the shower. She let the steady cool spray beat down on the tight muscles in her neck and shoulders for a good ten minutes. Then she dressed and went into the kitchen to make breakfast.

While the coffee was brewing, she popped a piece of bread into the toaster, finding comfort and reassurance in the familiar surroundings. She was home. She was safe. If she said the words enough times, maybe she would start to believe them.

She stiffened, hearing a key in the lock. She let out a breath of relief when her roommate, Kari, a petite brunette, entered the apartment. Kari was usually cheerful and energized, but today she looked decidedly weary, which was no surprise since she'd been on duty the last twelve hours.

"You're up early," Kari said in surprise. "Too hot to sleep?"

She nodded, happy to have the heat as an excuse. She

hadn't told anyone what had happened in Colombia, not Kari, or her family. While the Callaways were wonderfully supportive, she couldn't bring herself to talk to them about that night of terror.

"The E.R. was hopping all night," Kari continued. "People sure get trigger happy when the temperature rises."

Kari had no idea that her casual words set off another rolling wave of panic within Shayla. She was supposed to work in the E.R. on her next rotation. How was she going to handle gunshot wounds, stabbings and more violence? She'd always thought of herself as a strong person, until now…

Shayla tried to drive the anxiety away by changing the subject. "Do you want some coffee? I just made some."

"No thanks. The last thing I need is more caffeine. I'm going to try to get at least six hours of sleep before I go back to the hospital."

"You're working another double shift?"

"Yes, but it's fine. I'm leaving tomorrow for five days, so I'll have time to relax then."

She'd forgotten Kari was going away, and she dreaded the idea of five days alone in the apartment. Not that she needed to be alone. She could always go home to her parents' house or stay with one of her siblings, but that would require more explanations than she wanted to make.

Kari yawned. "I'm going to hit the sack. See you later."

As Kari left the room, the front door buzzer rang. Shayla almost jumped out of her skin. It was way too early for visitors. She walked over to the intercom and warily said, "Yes?"

"It's Emma. Can I come up for a quick second?"

Shayla inwardly groaned. She'd been avoiding

Emma's calls all week. She should have guessed her big sister wouldn't give up that easily. "Kari is sleeping. I'll come down." Maybe if she didn't let Emma into the apartment, she could get rid of her more quickly.

Shayla jogged down three flights of stairs and pushed open the front door.

Emma Callaway Harrison stood on the steps. Her big sister by six years, Emma was a slender blonde with short, angled, straight blonde hair and bright blue eyes that were often inquisitive. She was dressed for her job as a fire investigator for the San Francisco Fire Department, wearing black slacks and a white button-down blouse with the sleeves pushed up to the elbows in deference to the summer heat.

"What are you doing here so early?" Shayla asked. "Is something wrong?"

"Not with me. But we're all worried about you," Emma said pointedly. "You haven't returned anyone's calls since you got back from Colombia. Mom says she saw you for five minutes three days ago, and you looked exhausted and too thin." Emma's gaze swept her body. "I thought she was exaggerating, but she wasn't. When did you eat last?"

"I had a stomach bug, and I haven't felt like talking to anyone."

"But you're better now?"

"Getting there." She hoped her sister's sharp gaze wouldn't see the lie in her words. As an investigator, Emma was really good at spotting liars. "I'll call Mom later and reassure her."

"Maybe you should go see her." Emma's eyes filled with compassion. "We don't know the details of what happened to you in Colombia, since you haven't wanted to fill us in, but from what I've read online, it sounds like it was terrifying."

"It was, but I'm okay."

"Are you? You don't seem like yourself, Shay. And while you've looked exhausted for most of medical school, now you're almost a shadow of yourself."

She shrugged and pushed a strand of hair off of her face. "I'll admit I'm tired, but a few more days of rest, and I'll bounce back."

"Sometimes it helps to talk to someone. If not me, then someone else."

She wished she could talk to Emma, but even without the promise she'd made to Robert, she couldn't speak about what had happened. "I'll think about it. So, how is everything with you and Max? Is your husband still amazingly awesome?"

"Absolutely. Married life is better than I ever imagined." Emma's eyes sparkled with happiness. "We've started talking about kids."

"Really?" Her sister had spent the past decade focused on her career in the fire department, first as a firefighter and then as a fire investigator.

"We're not rushing into anything," Emma added quickly. "Just talking about it. Since I've been spending time with Sara and Aiden, I've gotten a touch of baby fever."

"I can totally understand that. Chloe is adorable."

"But first I have to figure out how to juggle my career with being a mother."

"Probably a good idea, although not your usual approach to life." While Shayla had always been a planner, Emma liked to leap first and think about how to land later.

"I'm trying to be smart. Anyway, I also came here to talk to you about Drew and Ria's wedding. We're meeting tomorrow at noon at the bridal boutique to try on our dresses and then we're going to lunch on Fisherman's

Wharf. It's going to be just the girls, and I want you there."

"I will be."

"Good. I better get to work. See you tomorrow."

As Emma walked out to her car, Shayla looked around the neighborhood. There was a woman putting out the trash a few buildings down, a man walking his dog by the corner, and another man trying to park his SUV in an incredibly tight spot.

It was a typical morning in San Francisco. She was a long way from Colombia, from the men with guns, but she still couldn't stop the goose bumps that lit up her arms. She walked quickly back into her building, making sure the front door locked behind her. As she walked up the stairs to her apartment, she wondered if she'd ever feel safe again.

Chapter Two

"So what's your plan, Becker?" Jared Stone filled a shot glass with Jack Daniels whiskey and pushed it across the bar.

Reid Becker sighed at the familiar question that seemed to come more frequently with each passing day. Since gunfire had shattered his left leg nine months ago, he'd been forced out of the Army where he'd spent the last sixteen years of his life, most recently on an elite tactical fighting unit. He still had his leg, and eventually he would be free of pain and able to live a normal life; he just wouldn't be able to do what he'd been trained to do, what he loved to do, *all* he knew how to do...

Which brought him back to Jared's question.

What the hell was he going to do next?

"Right now I'm just going to drink." He lifted the glass to his lips and enjoyed the warm, tingly slide of alcohol down his throat.

"Like you've done way too many nights for the last few months," Jared observed as he wiped down the bar with a towel. "As much as I appreciate your business, I'm concerned. You've never been a guy to do nothing. What's the deal?"

He had no answers. Everything Jared had said was true.

"Are you thinking you're going to find a way back into the Army?" Jared asked.

"No. That's over." He shrugged and smiled. "Maybe I'll open up a bar. It seems to work for you."

"It does work for me, and there are certainly worse things you could do, but I can't see you as a bartender."

"Because I'd drink all my profits?" he asked lightly.

"There's that. But you'd also be bored out of your mind in a minute. You're used to action, and while we have the occasional bar fight, most nights are pretty tame."

"Do you ever miss the action?" Jared had served with him for over seven years. He'd left the Army three years ago to take over the family bar after his dad had a heart attack.

"I miss the guys, but nothing else. I sure don't miss the desert, the bad food, or the threat of dying every day. I never lived for the adrenaline rush the way you did." Jared poured some peanuts into a bowl and pushed it across the bar. "Eat something. Soak up the booze."

"I'm not hungry. And I don't want to soak anything up."

Jared sighed. "You're damn stubborn."

"That's news?"

"Why don't you go to work for Matt? He's been trying to get you into his company ever since you got out of the hospital."

"I'm considering my options." Matt Kelton was another Army buddy who had opened a private security firm that apparently was booming with business. While investigative work could certainly be dangerous and challenging, Reid couldn't seem to get up the energy to have a conversation about it. He knew that eventually he had to dig himself out of the rut he'd gotten into, because Jared was right; he didn't like to do nothing. Unfortunately, there was nothing besides the Army that he really wanted to do.

"What other choice do you have?" Jared asked.

"Right now, my best option is to get drunk and see if I can pick up that redhead over there." He tipped his head toward the tall woman who'd been sending him a flirtatious smile for the past fifteen minutes.

Jared grinned. "That's not going to be a challenge. You used to like to push yourself, Becker."

"I'm not that man anymore." His words came out more serious than he'd intended. But they were all true.

"So be the man you are now."

"This is the man I am now." He tossed back the shot of whiskey. Then he headed across the bar, hoping to find more pleasant conversation.

* * *

Reid Becker was nothing like his brother. Shayla made that assessment in about ten seconds—the length of time it took for the man to settle on a couch between a pretty brunette and a busty redhead.

Reid was attractive in a scruffy, sexy, take-no-prisoners, don't-get-attached kind of way. Just the kind of man she would have expected to see in a bar called the Cadillac Lounge. His jeans were faded. His t-shirt had a guitar on the front, and he didn't look like he'd shaved in a day or two. He had penetrating eyes, green, she thought, and his thick, wavy, tousled brown hair looked as if someone had run their hands through it—maybe the redhead who was stroking his thigh while whispering something in his ear.

Reid laughed and gave the woman a quick kiss before calling the waitress over for another shot.

Shayla frowned. This was the man who was supposed to save Robert? He was either drunk or on his way to it. She really wished Robert had agreed to let her call Max. Emma's husband was a detective. Max could do more for Robert than this guy. But Robert had been insistent that she trust no one but Reid. Right now he seemed like the last man she should trust.

Someone bumped into her from behind, and she stumbled forward. Reid suddenly looked up, his gaze meeting hers. Then he gave a beckoning wave.

She started at the gesture and turned around to see if he was talking to someone behind her, but there was no one there. When she turned back to face him, she saw amusement in his eyes.

"You," he said, motioning her to come forward. "I could use a blonde over here."

She frowned at his suggestive and rude comment. As much as she wanted to blow him off, she couldn't. She'd promised Robert. So she stepped forward and gave him what she hoped was a serious and sharp look. "Are you Reid Becker?"

"Who wants to know, babe?"

"My name is Shayla Callaway." She looked for some sort of recognition, but there was nothing more than casual curiosity in his gaze. Apparently, Robert had never mentioned her to his brother. "I need to talk to you."

He patted his thigh. "I got a spot right here for you, sweetheart."

"It's about your brother."

His jaw tightened, and anger flashed through his eyes. "What about him?"

"Could we speak in private?"

"I'm not interested in anything Robert has to say."

"Robert isn't the one talking; I am. It will take just a few minutes," she added, feeling a little desperate. She'd expected Robert's brother to want to help her, but this man had gone cold at the mention of his brother's name. "It's important. A matter of life and death."

He stared at her for a long moment, his gaze searching her face as if to judge the sincerity of her words. Finally, he disengaged himself from the women and stood up. He was taller than Robert—taller, broader, stronger, sexier...

Her stomach tightened as he walked over to her.

"So, talk," he ordered.

"Outside," she said, not letting him intimidate her. She was used to strong men. She had five brothers and a father and a grandfather who were leaders among men. Not only that, she was a female doctor who'd taken a lot of crap over the years. She could handle this guy. At least she thought she could. She just needed to get past the unexpected nervous tingle running down her spine.

She turned away from Reid and walked toward the front door, hoping he would follow. After a moment's hesitation he did exactly that.

When they neared the door, Reid put a hand on her shoulder and said,

"This is far enough."

She glanced around, wanting to make sure there was no one close enough to hear what she was about to say. Then she looked back at Reid. While she could smell the liquor on his breath, the gleam in his eyes told her he was paying attention.

"I was working for your brother at a clinic in Colombia until a week ago. There was trouble. Some people were hurt—killed—and your brother went missing." She licked her dry lips. "This morning Robert called me. He said he was in danger and that only you could help him."

"Is this a joke?" Reid asked, disbelief in his eyes, eyes that were definitely green, a beautiful green, she thought, distracted by his gaze. "Well?" he prodded.

"No, it's not a joke," she said, forcing herself to focus. "Why would you ask that?"

"Because there's no way Robert could possibly think that I would want to help him."

She remembered what Robert had said on the phone— that he didn't know how long it would take her to convince his brother to meet him. "Look, it's not a joke. I don't know what's between you and your brother, but Robert said you are the only one who can save his life." She saw lingering doubt in Reid's expression and searched for another way to convince him. "It was on the news—the attack on the clinic—you can look it up online. I'm not lying about what happened. Your brother is in serious trouble."

Reid ran a hand through his hair, his jaw stiff with tension, his eyes glittering with emotions she couldn't begin to decipher.

"This doesn't make any sense," he muttered.

"Maybe it will make sense if we keep talking. Can we get some coffee?" She could see the indecision in his eyes, but she couldn't take no for an answer. "What do you have to lose by having a cup of coffee with me?" she asked. "Just give me fifteen minutes."

"Maybe tomorrow."

"It can't wait until then. Please." She was close to begging, but she didn't care. She'd been on edge for a week, and she wouldn't be able to stop the nightmares until Robert was back in San Francisco, living his life, and doing his job. "You have to help me. I don't know what else to do."

Her pending hysteria worked in her favor. Reid put his hand on her shoulder again. "Okay, calm down. We'll talk." He glanced at his watch. "There's a coffee house around the corner. It should be open for at least another hour."

"Perfect," she said with relief, following him outside.

The bar was in an industrial area that was fine by day but seedy at night, and while it was only a little after eight o'clock, she was happy to have Reid by her side.

They crossed the street at the corner and were only a few feet into the intersection when a car came speeding down the block.

She froze at the sudden, blinding headlights. Then Reid shoved her towards the sidewalk as the car screamed past, flying around the corner on squealing tires. She landed hard on the pavement, Reid's body adding more weight as he fell on top of her.

The shock of what had almost happened took her breath away. She was still trying to get it back when Reid jumped to his feet. He ran toward the corner, but the car was gone, and there was no one else around who could have seen what happened.

She was making her way to her feet when he returned to her, his expression grim.

"He almost hit us," she said, her lips trembling.

"Yeah." He gave her a hard look. "You asked me what I had to lose by having coffee with you—I think I just got an answer."

"That wasn't about me," she protested.

"Wasn't it? You tell me my brother is in danger and then someone tries to run us down? I don't think that's a coincidence. We need to talk. Did you drive here?"

"No, I took a cab."

He pulled out his phone. "So did I. I'll call a taxi.

We'll go to my place."

"Your place?" she echoed. "Isn't the coffee house down the street?"

"I'd like to get farther away from here. Is that a problem?"

She slowly shook her head, reminding herself that he was Robert's brother. She could trust him, couldn't she?

* * *

What the hell was he doing, Reid wondered as he ushered Shayla into a cab a few minutes later. He'd gone to the Cadillac Lounge to have some drinks and forget about everything that had gone wrong in his life—a few mind-numbing hours of nothingness. He certainly hadn't intended to follow a beautiful blonde out of the bar and almost get himself run over.

He glanced out the window of the taxi, seeing no sign of the vehicle that had narrowly missed them, not that he'd gotten a good look at the car. In fact, he couldn't have described one thing about it, and that bothered him. He used to be better at details, because details could save his life. It was another sign of how much of his edge he'd lost since he left the Army.

He couldn't imagine why Robert would think he could save his life or that he would even want to try. They hadn't spoken in eight years. They didn't know anything about each other now. And Shayla's story about Colombia, drugs, guns, raids… it was crazy, and it didn't sound at all like his academic, intellectual brother, who'd always been more interested in books than adventure.

Shayla tapped her fingers nervously on her thigh, drawing his attention back to her. Her fingers were bare of jewelry. She didn't appear to be married or engaged, and as she turned her pretty light blue, almost gray, eyes on him, his gut clenched. He'd noticed her in the bar long before he'd realized she had a more serious reason for staring at him than just to flirt. He wished now that had been her only reason, because she was a very attractive woman and just his type with long blonde hair that would probably look great out of a ponytail. Her eyes were fringed with dark lashes, and she had a killer mouth with soft, full lips. The rest of her body didn't look bad either in white jeans and a sleeveless tank top.

As she stared back at him, he realized she was younger than his brother, quite a few years younger, probably mid-twenties. "What were you doing for Robert?" he asked.

"I was working at the medical clinic that had been set up in El Catatumbo to facilitate the drug trial Robert was running and to bring health care to the surrounding villages, which are remote and extremely poor. I'm a doctor. I took the assignment as part of my residency program."

"You look more like a student than a doctor. How old are you?"

Her lips tightened and her eyes sparked with irritation. He had a feeling it wasn't the first time she'd heard the question.

"Twenty-six," she said tersely.

"Did you start college when you were twelve?"

"Three days before my sixteenth birthday."

He would have been more impressed at her early achievement if he hadn't grown up with Robert. "Not so young then. Robert started freshman year when he was fifteen."

She nodded. "I know. We met my first week of college. He was a guest lecturer in one of my classes. He took me under his wing and said he remembered what it felt like to be younger than everyone else. He gave me some advice on how to fit in, and over the years he kept in touch, checked in with me every now and then. He helped me out a lot."

There was a note of affection in her voice when she spoke of his brother, a note he didn't care for. "Are you and Robert sleeping together?"

Her eyes widened, and then she gave a quick and emphatic answer. "No. It's not like that. We're friends and colleagues. Robert has been a mentor to me, but that's all. And up until last year he was married."

"*Was* married?" Every muscle in his body stiffened at that piece of news.

"Robert and Lisa divorced right before Christmas." She gave him a thoughtful look. "Do you know Lisa?"

"I know her." He stopped there. He was not going to discuss Lisa. "So you and Robert were running a medical clinic in Colombia..." He still couldn't quite believe his brother would go to one of the most dangerous countries in the world. "Why there?"

"Because there's a cluster of early-onset Alzheimer's cases in the mountain villages, and some five thousand people in the surrounding areas who carry a similar genetic mutation. It was the perfect location for the drug trial. Abbott Pharmaceuticals, the company funding the trial, is very excited about a new drug they're developing. It could change a lot of lives for a lot of people, people like my grandmother. She's the reason why I wanted to go, wanted to help." Her voice faltered. "But everything changed last week when the clinic was attacked by gunmen, who not only stole the drugs but also destroyed the data and killed several people."

"And that's when Robert went missing?"

She nodded. "No one had heard from him until he

called me this morning, and he was adamant that I not tell anyone about that call except you. You have to help him, Reid."

"I don't have to do anything." He tried not to soften at the plea in her eyes. "My brother can get himself out of whatever mess he's in. Robert had always been good at escaping consequences. He's the *golden boy*. Why should this time be any different?"

She frowned at his harsh tone. "I don't think Robert can get himself out of this trouble. He was different on the phone this morning. There was real fear in his voice. After having seen what I saw in Colombia..." She drew in a quick breath. "I think Robert is caught in the middle of something very dangerous. I'm terrified for him. I need you to understand that this isn't some joke. It's very, very real."

"I get it."

"Then you'll help me save your brother?"

He hesitated. "That's still to be determined."

She gave him a frustrated look. "Why?"

"Before I can commit to saving him, I have to stop wanting to kill him."

Chapter Three

Reid's words hung in the air for a long minute. Shayla couldn't begin to understand the anger in his eyes, but she could only hope that he'd find a way to get over it, because if he didn't agree to help his brother, then she didn't know what to do next.

The bright lights of the Golden Gate Bridge distracted her from their conversation. "Where are we going?" she asked.

"My place. I live in Sausalito," he said, referring to the small town across the bay from San Francisco.

"Oh. I thought you lived in the city."

"I don't like cities. Too much traffic, noise, people."

"You didn't seem to mind the *people* in the bar. You were the center of attention."

He smiled. "I was hoping to take home a beautiful woman tonight. I just didn't think I was going to have to dodge a speeding car or knock her on the ground first."

"I've always been hard to pick up," she returned, happy to follow his flirtatious lead for a moment, because thinking about everything that had happened and might happen was making her way too anxious.

"I'll bet," he said. "You're way out of my league."

She wasn't at all taken in by his false modesty. This man would have no trouble getting a woman. Keeping one might be another story. He had an angry, bitter edge. But then, he probably wasn't interested in a relationship lasting more than a night.

The cab pulled up in front of the Sausalito harbor.

Reid paid the driver. Then she followed him onto the sidewalk.

"Where's your house?" she asked.

"My home is this way." He opened a locked gate, then headed down a narrow dock lined with houseboats. Reid paused by the second to last boat, which was aptly named *Lone Wolf*. "This is it."

"Seriously? You live on a boat?"

"It's great. The water rocks me to sleep at night."

She shook her head in amazement. "You are nothing like your brother."

His mouth curved into a smile. "That's the nicest thing you could have said to me."

"Why do you hate Robert?" She was getting really curious about what was between them.

"Right now we have more pressing things to talk about," he said, as he stepped onto the deck of his boat. Two beach chairs were set up on either side of a small table. A fishing pole and a tackle box were off to the side as well as a one-person kayak, obviously meant for solo trips on the bay.

Reid unlocked his front door, and as she followed him inside she was surprised at the spaciousness of the interior. They walked through a galley kitchen into a sitting area with a sofa, armchair, and a crowded bookshelf. On the walls were beer and whiskey placards and pictures of wild animals.

"The bathroom is there." He pointed to the hallway. "The bedroom is just beyond that."

"I must admit this is bigger and better than I thought," she said, sitting on the couch. "But the décor could use a female touch."

He grinned and his whole face lightened up with that smile, a smile that made her stomach do a little dance. He did have a sexy charm when he wasn't pissed off.

"I bought this boat and all the furnishings from a WWII vet named Walt Hopper," he said.

"And you haven't changed anything?"

"Why would I?" he asked with a shrug.

"To make it yours. I'm sure one of the women you were with tonight would be happy to help you redecorate."

"I'm not really interested in their decorating skills." He took a seat in the armchair across from her.

"Big surprise. Did you even know their names?"

"We hadn't gotten that far."

"The redhead was practically sitting in your lap."

"Jealous?" he challenged.

"Hardly," she said forcefully, feeling a need to convince herself as well as him. "How long have you lived here?"

"About seven months."

"And before that?"

"I was living on Army bases and traveling the world."

His tone turned cold, the light in his eyes replaced by dark shadows. She was suddenly curious about his story, why he'd left the Army, why he hated his brother, why he lived on a boat decorated by an eighty-year-old man, and why he seemed to wince with pain every now and then. Something bad had happened to this man, some kind of terrible pain that he tried to hide but couldn't quite cover up. Her nurturing, healing instinct wanted to help, but she doubted he'd be receptive. And she hadn't come here to help him but to help his brother. She needed to focus on Robert.

"Let's talk about my brother," he said, obviously coming to the same conclusion.

"All right." She paused. "I must say you don't seem as drunk as you did in the bar."

"Almost getting killed has a tendency to sober me up."

"I guess I should thank you for shoving me out of the way."

"You guess?"

"You're right. Thank you."

He gave a dismissive shrug. "I was saving myself. If you went down, I was going with you."

"Wow. First you want a thank you and then you don't. You're kind of being an asshole, you know."

"I know," he agreed.

"So what's your problem?"

"You're my problem. I was having a great time tonight and then you walk into the bar and mess everything up."

"Your brother sent me."

"Of course he did, because there is nothing my brother likes more than to screw up my life."

"Okay, that's it. We can't go any further until you tell me what happened between you and Robert."

"It's too long of a story."

"I've got time."

"Not that much time."

She stared back at him, thinking about what could possibly break the relationship between two brothers. All she could come up with was a woman. And while she couldn't imagine two men as different as Robert and Reid being in love with the same woman, it made the most sense.

"Lisa," she said abruptly, remembering the way Reid had reacted in the taxi when she'd mentioned Robert's ex-wife. "She came between you in some way, didn't she?"

"Why would you say that?" he countered.

"Because I have five brothers, and I know that it takes something big to break the bond."

"Five brothers? Big family."

"Two sisters, too."

"Your parents ever hear about birth control?"

Anger ran through her. He could throw darts at her, but her family was off limits. "My parents are two of the most incredible people in the world. Their first marriages ended badly, one with death, the other with divorce. They got together and blended two families, then they had me and my brother, Colton. We were all raised together in the most loving environment you could ever imagine."

He gave her a thoughtful look and then an unexpected apology. "Sorry."

"Anyway, we got sidetracked. Let's get back to you."

"Do you want a drink?" he asked.

"Haven't you had enough to drink? I need you to focus."

"Since we're about to talk about my brother, I will never have had enough to drink," he said dryly. "And you could use something to stop that incessant tapping."

She realized she'd been drumming her hands on her thighs ever since she'd sat down. She forced herself to stop, then said, "Fine, I'll take a beer. It's been a rough week."

He stood up, a grimace of pain crossing his lips at the action. Then he walked over to the refrigerator. He pulled out two bottles of beer, handed one to her, and then sat back down with another glimmer of discomfort in his eyes.

"You were injured, weren't you?" she asked.

"Yeah."

"Your leg?"

He took a swig of beer. "Yeah."

She'd obviously hit another closed topic. Fine. "So what's the story with you and Robert? Did you have a thing for Lisa?"

He tensed. "If you call an engagement a thing, then yes, we had a thing."

His answer surprised her on several levels. She couldn't imagine a woman turning away from Reid, who oozed sex appeal from every pore, to get to the intellectual Robert, who was attractive but not like this guy. She also couldn't quite get her head around the fact that Reid had been willing to ask a woman to marry him. He seemed more like a player to her.

"What happened?" she asked.

He sighed with resignation. "Lisa hooked up with Robert the night before the wedding, just after we'd finished the rehearsal dinner and practiced making our walk down the aisle." He took a long drink of beer as if to wash away the bad taste in his mouth.

His answer didn't make any sense at all. "I don't understand. You're saying that Robert and your fiancé hooked up at the rehearsal dinner?"

"Yeah, in the coatroom. I think they might have actually had sex on my jacket."

She was appalled. "That can't be true."

"Can't it?" he challenged.

"It's difficult to believe that Robert would do such a thing."

Reid took another drink of his beer. "Then you don't know him as well as you think you do. Before you start trying to find an excuse for him, I can tell you not to bother. I've heard them all before. And, no, it wasn't better to find out before the wedding. It would have been better if it never happened at all. That's the only way it would have been better."

"I wasn't going to make an excuse," she said slowly. Nothing could excuse what Robert had done, but she sensed there was more to the story than the little she'd heard.

"Really? You're not?" he asked, disbelief in his voice.

"No. That's a line a brother shouldn't cross. You were in love with Lisa, and your brother should have respected that."

"So tell me why the hell should I help Robert now?"

She drew in a breath, now realizing the enormity of the task before her. No wonder Robert had told her it might take a few days to convince his brother to help. It might take a lifetime, and she didn't think Robert had that much time. She searched for something to say, something that wouldn't sound inane and stupid.

"Because he's still your brother." It was all she could come up with, and in light of what he'd just told her, it was inane and stupid.

"And you think that makes me care about him? After what he did to me?" Reid shook his head and tossed back the rest of the beer, setting the bottle down with a thud on the nearby table. "That's ridiculous."

"No, it's not ridiculous. You still care," she said with growing certainty. "You wouldn't have left the bar with me if you didn't."

"I've always been a sucker for a blonde in trouble."

"So if I'd been a brunette, you wouldn't have gotten up?"

"I guess we'll never know," he drawled.

"Well, we're together now, for whatever reason, and Robert still needs your help. And it's not just him," she added quickly. "Whatever you think of him personally, whatever he did to you, that's not the sum total of who he is. He's brilliant at his job. His research is important. He needs to finish it. He's going to help a lot of people, people like my grandmother, maybe people you know and care about, too."

"Sounds like you've drunk the Robert Kool-Aid. My brother obviously chose the right person to help him."

"He did, because I care about your brother. Not in a romantic way," she added quickly. "But as a friend and someone who has done a lot for me. And for all the other reasons I just said."

"You want me to save Robert so he can save the world?" he asked sarcastically.

"Yes. Not because he can save the world, but because he can save a lot of people. He can make a difference in the lives of so many men and women who are suffering from Alzheimer's."

"The research goes on without him. You're obviously passionate about it. Why can't you take over?"

"Because I'm not a researcher. I'm better with patients than with drugs."

"Then someone else. No one is irreplaceable, Shayla, not even my brother. Someone else can do what he does."

"Maybe he's not irreplaceable in medicine," she acknowledged. "But you don't have another brother. He's it."

"Yeah, lucky me."

"You can fight me on this, Reid. But I want you to know that I'm not quitting. I'm not going away. I'm going to keep talking to you and trying to find ways to convince you to help, and if you kick me out, I'm going to come back tomorrow and try again. I've never been a stalker, but I'm willing to start now. According to Robert, you're his best hope of getting out of trouble." A wave of emotions ran through her as she tried to convince him to help her. "I need Robert back at his job, Reid. I need him to be okay. I need for all of this to be over. And it can't be over until he's all right." She blew out a frustrated, angry breath. "So what's it going to be?"

Reid's green-eyed gaze clung to hers for a long moment. She could feel the tension simmering between them. He wanted to say no, but she needed him to say yes.

"I don't know yet," he said.

Disappointment ran through her, but she told herself it wasn't a *no* so there was still hope. As a doctor, she didn't quit even when there wasn't hope. She kept going until there was nowhere else to go.

"I need more information," Reid said. He settled back in his seat. "I need to know exactly what happened that night in Colombia, every last detail."

Her heart stopped. "Robert wasn't there. At least I don't think he was. No one saw him."

"But you were there."

She gripped the bottle of beer more tightly. "Yes."

"So what happened that night, Shayla?"

Could she tell him? Could she take herself back to that place, to that horror? She hadn't told anyone the whole story, not the local police in Colombia, not the people from the State Department or the FBI, not her roommate or her family. She'd given out bits and pieces, the facts that everyone pretty much already knew, but Reid wanted more. She could see it in his eyes. He wasn't going to settle for half the truth. He wanted it all.

"Shayla," he said. "I won't help you unless I know the whole story. So you can tell me, or you can leave. Your choice."

Chapter Four

Reid had no idea what he was asking of her. She wanted to run home and bury her head under the pillows, the way she'd done every night since she'd come back to San Francisco. She'd been a coward before. She didn't want to be one now.

She opened her mouth, but no words came out. Her mind was spinning, and her heart was beating so fast she felt like she was going to pass out.

She wanted Reid's help. She *needed* his help. And she was angry with herself for letting her emotions get the best of her. She was a doctor. She was supposed to be able to deal with life and death situations. She was supposed to be brave and strong and unshakeable, but right now she felt every muscle in her body beginning to spasm.

"What the hell is wrong with me?" she muttered, waving a frustrated hand in the air.

"Why don't you tell me what happened to you?" he suggested, his gaze holding hers for a long second.

"Nothing happened to me. I wasn't shot. I wasn't killed. I wasn't even scratched. So why am I such a mess?"

Reid's eyes softened, and there was compassion in his

gaze. It was a change from the anger, bitterness and sarcastic amusement she'd seen most of the night. "Because you survived and others didn't. You feel guilty."

"I do feel guilty. I could have done so many things differently." She ran her fingers through her hair, tucking the strands that had escaped from her ponytail behind her ears. "I know I need to talk to you, but it's hard to find the words."

"Start with the last time you saw my brother."

"It was the afternoon of the attack. I had come back from giving flu shots to some villagers on the other side of the river. Robert was leaving. He seemed distracted, but that wasn't unusual. Robert always had a million things on his mind."

"Did you speak to him?"

"Briefly. He said he needed to talk to me but it would have to wait until tomorrow." She paused, thinking back to that day, wondering if she'd missed some foreshadowing detail of what was to come.

"What did he want to talk to you about?"

"He didn't say." She frowned. "Robert had a canvas bag in his hand, the kind of bag we often filled with medical supplies when we left to visit the more remote villages. But Robert never made those trips. He was either in the clinic overseeing the trial or out of the country entirely."

"So he came back and forth between Colombia and San Francisco?"

She nodded. "He was in and out every couple of weeks."

"All right, so let's move ahead a few hours," Reid said evenly.

The suggestion sent her heart racing again.

"What did you do the rest of the day?" he asked.

"I worked in the clinic. We had a lot of patients. One of the other doctors had recently left, so we were shorthanded."

He nodded. "Go on."

She drew in a breath for courage, telling the part of the story she'd already told. "A man came in around seven o'clock that night. He was one of the participants in the trial. He presented with a rash and respiratory problems. After examining him, I decided to take a chest x-ray. The x-ray machine was in the adjacent room. I walked to the door to see if it was in use, and then I heard the sound of gunfire." She licked her lips. "I didn't know what to think at first. I actually thought it was fireworks. And then I heard screaming. I turned around and..." She drew in a breath, willing herself to get through the story.

"And then what?" he prodded.

"A man came through the other door. He was shooting—a million shots a second it seemed like to me."

The sound of rapid fire ran through her head. She could feel her knees hitting the ground as she sought cover. Bullets whizzed by her ear. She cowered on the floor, knowing she was going to die. She waited for the hit, for the pain. It was coming...any second...

"Shayla!"

Reid's sharp voice cut through the haze in her head.

She stared at him in confusion.

"Stay with me, Shayla," he ordered. "What happened next?"

"People died."

"Your patient," he said, meeting her gaze.

She nodded. "He was shot numerous times. There was so much blood everywhere." Nausea ran through her at the memories. "I—I didn't try to get to him. I should have thrown my body over his. I should have done something.

But I just dropped to the ground. I saved myself, but I didn't save my patient. He came to the clinic for help, and I let him die." She couldn't believe she'd actually said the words out loud, but it was too late to take them back.

Reid got up from the chair and squatted down in front of her. He put his hand over hers and gently pried her fingers off the beer bottle. "Before you break it."

As the bottle slid from her grasp, her fingers tingled with pain. Another second, and she would have broken that bottle and cut her hand. She almost wished that had happened. Physical pain and her own blood would be easier to deal with than the terrible memories and regrets that kept running through her head.

"You didn't do anything wrong," Reid said, putting his hands on her knees. "You acted on instinct."

"The instinct to save myself."

"You were across the room, weren't you?"

"Yes, but I could have moved. I *should* have moved."

"And you think your body would have stopped those bullets from hitting your patient?"

"It's possible."

"Shayla, you know that's not what would have happened. You would have both died."

"But at least I would have tried."

"It sounds like it happened too fast for you to move a step. The brain's desire to protect itself is a powerful force. You know that. Your mind told you to dive for cover, and that reflex action saved your life."

"You're making excuses, trying to make me feel better, but nothing can make me feel better." She pushed his hands aside and got to her feet. "I need some air."

She walked out to the deck. The air had finally cooled after the long, hot day, and a brilliantly clear sky filled with stars eased some of the tightness in her chest. She stood there for several minutes just letting the breath move in and out of her chest, as she tried to clear her brain. She told herself to focus on the present, on the lights of San Francisco, the Golden Gate Bridge, the large cruise ship making its way across the bay.

A moment later she heard Reid come up behind her. For a moment she thought he might put his arms around her, and shockingly enough, she found herself wishing he would do just that. He had a broad chest, strong arms. A woman could feel safe in his embrace.

But he didn't touch her. He stood next to her, gazing out at the view, his hands tucked away in the pockets of his jeans.

There was silence between them now, the only sounds coming from the distant traffic and the soft lapping of water against the side of the boat. She was starting to understand why Reid liked living out here.

"Not so bad, is it?" Reid asked.

"Not so bad," she echoed. "Do you have neighbors?"

"A few. Some of the houseboats are used as vacation rentals. I rarely run into anyone."

"It doesn't get lonely?"

"I know where to find the action, if I want it."

"The Cadillac Lounge?"

"Among others." He fell silent, his gaze back on the view. Then he added, "It's going to be okay, Shayla."

"Is it?" she asked, not at all sure *okay* was even a remote possibility.

"With time, yes. You won't forget, but you'll find a way to go on. Because that's all you can do."

"You sound like you speak from experience."

He shot her a quick look. "Unfortunately, I do."

She stared back at him. "I have nightmares every night. I haven't slept for more than a few hours at a time since I got back. When I close my eyes, I see the gunman and the wide, shocked eyes of the man I was supposed to help." She bit down on her bottom lip. "Tonight was the first time I said any of that out loud."

"You need to talk, to let it out."

"Really? That doesn't sound like the kind of advice a man like you would take."

He tipped his head. "We're not talking about me."

"Why would I be different?"

"Because you are."

"The Chief of Psychiatry at St. Paul's, the hospital where I work, called me yesterday and said his door was always open. He had spoken to Tom, another resident, who was in Colombia with me. Tom had gone in for some counseling and suggested I might need some, too. But I couldn't talk to him. I said I'd think about it."

"Tell me about Tom. Was he injured in the attack?"

"No, he wasn't at the clinic at all. He was back in the apartment building where we were staying. He didn't know anything until the local police got him out of his apartment and took him to the embassy. They evacuated us out of the country the next morning."

"Just you and Tom?"

She nodded. "We were the only Americans besides Robert. The other members of our team were from Australia and Germany. They were also sent home, but not with us."

"Have you talked to Tom about your experience?"

"A little, but not the part about me failing my patient. I haven't been able to tell anyone that—until tonight, until you forced me to talk in exchange for your help, which you still haven't given me."

"I'm still thinking about it."

"I didn't realize you were such a thoughtful man. The

few times Robert spoke of you he described you as a man of action, a fearless, courageous warrior."

"That's what he said about me?"

"Pretty much in those words," she said. "But when I asked him more about you, he shut up. He certainly never told me what went down between you. I'm kind of shocked about all that. And Lisa never said a word to me, either. Not that I know her very well, but we've had a few dinners together."

"I don't want to talk about her."

She could understand that. "So, getting back to Robert…"

"Right. Tell me what Robert said to you on the phone this morning."

She tried to remember his exact words. "He wanted to know if anyone from the FBI or State Department had spoken to me. I said that I'd been interviewed by both agencies."

"What did they ask you?"

"They wanted to know about the attack, what I could remember, whether I could identify anyone, and I said no. The men had masks on. I didn't see their faces. They asked me about Robert, where he was, when I last saw him, where I thought he might be now. I said I had no idea. They also questioned me about the clinical trial, whether Robert had said anything to me about the data."

"Had he?"

"Not really. And since I only worked with bits and pieces of data, I had no idea how the trial was going. I wasn't seeing the whole picture, which is not at all uncommon by the way."

"Okay. What else did Robert say to you this morning?"

"He asked me to get him something from his office, to

make sure that no one saw me do it. He wanted me to give you the item and ask you to meet him on Sunday."

"Why Sunday? Why not tomorrow?"

"He said he didn't know how long it would take him to get there or how long it would take me to convince you to help him."

"And he thought three days would be enough?" Reid asked dryly.

She shrugged. "I guess."

"Where am I supposed to meet him?"

"I'm not sure. He said to give you this quote. *It is not the mountain we conquer but ourselves.* Do you know what that means?"

The spark in his eyes told her he knew exactly what it meant.

"Yes, I know what it means."

Relief ran through her. "Good."

"Did you bring whatever you're supposed to give me?"

She shook her head. "No. I was waiting until late tonight to go down to the hospital."

"What are you trying to get?"

"Well, it's kind of weird. Robert told me to get the present I'd given him last year for his birthday. He wouldn't let me say what it was on the phone. He was afraid someone might be listening in on our call, which sounds really creepy, but I'm hoping that wasn't the case. Anyway, what I gave him was a notebook, an artist's sketchpad. When Robert gets stressed, he likes to draw. It helps him to relax. He told me that when he was a little kid he would draw his own comic books."

A glimmer of something shifted in Reid's gaze, as if her words had touched a deeply buried nerve.

"I remember that," he muttered. "*The Amazing*

Adventures of Razor and Rocco." He blew out a breath. "I haven't thought about that story in years. Robert would spend hours on those pictures. It was the only thing he did that ever distracted him from his studies. Of course, he was as good at illustrating comics as he was at everything else," he added dryly. "My parents' pride in him knew no bounds."

"They must have been proud of you, too."

"I gave them more headaches than feelings of pride."

She wasn't surprised. She had a feeling that Reid had raised a lot of hell in his life. His hard edges had no doubt come from pushing the limits, which had probably made him a very good soldier. And that was probably why Robert wanted Reid's help, something he still hadn't promised to give.

"So Robert asked you to get this sketchpad and give it to me?" Reid asked.

"Yes, he must have written something down in it that's important."

"And he didn't have it in Colombia?"

She thought about that for a moment. She did remember seeing Robert working on something, but had it been that notebook? "I don't know. I don't think so."

"When was the last time Robert was in his office here in San Francisco?"

"He made several trips back here during the three months that I was in Colombia."

"It looks like our next step is to get that notebook. I'll get my keys."

"And you'll let me drive," she said firmly. "You've been drinking. I'm sober."

"Do you know how to drive a stick?"

"Of course, I do. Five brothers, remember? And a father who insisted I learn how to check the oil and change a tire."

"Fine. You can drive."

"Good." She paused, pleased by the sparkling light in Reid's eyes. "You're going to help Robert, aren't you?" she asked hopefully.

"We'll see," he prevaricated. "Right now I'm going to help you get that notebook. Let's take it one step at a time."

"You really don't like to make long-term commitments, do you?" she asked in frustration.

"No," he admitted. "Not anymore."

As he turned away, she realized that the last time he'd probably made a long-term commitment was when he had asked Lisa to marry him.

Chapter Five

He could make a commitment, Reid thought, as Shayla drove them to the hospital. He could commit to a plan of action, to his fellow soldiers and to his friends. If he said he'd do something, he did it. If he said he would go somewhere, he went. He prided himself on never making a promise he couldn't keep, which sometimes meant he didn't make promises.

He knew Shayla was frustrated by his unwillingness to commit to helping Robert. And he probably wasn't fooling her any more than he was fooling himself. At some point he would probably agree to meet his brother. He didn't want to. Robert's betrayal had been a knife to the heart, and he could still feel the pain. A part of him thought maybe Robert was just getting what he deserved.

His brother had always been self-absorbed. Everyone around Robert had treated him like a God. Shayla had had the same adoration in her voice when she spoke of her brilliant mentor. Robert had always been the bright light, the sun around which the rest of the world orbited.

As a kid, Reid had felt the same kind of amazement when it came to Robert, but as the years went by he saw

Robert start to believe in his own wonderfulness. His brother didn't have to clean his room or mow the lawn or do anything to get his allowance, because according to his parents Robert needed to spend his time on studies. In school Robert had been excused from classes like P.E. and ceramics because they would have slowed down his incredible pace toward an early high school graduation. With all the perks of being a genius, Robert's head, his ego, had swelled to a point where he thought he could do anything he wanted, and someone else would clean up his mess, because that's what people always did. Now, Reid couldn't believe he was actually considering being one of those people.

But it wasn't too late to back out. He hadn't made Shayla the promise she wanted. He was keeping his options open until he knew more about what kind of trouble Robert was involved in. If Robert was at all guilty, he was going to be out the door so fast Shayla's head would spin around.

"You can't bail on me," Shayla said abruptly, interrupting his thoughts.

He turned his head and saw the determination in her eyes. While he didn't care for her words, he appreciated the renewed fighting light in her gaze. It was far better than the hurt, bewilderment and agonizing pain he'd seen earlier when she'd told him what she'd gone through in Colombia. She was bouncing back. That was a good thing. What wasn't a good thing was that she'd read his mind.

"I'm not bailing," he said. "Not yet anyway."

"You always like to keep one foot out the door," she complained, as she stopped the truck at a red light.

"It makes for a faster getaway."

"I promised Robert that I'd get you to meet him."

"That was your promise, not mine."

She sighed. "You're really annoying."

"I've been called worse, sweetheart."

"And I don't like to be called sweetheart," she retorted. "Or babe, or chick, or whatever other word you use for females. I'm not some girl you picked up in a bar. I'm a doctor."

"Okay, Doc," he said with a smile tugging at his lips, because he hadn't felt so challenged or entertained by a woman in a very long time.

The light changed, and Shayla switched gears with an awkward rev of the engine. "Easy," he said. "You have to be gentle with her."

She shot him a quick look. "Seriously? You're worried about this truck? It's about a hundred years old."

"Fourteen years old," he corrected. "She's just coming into her prime."

"You're seriously equating this ugly ass truck with the dented fender and the peeling paint to a woman in her prime?"

He grinned. "I'm not coming off very well tonight, am I?"

"Do you ever?"

"Hey, I think this truck is a beauty. You're the one being judgmental."

Shayla probably would have had more to say if they hadn't reached their destination. She pulled into the parking lot and shut off the engine, all traces of humor fading from her expression as she stared at the hospital and adjacent medical building.

Reid put his hand on the door, but when she didn't make a move, he hesitated, shooting her a thoughtful look. "Are you okay?"

"Sure, of course," she said, her frozen posture not backing up her words. "Why wouldn't I be? I'm just going into Robert's office, like I've done a thousand times. What could be hard about that?"

"Two answers to one question isn't usually a good sign. Have you been in the hospital since you got back?"

"I was there for about an hour. I was having a panic attack for pretty much the whole time. Everyone thought I was sweating and pale because I'd picked up a virus in Colombia. It gave me a good reason to leave quickly."

"When are you supposed to go back?"

"Two weeks. I'll be in the E.R. again, and I'm not sure I'll be ready. I still feel jumpy and nervous. A car backfired the other day, and I thought I was being shot at again. I dove behind a garbage can, and a woman walking her dog looked at me like I was crazy. Maybe I am crazy."

"You're traumatized, not crazy."

She looked at him with frustration in her eyes. "I want to stop feeling so anxious, but I don't know how to get to a calmer place. I keep thinking that things will change when Robert comes back, when I know he's safe, and that whatever happened in Colombia is truly over. Not that I even know if the attack in Colombia and Robert's disappearance are tied together," she added. "He wouldn't tell me what's going on. He said he didn't want to involve me too much."

"You're looking pretty involved to me," he said dryly, thinking that if Robert had really wanted to keep Shayla out of it, he wouldn't have called her at all.

"I just have to get his notebook. That's not a big deal, right?"

"It's not. I find the best way to deal with dizzying panic is to narrow your focus. Don't think about tomorrow or next week. Stay in the present. All we have to do tonight is go into an office building, not even the hospital, right?"

"Right. His office is in the medical building next door."

"Great. There's nothing scary about a medical building. You've been in Robert's office before. You know where it is, what you'll see."

"That's true."

"Unless you want to tell me where the notebook is, and I'll see if I can find it on my own?"

Her lips drew together as she shook her head. "No, I'm not sure where it is, but I'll have a better idea where to find it. I can do this." She drew in a long breath and reached for the door handle. "I just have to get out of the truck."

"First step is the hardest," he said.

She opened the door and got out. He followed suit, meeting her at the front of the truck. Shayla was a fighter. No doubt about it.

* * *

Reid's advice about staying in the moment rang through Shayla's head as they walked down the dimly lit path to the front door of the medical building. She focused on what she needed to do: insert her I.D. card into the lockbox, press her finger against the fingerprint reader, and open the door.

Done.

They stepped into the empty lobby and walked over to the elevator. The doors opened immediately.

Two minutes later they were getting off on the third floor, making their way down another hallway to Robert's office. There were security cameras probably filming their every move, but Shayla reminded herself that she had every right to be in the building, and this wasn't the first time she'd gone to Robert's office after midnight. Robert had often worked late, and sometimes she'd come by to chat with him after she got off a shift.

But all the reason in the world did little to lessen her anxiety, and her pulse was racing by the time they got to the office of Dr. Robert Becker. Well, if she couldn't get rid of the panic, she just had to breathe through it.

She keyed in the code and opened the door, reaching for the light switch. The first office belonged to Robert's administrative assistant, who was a meticulously organized woman. Nothing was ever out of place. Behind her desk was the door leading to Robert's office, a door that was always closed and locked when Robert was away, but tonight it was open.

"The door is open," she muttered.

"Hang on," Reid said, grabbing her arm. "I'll go first."

That was fine with her, but she stuck close to Reid's back as he made his way into the room. The light from the outer office spilled into Robert's office, and Shayla's mouth dropped open when she saw the chaos inside.

"Someone broke in," she said, shocked to see Robert's files on the desk and floor, numerous papers spilling out of the manila folders. The bookshelves had been searched as well, dozens of books tossed haphazardly on the ground. Even some of the framed pictures were askew as if someone had been looking for a safe.

"Looks like someone conducted a thorough search," Reid said, a grim note in his voice as he wandered around the room. "And they didn't bother to hide that they were here."

"Who would do this?"

"I have no idea."

"And when did they do this?" She suddenly felt even more nervous about being in the empty building. What if whoever had done this was still around? "We should go. They might come back."

"We need the notebook, Shayla. Where did Robert keep it?"

"I think it was in his desk, but it looks like all his drawers were emptied."

"What does the notebook look like?"

"It's a spiral-bound book with a blue cover." She squatted down to dig through a pile of folders. Her pulse sped up as she saw a flash of blue. "It's here. They didn't take it."

She pulled it out from under some books and got to her feet, a little stunned that they'd actually found what Robert wanted. She flipped the notebook open. The first page was an illustration of a teenage boy with spiked hair and a spider tattoo on his right bicep. He wore ripped jeans, a t-shirt, and a backwards baseball cap. He was standing on a skateboard, about to head down a steep San Francisco hill. "This is it."

"Let me see it," Reid said, moving to her side.

She handed it to him. "I still don't know why he wants it."

Reid's frown grew as he flipped through several pages. "It's the story he drew when we were kids," he muttered. "I can't believe he's drawing the same pictures after all this time. Although, they're better than they used to be."

"But what value could this notebook have?"

His lips tightened as he thought about her question. "There's something hidden in here. Something that no one searching Robert's office would be able to figure out."

"Do you think this book was the target of the search?"

"It seems like a possibility." He paused, glancing around the room. "This had to have happened after the staff went home for the night. Otherwise, someone would have reported it."

Which meant it had occurred in the past several hours. She swallowed a growing knot in her throat. "Why tonight?" she asked. "What would have triggered someone to come here now? Robert has been in Colombia for months."

"But you said he came back here several times while you were out of the country."

"Yes, but my point is that the search could have been done any time before now. So what changed?" She asked the question, but she already knew the answer. "Robert called me today. That's what changed."

Reid stared back at her. "You said he was worried about someone listening in."

She nodded. "He wasn't on his phone though."

"No, but you were on your phone."

Her eyes widened. "You think someone is tapping my phone?"

"It would make sense. You talk to Robert. He asks you to get something out of his office. We show up here, and the place has been tossed. A coincidence? I don't think so. I am a little surprised there isn't more security around."

"This building is mostly offices; the lab work is done in the hospital, where there is a lot more security. I have seen a guard walk around this building after hours, but I'm not sure how often he patrols or where he comes from. There is a walkway between this building and the hospital on the second floor."

As Reid finished speaking, she heard the ding of the distant elevator. It could be the same security guard she'd just mentioned, or it could be whoever had searched the office was on their way back. "Someone is coming."

Panic ran through her as she flashed back on that moment in the clinic in Colombia when the door had burst open and the gunman had appeared.

Her breath came short and fast. She wanted to run, but where would she go? She'd have to pass whoever had just gotten off the elevator.

She told herself the person could be perfectly harmless. It was the security guard, or someone else who worked on this floor, but reason couldn't make a dent in her overwhelming and paralyzing fear.

Reid moved quickly out of the room. He turned off the light in the outer office, then came into Robert's office and shut and locked the door. Then he motioned for her to join him by the wall. If the door opened, they'd be right behind it. She doubted it would provide much defense, but it was better than nothing.

As thcy huddled together, she thought she heard footsteps, but maybe it was just the pounding of her heart.

Was that the outer office door opening?

She strained to hear, panic running through her veins. She had to get out of here. She couldn't breathe. There wasn't enough air. A scream welled up inside of her, but she couldn't let it out. She'd get them both killed.

Reid suddenly turned and put his arms around her, obviously sensing her distress. "It's okay," he whispered in her ear. "We'rc going to be fine."

She didn't believe him. She *couldn't* believe him. Fear swamped all of her senses.

A small click made her jump.

Had someone turned the doorknob?

She wrapped her arms around Reid's neck and pulled his head down to hers, needing something to do, some way to distract herself from her terrifying thoughts. Reid was the perfect life buoy in her stormy sea. She pressed her lips against his and held on to him for dear life.

Reid seemed startled at first, but soon he was kissing her back, stealing the scream from her lips. The firm pressure of his hot mouth gave her something else to think about. Her lips parted, her tongue tangling with his. She wanted to take him into her soul so she wouldn't be alone, wouldn't be afraid. She wanted to soak up his strength, his calm, to lose herself in his arms.

As the seconds passed, as a sensual haze enveloped her, she lost track of time. How long they kissed, she couldn't say. Was it seconds? Minutes? An hour? She just knew she didn't want it to end. She felt good, safe, protected, and she hadn't felt like that in a very long time.

Eventually, Reid lifted his head, the sparks of gold in his green eyes glittering in the darkness. His warm breath caressed her cheek as they clung to each other.

"I think they're gone," he murmured. "I'm going to check."

She grabbed his arm. "No, not yet. Please don't let go of me," she whispered.

She was such a freaking coward, she thought. She'd never been clingy in her life, but tonight she couldn't let go of a man she barely knew, a man she'd kissed with more intensity and passion than she'd ever kissed anyone in her life.

Reid held her for another minute. As the quiet built around them, her pulse slowed down, and she began to believe that whoever had gotten off the elevator had gone. When Reid edged toward the door, she finally let him go.

He pushed open the door a few inches, then said, "All clear."

They walked into the admin's office. It was quiet, empty, and the door was closed to the hallway. If someone had opened it, they'd gone now.

Reid opened the outer door and peered down the corridor. "I don't see anyone. Let's get out of here." He shoved the notebook under his shirt. "In case anyone is looking at the security video tomorrow."

"Oh, my God, they'll think we did this," she said.

He met her gaze. "It's possible."

"I should report it. Shouldn't I?"

"Let me think about that. For now, I think we should go."

She was torn. She didn't want to leave the safety of the office, but she also didn't want to stay in the empty building any longer. Trusting Reid's instincts, she followed him down the hall and into the elevator. They made their way out of the building without running into anyone, but she didn't take a full breath until they were in the parking lot.

Reid took the keys out of her hand as they approached the truck. "I'm driving."

She didn't argue. Her hands were shaking, and Reid was stone cold sober now.

"What's your address?" Reid asked, as he pulled out of the parking lot.

"1210 Stansbury," she said, her teeth chattering. The night was still warm, but she was suddenly shivering, a reaction to the terror-filled adrenaline still running through her body. "Take a right at the next corner. I'll direct you from there." She paused. "Who do you think was in the building?"

"Any number of people including the security guard you mentioned."

"I thought I heard the door handle turn."

"Someone checked to see if it was locked, which seems like something a security guard would do."

"So I overreacted."

"Possibly. But someone did search Robert's office. That's an undeniable fact."

She thought about that. "Have you ever seen the

results of a search warrant?"

He shot her a quick look. "You think that search was done by the cops?"

"Or the FBI or the State Department, who both interviewed me in regards to what happened in Colombia and Robert's disappearance. Maybe they went through Robert's office looking for clues."

"At this point, we can't rule anything out, but did either agency give you any indication that they thought Robert was involved in something illegal or criminal?"

"No, but they were more interested in asking questions than answering them." She paused as Reid drove through the intersection near her house. "It's the white building in the middle of the block. You can drop me off out front."

"Do you live alone?"

"I have a roommate, but she's working tonight. She won't be home until the morning."

"I'm going to park," he said decisively. "I'll walk you in."

She didn't argue, happy about the thought of not going into a dark building alone.

After entering her apartment, Reid followed her down the hall. She took a quick look in each of the bedrooms and bathrooms, and everything looked exactly the way she had left it.

"It's all good," she said, blowing out a relieved breath as they returned to the living room. "As it would be. I've been letting my imagination get the best of me. You must think I'm a lunatic. Jumping at every noise, every imagined footstep." She licked her lips, thinking maybe she should also apologize for kissing him.

"I'd rather you were crazy than not aware of what's going on around you."

Nodding, she drew in a deep breath and let it out, starting to feel her pulse returning to normal. "I guess you can go now," she said a little half-heartedly. The long night loomed ahead of her, and she was way too wound up to even contemplate being able to sleep.

"Not quite yet," he replied, taking a seat on her sofa. "Do you have anything to drink?"

"Nothing alcoholic."

"Juice?"

"Probably," she said.

"Orange?"

"Yes."

"I'll take a glass."

"Okay." It seemed strange to be talking about juice after everything that had happened. But going to the refrigerator, pulling out the orange juice and pouring Reid a glass helped to settle her nerves, and she quickly realized that had no doubt been Reid's intention.

She set the juice on the coffee table in front of Reid. "Should I call hospital security and tell them what I saw?"

"Yes. Put it on speaker so I can hear."

She pulled out her phone and punched in the number.

"Security," a man answered.

"This is Dr. Shayla Callaway," she said, adopting her most professional tone. "I was just in the office of Dr. Robert Becker, and it looks like someone broke into the office."

"Is anyone hurt?"

"No, there was no one in the office. I'm not sure if anything was taken. It was a big mess."

"Are you still there?"

"No, I went home. I didn't see anyone, but I was afraid to stay in the building, so I left. I'm sorry. I probably should have gone straight to your office. I wasn't thinking straight."

"We'll check it out, Dr. Callaway. Do we have your number?"

"Yes, it's on file."

"Have you been in contact with Dr. Becker?"

"No, I haven't. I don't know where he is." She wasn't sure if the man in security knew anything about Robert's disappearance, but she wanted to make it clear that she didn't know anything.

"We'll be in touch."

"Thanks." She hung up the phone and looked at Reid. "Was that okay?"

"Perfect," he said with a reassuring smile. "That should get you off the suspect list."

She frowned at his use of the word *you*. "Damn. I just realized I didn't mention that I was with you."

"It's fine."

"But you're Robert's brother. It would make it seem less likely that you and I would have tried to steal something from his office."

"We'll save that for another day—if we need it. Right now I want to see if I can figure out why this notebook is important."

"Okay." She sat down on the couch next to him.

As Reid looked through Robert's drawings, she studied his profile, and her lips began to tingle in memory of their kiss. She could still feel the rough burn of his scruffy beard against her cheeks, the demanding force of his mouth, the solid feel of his chest against her breasts. She'd never had such an intense reaction to a man. She'd felt out of control, wild, and while she could chalk it all up to her panic in the moment, that didn't explain the butterflies dancing through her stomach now, or why she felt like she was both a little too close to him and not close enough at all.

She got up and moved around the table, taking a seat in the uncomfortable armchair her roommate had picked up at a garage sale. She liked the stiff, unyielding seat and back; it grounded her. Made her feel like her feet were settling back on the ground and that she wasn't caught up in a billowy cloud of emotions.

She'd always been good at putting distance between herself and temptation. When she was a kid and she needed to study, she'd close her bedroom door, put on her headphones and shut out the world, focus on what she needed to do, which was what she needed to do now.

But she found her gaze drifting back to Reid. She wondered what he'd thought about their kiss. Probably nothing. In fact, he'd no doubt forgotten all about it. He certainly seemed to be engrossed in Robert's comic book illustrations.

That was fine. Better to have his attention directed toward his brother than her.

She tapped her fingers nervously on her legs, wondering how long he planned on staying. Again, she was torn between wanting him to go and not wanting to be alone.

What a basket case she was. She normally liked being on her own, independent, doing her thing, living her life. But ever since the guns had gone off in Colombia, she'd become fearful of everything.

Robert's call hadn't helped. Nor had almost getting hit by a car or finding Robert's office in disarray. Were the events connected? Or was she once again leaping to illogical conclusions?

"You need to relax, Shayla." Reid's voice cut through the tense silence that had fallen between them.

"I'm trying."

He lifted his gaze to hers, a smile playing around the curve of his mouth. "Do you want to kiss me again? Take the edge off."

She should have realized he wasn't going to let that kiss go without a comment. "No, thanks. I'm good."

"Too bad."

"That kiss was…" She didn't know what it was.

"Really interesting," he finished.

"I was having a panic attack. I shouldn't have grabbed you like that. I'm sorry."

"You don't ever have to apologize for kissing me, Doc. But next time I'd prefer it if you weren't scared for your life."

"There's not going to be a next time."

"You never know."

She didn't like the wicked sparkle in his eyes or the fact that it made her want to make the next time now. She got to her feet, too restless to sit. "I'm going to use the bathroom."

"Most women run toward me, not away, Doc."

She paused, frowning at his cocky drawl. "You're incredibly arrogant."

"I'm incredible at a lot of things. Just give me a chance to show you." His sexy grin made her nerves tingle.

She practically ran down the hall to her bedroom, knowing that if she didn't put a few more feet between them, she might give in to his invitation, and that would be her worst mistake yet. She already had enough problems without getting involved with one moody, know-it-all, sexy-as-hell man.

Chapter Six

Reid's smile faded as Shayla left the room. He'd tried to distract her with his comments, because her nervous tension was still palpable, but teasing her about the kiss they'd shared in Robert's office had been a bad idea. He could still taste her on his tongue, feel her soft curves in his arms and smell the scent of lavender that seemed to linger in her hair and on her skin.

Lavender was supposed to be calming, but when he got near Shayla, he felt nothing close to calm. When she'd first shown up in the bar, he'd been intrigued. When the car had almost run them down, he'd been worried and wary. When they'd hidden in Robert's office, he'd been tense and incredibly turned on. Now...Now, he just felt alive, and it felt good.

He tried to convince himself that it wasn't just having a beautiful blonde in his arms that had woken him up but also the threat of danger, discovery. He'd always been a man to live on the edge of life, to push the limits, to test himself, but for the past six months he'd been living in a fog. Tonight's events had blown through that fog, and he felt like he was seeing clearly for the first time in a long time.

Unfortunately, his new awareness and clarity was not helping him figure out why his brother wanted this notebook of sketches, most of which Robert had originally drawn in his youth, although there appeared to be some newer sketches toward the back. But why would any of this be important to Robert now?

If he didn't know his brother that well, Reid might have said the illustrations had some sort of sentimental value, but Robert wasn't sentimental. He was logical, analytical, ambitious and driven. He didn't waste time on emotions or even on people. He was always in pursuit of his next goal. His only real detour had been Lisa.

Even said in silence, her name tasted bitter. He downed the orange juice, then got up from the couch and went into the kitchen to refill his glass. On his way back to the couch he wandered around Shayla's apartment, a little curious about the woman who had shown up in his life a few hours ago and turned everything upside down.

Had it really only been a few hours since they'd met?

It seemed like they'd known each other for years.

After she'd shared her intensely personal and terrifying experience with him, he'd felt a connection to her. He'd been through similar raids as the one she'd described, although he'd always had a gun, a way to defend himself. He could only imagine what Shayla must have felt when faced with automatic gunfire and almost certain death.

Why she hadn't died was a mystery, and he'd been trained in war games long enough to know that that probably wasn't just luck.

Why kill some people and leave others completely alone? He needed to know more about the individuals who had been killed. Was there a common link between them?

Perhaps Shayla had been spared because she was a doctor. She might have tended to the sick in the very village where the gunmen had come from. Maybe that had been her saving grace.

As he paused in front of a bookcase and saw the numerous medical books on the shelves, he was reminded that Shayla was a lot like his brother when it came to academics. No wonder they'd become friends.

What was more curious was why *he* liked her so much.

While he had no problem with smart women on the job, in fact, he preferred a high level of intelligence in the people he worked with, when it came to the bedroom a high IQ wasn't a prerequisite, nor was it even preferred. Smart women tended to ask more questions, have more demands, and want more from him than he wanted to give. Which was why he needed to keep his hands off of Shayla, because she was probably the smartest woman he'd ever met.

Shaking that thought away, he browsed the notes on her bulletin board. Judging by the miscellaneous take-out menus, Shayla and her roommate didn't cook often. There were also slips of paper with scribbled phone messages and reminders to buy milk and bread as well as a couple of photographs. One pictured Shayla with another woman. They had on white coats with stethoscopes around their necks, and he assumed the other female was probably her roommate or another medical resident. It was interesting to see Shayla actually dressed as a doctor. She looked a little older in the white coat, but there was no denying the bright, youthful sparkle in her eyes.

He was only eight years older than her, but he'd had to grow up really fast once he joined the Army. His experiences there, the things he'd seen, the things he had to do, had changed him in ways he could never change back. He didn't regret those years. He'd loved being a soldier, fighting for his country, for what was right, but over time the lines of war had gotten blurry and sometimes he'd questioned what he was fighting for.

In the past few years, cynicism had settled over him like a heavy, scratchy coat that was both familiar and uncomfortable. The coat had gotten tighter since he'd been injured. He didn't think he could get it off now even if he tried. And he hadn't wanted to try. He hadn't wanted to do anything—until now.

Now he wanted to help Shayla. She was the real reason he'd come this far with her. It wasn't about Robert's need to get out of trouble that had gotten him out of the bar; it was about the look of fear and desperation in Shayla's blue eyes. She needed to move on with her life, but she couldn't get closure until Robert was safe.

So he would save his brother, not for Robert's sake, but for hers.

Then she could move on, and he could do the same. Because being with Shayla was already setting off alarms in his head. She was not the woman for him. He didn't make promises or do forever and Shayla was the kind of woman who deserved both.

The next picture only reconfirmed that thought. Shayla stood in the middle of a huge family that seemed to boast far more members than the seven siblings she'd told him about. The ages ranged from a baby in arms to toddlers, teenagers, adults and several white-haired individuals. There were smiles on every face and an obvious love radiating from the group like a warm golden glow of happiness.

He couldn't remember the last family photo he'd been a part of. And if there had been a photo, he doubted there'd been many smiles. His small family of four individuals was completely disconnected. Although, that wasn't completely true. The other three were in sync; he was the odd man out.

He glanced away from the board as Shayla reentered the room. She looked more composed now, less agitated and fearful. Her cheeks held more color, and judging by the damp strands of hair around her face, she'd obviously splashed on some cold water and taken a moment to pull herself together.

"Is this your family?" he asked.

"Yes, that was taken at my cousin Maya's twenty-first birthday a few years ago. That's about eighty percent of the family that lives here in the city."

He raised an eyebrow. "Eighty percent? There are at least thirty people in the shot."

"I think it's closer to forty if you count all the little kids. Some of my cousins have been prolific at procreating." She paused, smiling fondly at the picture on the board. "My family is really big on celebrating every event in life. Sometimes it seems like a pain to get everyone together. There's always some bickering. We have a lot of strong personalities in the group. But I feel very lucky to have them all in my life."

"Who's the woman you're standing next to?"

"That's Emma. She's older than me by six years. She's an arson investigator with the San Francisco Fire Department."

"An unusual job for a woman."

"Not for a Callaway woman. I come from generations of firefighters. My great-grandfather, my grandfather, my father, brothers, uncles, and cousins are all in the department. It's a family tradition. My father is deputy chief of operations, number two in command. His father was the Chief of Department back in his day, so I come from a long line of leaders."

"But you didn't follow in that tradition."

"No, and I think my dad was actually a little relieved. He wanted the boys to go into firefighting, but he's very protective when it comes to his daughters. He hated every second that Emma was working on the line. But she proved herself to him and everyone else who ever had doubts that she could be as good as any man."

"Sounds like strength runs in the family," he commented.

"It does. My other sister, Nicole, is also very tough. She's not a firefighter, but she's a teacher and the mother of an autistic six-year-old child. She's a warrior on his behalf."

"That's rough."

"Very rough, but Brandon has been making strides the last few months, since he was reunited with his twin brother."

He raised an eyebrow. "That sounds like a story."

She nodded. "A long one. The short version is that Brandon and Kyle were separated at birth and adopted out to two different families. Neither family had any idea there was a twin until the boys were kidnapped last year."

"Seriously?"

She nodded. "Yes, but thankfully they were rescued and everything ended well. Now the two families are working on co-parenting, because it's really important for the boys to stay together. Kyle, who is perfectly normal, has a way of communicating with Brandon that no one else has, and Brandon has been slowly improving since he got his brother back."

"That's quite a story."

"My family has its share of drama. What are your

parents like, Reid? Robert hasn't told me much about his family over the years. I met your parents once at a party. Your father was polite but a little cold."

"A little?" he muttered, thinking that was an understatement. "The man is made of ice when it comes to me. For Robert, he used to thaw every once in a while."

"What about your mom?"

"She's warmer," he conceded. "But both my parents were always busy with work. I often wondered why they bothered to have children. They didn't seem to know what to do with us. Of course that changed when they found out Robert was a genius. That they could relate to. They treated him like a little adult."

"And you?"

He shrugged. "I'm sure they loved me in their own way. But we had nothing in common." As he finished speaking, he headed back to the couch.

Shayla followed him, but once again settled herself on the very uncomfortable-looking chair by the fake fireplace.

"There's room for you here," he said, patting the soft cushions next to him. Her eyes sparkled at his suggestive words, and he smiled. "Unless you don't think you can control yourself when you're sitting this close to me?"

"Maybe you can't control yourself."

"I'm always in control." While his words were meant to be teasing, they were in fact the truth. He'd taken control of his life a long time ago, and he liked calling the shots. The one time he'd let himself get too caught up in what someone else wanted had ended in disaster.

"So let's get back to your family," Shayla said. "Your dad is a teacher, right?"

He let her change the subject, because he thought keeping Shayla on the other side of the coffee table was a better idea than putting her within arm's reach. "Yes. He teaches economics at Stanford. My mother runs the music program at a private school."

"How often do you see them?"

"I never see them."

"Why not?" she asked in surprise.

He shrugged. "I told you, we have little interest in each other. Robert is their favorite son, the one they understand and respect."

"Even after what he did to you?"

He stiffened, her question taking him back to a place he didn't want to go. "Yes," he said tersely. "Even after that."

"I don't understand."

"Join the club."

"They must have been angry with Robert. They must have realized that he hurt you."

"Who the hell knows what they thought? It was a long time ago. I'm over it."

"Are you?"

"Yes."

"I don't believe you."

"Well, what you believe doesn't really matter to me."

He didn't usually speak so harshly to a woman he barely knew, but she'd touched a nerve. It wasn't just Robert's betrayal that had hurt, it was also the way his parents had tried to make excuses for his brother that had told him just where he stood in the family.

"You like to say that a lot," Shayla said. "That things don't matter to you. That you don't care about anyone or anything and that no one cares about you in return. You even bought a boat called the Lone Wolf. I don't think that was a coincidence."

"I did like the name."

"Where did you and Lisa meet? What brought you

together? What made you fall in love with her?" Shayla asked.

He could see her curiosity growing with each question. "I don't want to talk about Lisa."

"Did you have a long engagement or one of those whirlwind romances?"

"What part of *I don't want to talk about Lisa* don't you understand?" he asked with annoyance.

She brushed off his question. "I know Lisa and Robert got married seven years ago, because I went to their anniversary party, which took place about a month before they separated. So I'm guessing you were with her at least eight years ago. That would have made you how old?"

"Twenty-six," he bit out.

Surprise flashed in her eyes. "Twenty-six?" she echoed. "Really?"

Her gaze narrowed as if he'd presented her with an equation that didn't add up.

"Yes. Why so surprised?"

"How old are you now?"

"Thirty-four."

"But Robert is thirty-four. How are you the same age?"

"You're the doctor. I'm sure you can figure it out."

"You're twins?"

"Bingo. I beat Robert out of the womb by one minute. It was the last time I was ahead of him."

"That is crazy," she muttered with a disbelieving shake of her head. "I had no idea Robert was a twin. Why didn't he tell me?"

"Why would he tell you?" Reid countered.

"Because I'm a twin, and we've had many conversations about the role genetics plays in disease. It seems strange that Robert wouldn't tell me he was also a twin."

"He probably forgot he had a twin," he said dryly.

"You don't seem very forgettable." She paused, compassion in her gaze. "Now I know why Robert's betrayal cut so deep. You aren't just brothers; you're twins. There's a difference."

"Is there?"

"Of course. My brother, Colton, and I have always shared a deep connection. We're much closer to each other than we are to our other siblings."

"Well, I don't have any other siblings, so I wouldn't know the difference."

"Were you and Robert close when you were young?"

"When we were really young," he admitted. "Once we hit school, Robert sped ahead. He wouldn't just jump one grade at a time; he'd skip two. I'd be struggling with basic math, and he'd be doing algebraic equations in his head. By the time we were ten, we were living very different lives. While I was figuring out high school, Robert was off to college at fifteen."

"Very few people are as smart as your brother."

"Apparently you come close."

She gave a self-deprecating shrug. "My IQ is nowhere near Robert's level. But there's book smart and street smart, and I have a feeling you would beat your brother when it came to street smarts any day of the week." She cocked her head to the right, giving him a thoughtful look. "Did you ever want to go to college?"

"Never. School was Robert's world, not mine."

"Did you always want to be in the Army?"

"No. I didn't know what I wanted to be. The Army seemed as good a choice as any at the time. In the end, it turned out to be the best possible place for me."

"You were a baby when you enlisted."

"I didn't think so at the time. In fact, I thought I had it all together, that I knew everything."

"Funny how that hasn't changed," she said dryly.

He smiled and tipped his head. "Fair point."

"So you were in the Army a long time."

"Sixteen years. I'd still be there if I hadn't almost gotten my leg blown off."

She winced, her gaze narrowing with compassion. "What happened, Reid?"

"I don't want to talk about it."

She sighed. "You brought it up."

"Now I'm dropping it."

"There's a lot you don't want to talk about."

"Then maybe you could do me a favor and stop asking me questions."

Her response to his words was a smile, and that irritated him even more. Not only was she not taking him seriously, she was damned beautiful when she wasn't terrified for her life. "What's so funny?" he demanded.

"You. You're like a grumpy bear who caught a nail in his paw and wants to bite anyone who tries to get close enough to take it out."

He stared back at her. "Is that what you think? That all I need is someone to pull out the nail? Maybe someone like you? You can't heal me, Doc. So don't even think about trying."

Her smile disappeared. "I wasn't trying to diminish your injury, Reid. I'm sorry if you took it that way."

"It's fine." He picked up Robert's notebook. "Let's get back to business. What can you tell me about these sketches?"

She hesitated, as if she didn't quite want to let the personal conversation drop, but in the end, she went along with him. "I don't know if I can tell you anything. I've seen

Robert drawing, but he's never shared the illustrations with me."

"Why don't you take a look at them now?"

She hesitated. "Do I need to? You have the notebook. You know where to meet Robert. Do we need to decipher the sketches?"

"I'd like to know what I'm heading into and I think this notebook holds a clue."

"Does that mean you've finally decided to help your brother?"

"First, I want to figure out why these sketches are important. If Robert is in trouble, I'd like to know what that trouble is before I get down in the quicksand with him."

She stared back at him. "I suppose that makes sense."

"Of course it makes sense. You don't go into battle without a plan."

"I don't want to go into battle at all."

"Then you shouldn't have told Robert you'd help him."

"I couldn't say no. He's my friend." She paused. "Even if you won't make me a promise, I know you're going to help Robert, because he's your brother, your twin brother. No matter what he's done to you, he's blood, and you're a loyal man."

He stared back at her. "I hope you're wrong."

"But I'm not, am I?"

Chapter Seven

Reid didn't answer her question, which was fine, since she already knew the truth.

"I'll take a look at the sketches with you," Shayla said. "But, first, I'm going to make some tea. Do you want some?"

"No, thanks."

She took her time in the kitchen, letting the water come to a full boil before finally pouring it into a mug. She let the bag steep for a couple of minutes, stirring every now and then. As she watched the color change from clear to amber, she contemplated all the twists and turns her life had taken in the past few weeks. Just when she'd thought her road had straightened out, another curve tossed her off course.

The latest curve was Reid. He had a presence about him that demanded attention. In that way, he was a little like Robert. But Robert commanded people with his mind. With Reid, it was physical. He had strength and confidence. He was the kind of man you wanted by your side when a fight broke out, the kind of man you could lean on and be certain that he would protect you with his life.

How hot was that? Didn't every woman want that kind of man?

And then there was the whole sexy, scruffy thing Reid had going on. She could still feel the rasp of his five o'clock shadow against her cheeks as he slid his tongue into her mouth.

She tried to shove the memory of that kiss to the back of her head, at least for now. Maybe later, in the dark, when she was alone, she'd let herself remember…

She took the teabag out of her mug and headed back to the couch, settling in next to Reid. "So what have you figured out?"

"That Robert has a very good memory. He recreated a lot of our childhood in this comic book, but I don't understand why." He looked at her with confusion in his eyes. "You said you gave him the notebook last year. Why didn't he draw something new, something different? Why rehash what he wrote when he was twelve or fourteen?"

"Maybe there was comfort in the familiar. What's the story about?"

"The adventures of teenage daredevil Razor and his trusty sidekick, Rocco, a golden retriever. They have superhuman skills with which they fight crime, search for treasure, and save lives." He slid closer to her and flipped through to the third page.

She had to fight the urge to move away. She told herself not to be ridiculous. She should not be so affected by the simple brush of his leg against hers.

"This is our house," Reid said, not at all as distracted as she was, which was a slight blow to her ego.

She forced herself to focus on the sketch, curious to see where Reid and Robert had lived as kids. The two-story house looked like a typical suburban home for a young family, but the action in front was far more disturbing. On the porch swing, the dog, Rocco, watched the teenaged Razor sail a skateboard down the front steps toward two hideous looking demons. In Razor's hand was a mighty sword, apparently to be used to vanquish the evil in front of him.

There was something very familiar about Razor. "That's you," she said, suddenly realizing the truth. "You're Razor."

Reid frowned as he gazed at the sketch. "I don't think that's true."

"Come on, it looks just like you."

"I don't see it."

"The kid is a warrior about to do battle, and if that isn't you, I don't know who it is."

"Maybe it's Robert living out some fantasy," he suggested.

She thought about that. It would make sense for a young artist to put himself in the story, but this sketch didn't feel like Robert. As she took a closer look, she saw a face in the upstairs window. "Hang on. I think I found Robert." She pointed to the figure barely visible behind a curtain.

Reid slowly nodded. "Yeah, you're right. That's Robert. That was his bedroom window. I used to see him sitting up there studying at his desk when I was outside playing with the other kids."

"Robert didn't join you?"

"Almost never. He was always about the books."

As she stared at the face of the little boy in the window, she felt a little sad. "It's like he's in prison. The square panes of glass look like bars, don't they? The boy seems trapped."

Reid frowned at her analysis. "I think you're reading

into it, Shayla."

"Am I? Didn't your parents put a lot of pressure on Robert to succeed?"

"No more than he put on himself. They did encourage him to be the best, but even if they hadn't, Robert would have done it on his own. He was self-motivated. He'd race home from school to do his homework. He wasn't a prisoner in the house. He could have left. He could have come outside with us. He didn't want to. He always said no when I asked, and after a while, I stopped asking.

"Well, prisoner or not, it's clear to me that Robert made you the hero of his graphic novel. And your dog," she added.

"We didn't have a dog. I always wanted one, but we couldn't get one because Robert had allergies."

She smiled at Reid. "Robert made you a superhero and gave you the dog you always wanted. You've got to like him for that."

"I don't know if that was Robert's thinking."

"Well, it makes sense to me."

"Let's move on." Reid flipped through a couple more pages of Razor and Rocco battling demons, robots, and other supernatural characters, the setting changing from the suburbs to the woods, a lakeside pier, and then the rooftop of a skyscraper.

"Razor and Rocco certainly get around," she said.

"Yeah." He paused on a page that brought the story back to suburbia.

She studied the drawing which showed Rocco in the back of a car, gazing longingly back at someone, the illustrator perhaps. There were two figures in the front seat, and in the distance was what appeared to be a university. "Rocco goes to college, but there's no sign of Razor." She paused, trying to put herself into Robert's head. "It's almost like Rocco is your brother. He's going to college. He's being taken away from his best friend, Razor." She touched Reid's shoulder in excitement. "I get it. Rocco is really Robert. This whole book is about the relationship between you and your brother."

He stared at her like she'd completely lost her mind. "I don't know…"

"I'm right, Reid."

"Now who's being cocky?"

She shrugged. "I know what I'm good at, and I'm good at figuring things out. Plus, I know Robert, and I'm getting to know you. From what you've told me about your relationship with your brother and your family, it all makes perfect sense."

"It's possible," he conceded. "But let's bring it back to what's happening now. If you're so smart, tell me why Robert wants this notebook."

She sighed. "I don't know. Maybe we haven't hit on the right sketch yet. How many more pictures are there?"

"A lot. Almost every page has been used. My brother certainly spent a lot of time drawing the past few months."

"This could take some time then."

"I think so," he agreed.

She settled back more comfortably on the couch, suddenly feeling incredibly tired. It had been a long day and an even longer week. Reid said something. She couldn't really comprehend the words, but the tenor of his voice was very soothing. Her eyes felt dry and heavy; she she couldn't keep them open for another minute. For the first time in a long time she felt safe.

* * *

Shayla was asleep, a sweet sexy angel. Reid watched the whisper of breath pass through her parted lips, the sweep of dark lashes that framed her eyes, the soft pink luster of her skin. She'd pulled the band out of her hair when she settled back against the couch, and now her long blonde hair tumbled over her shoulders in silky waves.

He wanted to run his fingers through her hair, lean over and frame her face with his hands and kiss her until she came awake in his arms.

But that would be more than selfish, he thought, trying to put on the brakes. Shayla was exhausted. She hadn't slept since she'd gotten back from Colombia, and she needed to rest, to let her mind take a break from all the fear and the worry.

He suspected that she'd been pushing herself hard for a long time, even before Colombia. Like his brother, she'd started college at a young age and had been in dedicated pursuit of degrees since she was sixteen. Had she even had a childhood? Had she dated in high school? Or, like his brother, had she been isolated and awkward?

As the questions ran around in his mind, he realized it was the first time in maybe ever that he'd thought so much about a woman he wasn't sleeping with.

He smiled to himself. Life would have been a lot easier if he'd gone home with one of the women from the bar tonight. If he hadn't been at the Cadillac Lounge when Shayla arrived, then he wouldn't be here now. Although, Shayla would have no doubt come looking for him again, and she would have eventually found him. She didn't quit easily. That much he knew. She was a fighter, and she was battling now for his brother, of all people.

He wondered again about their relationship. Shayla had been emphatic that there was nothing between her and Robert except friendship. He hoped that was the truth. But he couldn't help wondering if Robert felt differently about Shayla than she felt about him. The two of them certainly had a lot in common with their backgrounds, their careers, and their interests. His brother might have been an obsessed intellectual most of his life, but he wasn't blind when it came to women.

Which brought him back to Lisa.

With a sigh, he shoved Lisa's face out of his head. He'd told Shayla he was over her, over what had happened, and that was mostly true. He hadn't thought about Robert or Lisa in years.

Sighing, he shifted positions as his bad leg began to ache. He should go home, but his houseboat seemed very far away at the moment. Like Shayla, he hadn't been getting a lot of sleep lately between his healing injuries and the nightmares that often plagued his dreams. But tonight he felt far too comfortable to move.

Kicking his legs up on the coffee table, he set the notebook down, leaned back against the pillows and closed his eyes. He'd just take a little nap. Then he'd go home. Then he'd figure out what to do next.

As he sought the welcome oblivion of sleep, the pictures from Robert's notebook began to run through his mind, some of them bringing back really strong memories, especially the one of the dog in the back of the car going off to the university.

"Reid, are you coming?"

He heard his mom's voice, but he ignored her question, focusing instead on the video game playing on the television in his bedroom.

"Reid, come down and say goodbye," she yelled. "We need to get on the road. Robert has freshman orientation at three o'clock."

He didn't want to say goodbye to his brother. He couldn't even believe Robert was going to college at fifteen. It seemed like a joke to him. Sure, Robert was smart, but college? He was going to be a nerd freak among a bunch of eighteen-year-olds who wanted to party and have sex. Why his brother had agreed to go was beyond him.

"Reid," his mother said, appearing in his doorway. There was frustration and anger in her eyes. "Didn't you hear me calling? You need to say goodbye to your brother."

"I already said goodbye," he lied. Actually, he'd been avoiding Robert all day and most of the past week. He didn't know what to say to his twin. He hadn't known what to say for a long time. They'd once been super close but now they were strangers.

"Robert needs you," she said. "You think he doesn't care, but he does, much more than you know."

His brother didn't care. Robert barely spoke to him. His head was always buried in a book. He turned his attention back to the video game, hoping his mother would just go away.

He heard her angry breath for another second, then her footsteps going down the stairs, the sound of the front door closing and a car driving away. They were gone. He was alone.

And then a voice rang through the quiet.

"You should have said good-bye, Reid."

He jumped to his feet and whirled around to see a beautiful blonde sitting on his bed. Suddenly he wasn't fifteen anymore. He was all grown up. "It didn't matter, Shayla."

Her blue eyes scolded him. "Of course it mattered. You're his brother. He was moving away from home, and he was scared."

"You don't know that he was scared."

"I do. He told me."

"That was years later," he reminded her.

"That doesn't make it not true." She paused. "Robert needs you now. This time you have to go to him. This time it matters a lot."

"What has Robert ever done for me?" he countered. "Why is it always about him?"

"I don't know about always. I just know about now. You need to stop fighting yourself, Reid. You want to help him. You just don't want to admit it." She took a breath, then said, "Saving him doesn't have to mean you forgive him."

He stared at her in amazement. Was she reading his mind? "You're crazy."

"And I'm right," she said, getting up from the bed. "You're dreaming about me now, because you want me to tell you what to do. Then the decision won't be yours, it will be mine."

"I don't think that's why I'm dreaming about you," he said as she came closer, so close he could smell the lavender scent in her hair. He took a breath so deep it made his head spin. Or maybe it was just being near her. She made him feel like he was about to fall, and he never fell...

"What other reason could there be?" she asked.

"You have no idea how beautiful you are, do you?"

Her cheeks turned pink as her blue eyes brightened like a summer sky. "Everyone is beautiful in a dream."

He smiled, her modest words confirming what he'd just told her. "You don't see yourself as I see you."

"And how is that?" she asked softly, her lips so inviting, so kissable.

"Naturally pretty with smart eyes, an even smarter mouth, and a pair of beautiful breasts."

She subconsciously crossed her arms in front of her

chest. *"They're not that great. And you wouldn't know, because you haven't seen them."*

"In my imagination I have."

"We only met a few hours ago."

"And I was imagining you naked about five minutes after I saw you." He put his hands on her hips, leaned in and took the kiss he was hungering for.

Her lips opened like a flower to the sun. He tasted her warmth, letting her heat chase away the cold chill that had surrounded him for months. He raised his hand to her head, cupping the back of her neck, bringing her in even closer. Her hair fell in silky strands over his hand. He twisted his fingers in the soft curls as he took the kiss even deeper, as he let the spell that she had cast over him take hold.

She was everything that he'd ever wanted, and he was suddenly scared that she would slip away. Her scent was already fading. A chill filled the air between them as her features began to fade into the light.

"Don't go," he pleaded. *"I need you."*

God, where had that come from? He'd never told a woman that before, not even Lisa. He'd told Lisa he loved her, but he'd never said he needed her. Maybe that was why she had left...

But he didn't care about her anymore. It was the beautiful blonde with the haunted innocent blue eyes, the woman whose heart was just begging to be broken. But he didn't want to be the one to break it. He'd seen so much pain, so much suffering, and felt so much loss in his life. He didn't want that for her. He wanted to hold Shayla in this perfect dream where nothing bad could ever happen.

He reached for her as a voice rang through the haze in his head.

"Reid!"

Shayla?
Was he still dreaming?
"Reid, wake up."

Shayla's tone was sharper now. He blinked, opening his eyes. They weren't in his old bedroom anymore. They were in Shayla's apartment, on her couch, and he was sprawled on top of her, his legs pinning her down, his right hand tangled in her hair, his left hand remarkably close to the swell of her breast.

"Reid?" she said again, a catch in her voice as they gazed into each other's eyes. "What were you dreaming about?"

"You," he said huskily. "I was dreaming of you."

Awareness and desire flared in her eyes. She might not have been dreaming about him, but she wanted him as much as he wanted her.

"You kept telling me to stay," she murmured.

"But you weren't listening," he said, his gaze holding on to hers. "You were leaving me."

"Really, because right now I can't imagine why I'd want to go."

"I can't either."

He started to lower his head, but she put her hand against his chest, stopping his progress. "We probably shouldn't," she said.

"You really are the good girl, aren't you?"

"More like the smart girl."

"Don't you get tired of being smart?"

She let out a soft sigh. "More than I could ever say."

"Once in a while you have to do something, not because it's good or smart or right, but just because you want to. But you never do that, do you?"

"Almost never," she whispered. And then she flung her arm around his neck and brought his mouth down to meet hers.

There was no gentle tenderness between them, no slow exploration of the senses. His dream had already fueled the fire, and the feel of her body under his was enough to drive any sane man out of his mind. He kissed her with a fever that couldn't be contained, and she met him kiss for kiss with the same amount of passion, the same level of need.

He searched for bare skin, feeling a little thrill when he found the edge of her shirt, when his hand came to rest on her abdomen.

Shayla moved restlessly against him, shifting as he sought the curve of her breast, sighing a little as his fingers slid under the edge of her bra.

He raised his head and met her gaze, and saw that she was right there with him. Thank God!

He moved on to his side, helping her pull the shirt over her head, revealing a lacy black bra barely containing her beautiful breasts. The sight was even better than he'd imagined. His heart hammered against his chest. Blood thundered through his veins. And he was about to bury his face in those soft, enticing curves when the front door opened.

A female voice said, "Whoops! So sorry!"

Shayla shoved him away.

He sat up in confusion as Shayla immediately put her hands over her breasts.

"I'm not looking. I swear I'm not looking," the woman said, holding a hand over her eyes as she took a wide berth around the couch to get to the hallway. "I'm going into my room, putting on my headphones," the woman added as she hit the hallway, and the next sound was her bedroom door closing.

"Oh, God," Shayla muttered, grabbing her shirt off the

floor. She quickly pulled it back over her head.

He stared at her in bemusement. The switch from passion to off hadn't quite resonated in his brain. But Shayla was clearly moving on. Her face was red, her hair a tousled mess, her lips swollen from his kisses. And her eyes were a mix of frustration and embarrassment.

He wasn't embarrassed, but he was frustrated, especially when he shifted uncomfortably in his now too tight jeans. He didn't really care what her roommate had seen. He only regretted the fact that she'd come home.

But it was morning, he realized. They'd slept all night. There was sun coming through the slit in the curtains. He hadn't realized how long he'd been asleep. He'd only closed his eyes for a moment.

"I can't believe Kari saw us," Shayla muttered, running her fingers through her hair.

"A few minutes later, and she would have seen a lot more of us."

"Maybe it's good she came home, before we did something stupid."

"You mean something amazing," he countered.

"Amazing sometimes turns to stupid a few hours later. You and me— we're not together. We barely know each other. I don't do this. I mean I really don't do this."

"I believe you," he said.

"I was half asleep and so were you. It was a moment of madness."

He settled back against the couch. "And that moment has passed."

"Yes."

"Got it."

"It's not that I don't like you," she said a moment later. "And obviously I'm attracted to you."

"Obviously," he said dryly.

"But this can't happen again."

"Are you sure about that?"

"I don't even know you."

"You don't have to know someone to want them."

"I do. I have to know them. Or at least I did." She rubbed her temple. "I'm…confused."

"Well, don't sweat it. Nothing happened. You're still the good girl." He grabbed the notebook off the coffee table and stood up. "I'm going to head out."

She got to her feet. "You're still going to meet Robert on Sunday, right?"

"I'm considering it."

"Why can't you give me a straight answer?"

"That is my answer. Robert gave me three days to figure out if I want to meet him, and I'm going to take all the time that I have." He handed her his phone. "Put in your number in case I need to call you." Then he grabbed her phone off the table and put in his number.

After putting her number into his contacts, she handed it back to him, and said, "Will you let me know if you're not going to meet Robert, because if you don't want to help him, then I will. You can give me the notebook and tell me where to go."

"I'll let you know." There was no way in hell he was going to let Shayla go off on some suicide mission to save his brother.

"I mean it, Reid."

"I believe you." He lowered his head and gave her a quick kiss. It was a brief connection but it packed a big jolt. He smiled at her startled expression. "You can think it's never going to happen again, but I wouldn't bet on it."

"Goodbye, Reid."

"See you later," he said, his words barely getting out before she slammed the door behind him.

Chapter Eight

Shayla took a cold shower, feeling frustrated and angry, not just with Reid, but also with herself. Why couldn't she let go once in a while? Why did she have to worry so much about every little thing? She hated being the good girl. She'd heard that sneering comment more than once in her life. Not that Reid had been sneering. No, he'd been more amused and a little bewildered, as if he hadn't run into too many women who said no.

And why would he? He was attractive, sexy, strong, powerful, and he'd aroused feelings in her she'd only imagined feeling.

If Kari hadn't walked in, she would have had sex with him, and it probably would have been amazing.

But it was better this way. Smarter. Safer. Being with him would only complicate her life more, and she already had her hands full with one Becker brother. How could she handle both of them?

Shivering, she stepped out of the shower and dried off. Then she threw on shorts and a tank top and went into the kitchen where she found Kari making scrambled eggs.

Judging by the amusement and curiosity in Kari's

eyes, she was going to have some questions to answer.

"So..." Kari said, flipping the eggs over with a spatula. "I didn't know you were seeing anyone. Who is the hot guy? And why did you let him leave? I hope it wasn't because of me, because heaven knows you could use some sex in your life. You've been all work and no play for a long time." She paused. "By the way, do you want some eggs? I made too many."

"Yes, I would like some eggs. I actually feel hungry for the first time in a while."

Kari gave her a teasing look. "Sex will do that."

"We didn't have sex," she muttered.

"Why not? Was it because I came home? Damn, my timing sucks."

"No, your timing was perfect. That wasn't a date, Kari. That was Robert's brother. We were talking about Robert late into the night, and we fell asleep on the couch. When we woke up we were a little disoriented."

"And completely hot for each other," Kari put in with a knowing gleam in her eyes. "That guy is really Robert's brother? Robert Becker, the skinny, pale doctor who looks like he hasn't ever seen a gym?"

She frowned. "Robert is not unattractive."

"Well, no, that's true. He's handsome, but he's not *that* guy. What's his name? What does he do besides look hot?"

"His name is Reid, and he's a soldier, or he used to be. He got injured several months ago and was discharged from the Army."

Kari nodded. "That makes sense. He looks like a man whose body could be a weapon." She grinned. "A weapon of love."

Shayla rolled her eyes. "You're bad."

"And I can't believe you really stopped in the middle of whatever you were doing and kicked him out."

She sighed. "I know. I'm crazy."

"Certifiable."

Turning away from Kari, she grabbed the loaf of bread and put two pieces in the toaster. While she was waiting for it to toast, she got some butter out of the refrigerator.

"So what's the latest on Robert?" Kari asked. "What brought his brother over here?"

She couldn't tell Kari about Robert's phone call. "Reid is concerned that no one has talked to Robert in over a week."

Kari scooped the eggs out on to two plates. "You don't think he's still in Colombia, do you?"

"I don't know where he is." That much was the truth.

"I wish you'd tell me what happened down there. I read what I could find on the Internet, and the hospital gossip mill has been churning like crazy, but I don't know that anyone who wasn't there knows the truth." Kari gave Shayla a pointed look. "Do you feel like talking yet?"

"I really don't," she said apologetically. "I'm sorry."

"No, it's fine. When you're ready, I'm here, or at least a phone call away. I don't know if you remember, since you've been out of it lately, but I'm leaving this afternoon to spend some time with my new niece while my sister recovers from surgery."

"How long will you be gone?"

"I'll be back Wednesday at the latest, maybe Tuesday night, depending on how things go." She set the plates down on the small kitchen table. "Is the toast ready?"

"It is," she said, buttering the bread.

She was both sorry and somewhat relieved that Kari would be out of town for a few days. It was hard to spend time with her best friend and roommate without telling her what was going on. But she didn't want to break her promise to Robert, nor did she want to get Kari involved in whatever was going on.

She carried the toast to the table and sat down across from Kari. "I hope your sister will be all right."

"She's going to be fine, but the appendectomy and C-section were not the uneventful birth she was hoping for. While her husband is wonderfully supportive, he needs to take care of their oldest child, so it's Kari to the rescue."

Shayla smiled, knowing that there wasn't much Kari wouldn't do for a friend or a relative.

"So tomorrow is the wedding, right?" Kari asked.

"Yes, but the events begin today. We're meeting for a final dress fitting and lunch."

"No rehearsal dinner?"

"No. Ria said she doesn't need to practice walking down an aisle, and Drew was very happy with that decision."

"I'll bet. I'm actually surprised they're even having a wedding. From what I know of Ria, she seems to be a free spirit."

Shayla nodded. Her future sister-in-law definitely marched to her own beat, which Shayla really liked. "Ria is doing the big wedding for Megan. She really wanted to be a bridesmaid in a formal ceremony, and Ria and Drew want her to feel like she's part of it, that she's not losing yet another family."

Megan was actually Ria's niece and had only come to live with Ria after she'd lost he parents.

"Didn't Megan just graduate from high school?" Kari asked, munching on her toast.

"Yes, she's going to college in the fall, although she's doing an internship or something this summer, so she'll be leaving for Los Angeles on Monday while Ria and Drew take off on their honeymoon."

"So your brother doesn't have to be much of a stepdad; Megan is pretty much grown."

"She is, but I can tell that Drew loves her a lot. Seeing him with Megan makes me realize that he is going to be a great dad."

"Are they planning to have kids right away?"

She shrugged. "Who knows? Drew is the last person to share his plans, and Ria is pretty tight-lipped as well. But I know my mom would love to have a few more grandchildren."

"And you're certainly not helping with that," Kari teased.

"Hey, I'm the youngest. There are other people in front of me who should be feeling the pressure."

"Like your oldest brother, Burke. I do not understand why that man is still single."

"He had his heart broken when his fiancée died."

"That was like four years ago, wasn't it?"

"Everyone grieves in their own time. But I hope that Burke can find someone else to love."

"It's not that easy to find the right person," Kari said, a more somber note in her gaze.

Shayla studied her friend, whose usually happy smile now appeared to be strained. "Has something happened between you and Paul?" she asked, referring to the medical resident Kari had been seeing the past few months.

"Not really, but our schedules haven't been meshing very well. We can't seem to make time for each other and that's not a good thing."

"So make time when you come back next week. I think Paul is a good guy."

"He is a good guy, but is he good for me? That's what I don't know."

"You'll figure it out."

"I will." She set down her fork. "So I have to ask a question."

"Okay," Shayla said warily.

"Did you kick Reid out because you have feelings for his brother?"

She looked at Kari in astonishment. "Of course not. I don't have feelings for Robert."

"Really? Are you sure? You've always been pretty close. He has looked out for you for years. And now he's divorced."

"I've never felt that way about Robert. I care about him as a friend and I look up to him and respect him, but that's all."

"If you say so."

"You don't sound convinced. Does anyone else think that Robert and I—"

"Have hooked up?" Kari finished. "Sure, lots of people. You know how gossipy the hospital staff can be."

"I can't believe it."

"Don't worry about it."

"I don't want anyone to think I've used Robert to get ahead."

"No one thinks that. It's not like anyone else wanted to go to Colombia. Most everyone thought you were crazy or maybe crazy in love with Robert."

"I went to Colombia, because I wanted the global health experience and a chance to work on a drug trial that might one day benefit my grandmother. The fact that Robert was running the trial was secondary."

"Okay, sorry. I didn't mean to get you all worked up."

"I hate it when people gossip about me. It's been happening my whole life. I was always the odd girl out."

"That's because you're a genius," Kari said matter-of-factly. "But that's a good thing. When people are sick, they want the smartest person in the room to be diagnosing them." She got up and took her plate to the sink. "I'm going to sleep for a few hours before I catch my plane."

"Have a good trip."

Kari paused in the doorway. "You know I don't like to give advice."

"And you know I don't like to take it," Shayla said pointedly. "I grew up the youngest of eight kids. I've had two parents and seven siblings telling me what to do every day of my life."

"Then don't take this as advice. Think of it as a comment, an observation."

"Fine, say what you want to say."

"Sex doesn't always have to mean something. Sometimes you can just have a good time."

"That's your big observation? I've been watching you have fun, casual sex for years. I'm very aware that sex doesn't have to mean something."

"And I've been watching you study and work for the same amount of time, Shayla. I get that you're an overachiever. You have to be perfect. You have to be the best. That makes you a great doctor. But there's more to life, and sometimes I think you forget that."

"I haven't forgotten, but we're so close to the end. One more year of residency, and we're done. It's been a long haul. I don't want to mess it up now."

"You won't mess it up. You're great. Everyone thinks so."

She used to think so, too, but her confidence was shaken now. She couldn't tell Kari that. She could only smile and say, "I'll think about your advice."

Kari smiled back. "My advice is actually *not* to think. Just live a little."

* * *

After leaving Shayla's apartment, Reid drove home feeling more emotion than he had in a very long time. He was pissed off at himself for a lot of reasons, starting with not going home the night before, then for letting down his guard when it came to his family, and most of all for not finishing what he'd started with Shayla. Not that he'd had a choice. As soon as her roommate walked in on them, it was over. Shayla had immediately lost the delicious lazy blur of sleep and her brain had gone into overdrive, coming up with a million reasons why they should not have sex.

He couldn't deny that all those reasons weren't valid, but that didn't make them easier to take. He should be grateful she'd stopped things, but gratitude was not the emotion he was feeling. Maybe that would come later when he had a chance to regroup and realize he'd probably had a narrow escape from a hookup that would have been filled with all kinds of emotional consequences that he did not want.

Once he got home, he took a long shower, dressed and poured himself a bowl of cereal, adding in some bananas and blueberries. Then he sat down in front of his computer. While he ate, he ran a search on his brother's name as well as Colombia and drug trials. A list of articles came up, and he skimmed through them. He wasn't as interested in the medical aspects of the trial as he was in the raid on the clinic.

As Shayla had said, there were several news reports on the incident, but none of them were particularly detailed or enlightening. Colombia was a violent country with numerous drug cartels fighting for power, and raids on medical clinics were not uncommon, despite the fact that many of the people in the remote villages were desperate for some kind of health care.

Despite what he read, his gut told him that the assault on Robert's clinic was not just a random grab for drugs and turf, because if that were the case, why would Robert be in hiding? Why would he tell Shayla that he was in danger? Why would he want a notebook of illustrations?

Reid glanced at the pad he'd tossed onto the couch, knowing that there had to be a clue in there that he was missing. But rather than spend the rest of the day on that, he was going to take a more proactive approach.

Turning off his computer, he grabbed his keys and headed out the door.

As he drove back across the Golden Gate Bridge, he realized that today was the first day in months where he actually had something he needed to do, something that didn't involve seeing a doctor or struggling through a painful rehab session. Today, his focus wasn't on himself, and it felt good to get out of his own head.

Kelton Security was located in a three story brick building in a newly renovated area south of Market Street in San Francisco near the Embarcadero and the baseball stadium. There was no sign on the door; no indication of what kind of business took place behind the door.

Reid pushed the doorbell, gave his name, and a moment later was buzzed into the lobby. The interior was much more welcoming than the outside with hardwood floors, soft lighting, paintings on the wall and a narrow desk at which sat a young woman in her early twenties. She gave him a smile and told him that Mr. Kelton would be down to get him in a moment.

The idea that Matt was Mr. Kelton to this young woman made Reid feel old. It also reminded him how much Mr. Kelton had probably changed since he was Lieutenant Kelton.

Matt had left the service four years ago, and he'd definitely made a life for himself outside of the Army. That life appeared to be fairly successful, if not a little pretentious Reid thought as he stared at a painting that was probably very expensive and incredibly meaningful. All he saw was smeared lines and colors that reminded him of a chaotic mess, which in a strange way resonated within him. His life felt a little like that red, blue and orange blob of dashing paint strokes and blurry lines. The longer he looked at the picture the more he felt like he was looking inside his head, which was a disturbing thought.

He'd always considered himself to be clear-minded, focused, determined...not really so different from his brother in some ways. But that had been before his leg had been blown apart. Still, it was only his leg that had been injured, so why was his head so screwed up?

Before he could come up with an answer, the elevator doors opened, and Matt stepped off. He wore jeans and a light blue button-down shirt. There was an eager light in Matt's brown eyes, and Reid had a feeling a sales pitch was coming, but he wasn't here to get a job but rather to give one.

"I cannot believe it," Matt said, slapping him on the shoulder. "I figured you needed at least another month to come to your senses and agree to work with me."

Reid immediately held up a hand. "Don't get excited. I'm not here about your offer. I need some help."

"With what?"

"Robert."

"That's the last name I expected to come out of your mouth."

"And yet it did."

Matt met his gaze, then nodded. "All right. Let's go up to my office." As they walked toward the elevator, he added, "Can I get you a drink or anything?"

"No, I'm good."

The elevator took them to the top floor. The doors opened onto a luxurious space of glass-walled offices, colorful throw rugs warming up the wood floors, and even a pool table in one corner. He could see a couple of individuals in one of the conference rooms, a presentation of some sort in progress.

Matt led him into the executive office, which was more impressive. A massive oak desk sat in front of a floor to ceiling wall of windows overlooking the San Francisco Bay. A flat screen TV hung on one wall with a security bank of smaller monitors on the other wall.

Matt waved him toward the sitting area, which was comprised of a couch, two chairs and a glass coffee table. "Have a seat."

"Thanks. You've done well for yourself, Kelton."

Matt gave him a smug smile. "That's what I've been trying to tell you. I can give you the tour later if you want. You'll see more than a few familiar faces. The United States Army provided a great pool of talent for me to pick from."

"And all trained on Uncle Sam's dime," he drawled.

"You know it," Matt returned. "But we also provide training. We're now working on some of the most advanced technology systems in the world."

"I guess this isn't the bodyguard business."

"It can be at times, but it's a lot more than that. We've got our fingers in a lot of pies all around the world."

Reid stared at the man he'd known since he was nineteen years old. Matt had always been smart and aggressive and good at his job, but he'd never been rich. "Who bankrolled all this?"

"My father," Matt said, the humor fading from his

eyes.

Reid frowned. "I thought your dad was out of the picture."

"Oh, he was, until he died. Then I got a letter and a big fat guilt check."

"Must have been really big."

"Yeah, it turns out dear old dad was a loser father but a brilliant businessman. I thought about ripping up the check. But my mom told me I should spend every cent of it on something that would make me happy, that my father owed me that. So, Kelton Security was born."

Despite the bravado in Matt's tone, Reid suspected that his friend had gone through a lot more emotional upheaval than his words indicated. But he'd never been one to pry into someone's life. If Matt wanted him to know something, he'd tell him.

"So what can I do for you?" Matt asked.

"I need a favor."

"You don't ask for favors."

"I don't have a choice. I don't have access to the resources I used to have, but you do."

"Actually, I have resources beyond what you used to have," Matt said with an arrogance that made Reid laugh.

He and Matt had always competed with each other. In the old days, he'd usually won those competitions, but that was the old days. He shrugged off the past. He needed to stay in the present. "Great, then my favor won't be a problem."

"What do you need? You said it had something to do with Robert?"

"Yes. My brother was running a clinical drug trial in Colombia. Last week there was an attack on the clinic. All of the medical personnel were evacuated with the exception of Robert, who went missing."

"And you want me to find him?"

"No, I've got that covered, I think."

"So, he's not missing?"

"I think he's hiding," Reid answered. "He wants my help, but before I agree to give it, I need to know what he's involved in."

"Do you have any theories?"

"Unfortunately, no. This was all brought to my attention last night. So I'm still working in the dark." He leaned forward, resting his forearms on his thighs. "What I do know is this: Robert works for Abbott Pharmaceuticals. They have been funding his research for years, including his most recent project, which involves a possible miracle-making drug for Alzheimer's. The trial in Colombia involved a genetic cluster of Alzheimer cases. After the raid on the clinic, much of the data from the trial was lost, so the trial will need to be restarted or run somewhere else. Whether that has anything to do with Robert's disappearance I don't know. It could be something else entirely, but my gut tells me that the events are connected."

"Anything else?"

"I know that both the FBI and the State Department have sent agents to talk to the people on the medical team that returned from Colombia. Their questions were focused on Robert and his whereabouts."

Matt nodded. "And you want to know what their interest is in your brother?"

"Besides the obvious fact that no one seems to know where he is."

"I have some contacts in both agencies."

"Good."

"But first I have to ask you something," Matt said.

Reid knew what was coming, but he managed a nod.

"Go ahead."

"Why the hell would you want to help your brother after what he did to you?" Matt waved a disbelieving hand in the air.

"I've been asking myself the same thing," he admitted. "I haven't come up with an answer, but I'm thinking that maybe once I know what's really going on with him, I'll know what I have to do."

"I think you should leave him to rot in whatever hole he's crawled into."

Reid wasn't surprised by Matt's attitude. Matt had been one of the ushers in his ill-fated wedding. He'd seen the destruction first hand.

"I may still do that," he said. "It depends on what you find out."

"Is this request coming from your parents? Are they pulling some family guilt trip on you?"

"No. I'm not sure what they know. I haven't spoken to them in years."

Matt stared back at him. "Really?"

"Really," he echoed.

"Then was it Lisa who asked you to help?"

"No, it wasn't Lisa," he said. "Apparently, she and Robert divorced a year ago."

"Divorced, huh? Well, I can't say I'm surprised. Lisa didn't have a long attention span when it came to men. Sorry if that's too brutal."

"It's the truth," he said with a shrug.

"So if it wasn't Lisa or your parents who asked, then who was it?"

"That's not important," he replied, wanting to keep Shayla's name out of it. "Can you help me or not?"

"I can help."

"I'll pay you for your time."

"Don't worry about that. I'll collect when you come to work for me."

"That might be never."

Matt smiled. "Yesterday I would have believed that. Today, I'm not so sure. You look a lot different than you did last night in the bar. It's amazing what twenty-four hours can do to a man."

He couldn't argue with that. Shayla had certainly turned his life upside down. He got to his feet. "You still have my number?"

"Of course. And even if I didn't, I could find you. I'm that good."

"You were never short on confidence."

"Neither were you, Becker." Matt stood up to face him. "I know this isn't the Army, but we're doing some good things. We're making a difference and we're playing by our own rules. That has to appeal to you."

"I'll think about it. That's all I can say right now."

"I'll take it." Matt walked him to the door. "While I'm not thrilled about helping your brother, I have to say that I'm glad Robert got you off your favorite bar stool."

He smiled. "It wasn't Robert; it was a beautiful blonde."

Matt grinned, a gleam in his eyes. "Ah, now it all makes sense. What's her name?"

"That's on a need to know basis. Right now, you don't need to know."

Chapter Nine

"So what's his name?" Emma asked as she zipped Shayla into her bridesmaid's dress in the dressing room of the Beautiful Bride Boutique.

Shayla looked at her older sister's face in the mirror and saw the curious smile in her blue eyes. "What are you talking about?"

"I'm talking about whoever put the pink back in your cheeks. Yesterday you looked like death. Today, you're practically glowing."

"I'm just hot. When is this heat wave going to break?" She fanned her face with her hand.

"I don't know, but I like it. Summer is my favorite time of the year, and usually it's cold and foggy. But weather aside, I don't think you're telling me the truth, Shay."

"What isn't Shayla telling you?" Nicole asked.

Shayla sighed as her oldest sister stepped up next to her in a matching gold strapless cocktail dress.

"I asked her if there's a guy in her life, and she's avoiding the question," Emma said.

"Is it that doctor you're always talking about? The one

you went to study under in Colombia?" Nicole asked.

"Study under? Is that what they call it these days?" Emma joked.

Shayla frowned at both of her sisters. Apparently, the gossip about her and Robert had extended beyond the hospital to her own family. "I am not involved with Robert, and there is no guy," she said, even as images of Reid's penetrating green eyes flashed through her head. But Reid was just... She couldn't finish that sentence, so instead she said, "I'm too busy to date."

"You've been saying that for years," Emma said.

"Well, that's how long I've been busy," she returned with annoyance. She loved her sisters, but she was not like Emma or Nicole. She wasn't good at relationships. And it wasn't just due to lack of time; she'd always been socially awkward. It had been difficult to fit in with kids so much older than she was, so was it any real surprise that she'd spent more time with her books than with actual people?

"Relax Shayla, I'm teasing you." Emma gave her an apologetic smile. "I know how hard you've been working the last few years, and I admire and respect you so much."

"Me, too," Nicole said.

"Thank you."

Another female appeared in the mirror, her sister-in-law, Sara, whose dark brown hair stood out in the sea of blondes. Sara was married to her brother, Aiden, and the mother of a nine-month-old daughter, Chloe. Sara had grown up next door and had been best friends with Emma since they were in elementary school, so Sara had felt like a sister to Shayla for far longer than she'd actually been one.

"What are you giving Shayla a hard time about?" Sara asked, a curious light in her brown eyes.

"My lack of a love life is very disturbing to my

sisters," Shayla answered.

"Well, they have to live vicariously through someone. And you're the only one left," Sara said.

"Another reminder that my shelf date is close to expiring," she said dryly.

"Don't be ridiculous," Sara said. "You have lots of time to have everything you want. I know how difficult it is to juggle school and men. I don't think I had more than one date the entire time I was in law school."

"It is difficult. Men have always been a distraction I couldn't afford." Her mind returned to Reid, her lips tingling at the memories of their kiss. Since he'd left her apartment, she'd actually found herself missing him, which was crazy, since she'd only met him the night before. Maybe her sisters were right. Maybe she needed to get out more.

"We look good," Sara said, drawing Shayla's attention back to the full-length mirror.

"We do look good," Emma echoed. "But where is Jessica?"

"She had to work," Nicole said, referring to their brother Sean's girlfriend. "One of her teachers called in sick, and she didn't want to cancel classes. The dance studio is starting to take off, and she wants to keep it going. She already has her dress, and it fits perfectly, so all is good."

"She's not going to make lunch either?" Shayla asked.

"I don't think so," Nicole replied. "She said she'd try to stop by but not to wait for her."

"I wonder when Sean and Jessica will get married," Emma said.

Nicole shrugged. "I have no idea, but they act like they already are. Sean has become quite the family man since he fell for Jess."

Emma smiled. "Who would have thought our rebel musician brother would settle down in a condo with a woman and her kid?"

"Not me," Nicole said. "I thought he'd be the last of our brothers to fall in love."

"I think the last one will be Colton," Shayla said, although she couldn't really imagine her wild twin brother settling down with one woman.

"He is the youngest," Nicole said.

"Maybe the youngest," Emma conceded. "But not the most entrenched in bachelorhood. That would be Burke. I wonder if he'll ever let himself fall in love again."

"He just has to meet the right person," Sara interjected. "Then everything changes."

"You guys look amazing."

They all turned around as Ria's niece Megan came into the dressing room.

At seventeen, Megan was a beauty with black hair and olive skin. As the maid of honor, she would be wearing a slightly different version of the gold bridesmaid's dress, but today she was dressed in a layered tank top, short white denim skirt with four-inch heels that showed off her long legs."

"We look good, because you picked out some fantastic dresses," Shayla said. "Thank you for not making us look like hideous bridesmaids."

Megan grinned. "I would not let that happen. I'm glad you're happy. Does anyone need an alteration? Mrs. Valensky is finishing up another fitting, but she said she'd be right in to make any adjustments you need."

"I think we're good," Shayla said, everyone else nodding in agreement.

"Great, I'll let her know. After you all change, we're going to lunch." She checked her watch, then frowned.

"Ria was supposed to be here by now. I wonder where she is."

"I'm here," Ria announced, rushing into the room with an apologetic smile. Ria had light brown hair streaked with gold, her skin tan from all the hours she spent teaching sailing on the San Francisco Bay. While Ria usually preferred jeans and t-shirts, today she'd put on cropped turquoise blue pants and a loose-flowing floral top.

"Sorry everyone." Ria paused, emotion filling her eyes as she took in the sight before her. "Wow. I have the most beautiful bridesmaids in the world." She put her arm around Megan and gave her niece a hug. "Nice job on the dresses."

Megan beamed. "I told you they would be perfect."

"You were right."

"I want the wedding to be everything you ever dreamed," Megan said, her eyes filling with moisture. "You deserve it, Ria. You saved my life. I wouldn't be here if it weren't for you. And I wouldn't have a family like this if it weren't for Drew, and..." She paused, her voice choking with emotion. "I'm just so happy for you. I only wish Mom could see you now."

"I think somewhere she can," Ria said, giving Megan a quick hug. "But she wouldn't want either of us to be sad or to look back. We have a really bright future ahead of us—all of us. You, me and Drew are family now."

"Hey, don't forget about all of us," Emma cut in. "You're going to be Callaways. Not that you aren't already. From the first minute Drew brought you to the house, I knew you were both going to be a part of our lives forever."

"I knew it, too," Shayla said, not wanting Emma to take all the credit. "The way Drew looked at you made me want to cry."

"Someday a man will look at you that way," Ria assured her.

"I hope so." She shivered at the thought of Reid looking at her that way, but that was crazy. She wasn't even sure she was ever going to see him again. She'd done what Robert had asked. Reid had the notebook and he knew where to find his brother. Her part was done.

She wanted to be happy about that, so she forced a smile on her face as she changed the subject. "Are we meeting everyone else at the restaurant?"

"Yes, and we have to leave soon," Megan said, resuming her role as wedding coordinator. "I'll tell Mrs. Valensky we don't need alterations and meet you out front after you change."

"That girl is going to run the world," Nicole told Ria as Megan left the room.

Ria smiled. "No kidding. I'm going to miss her so much. I can't believe she's already leaving for college."

"She'll come home," Nicole said, putting her arm around Ria. "She's just ready to start her own adventure."

"I know, and I'm thrilled that she was able to get into college after missing so much school over the past ten years." Ria paused, looking around at the group. "I want to thank you all for going along with Megan's plans. Drew and I really wanted Megan to be a part of the wedding, to feel like she's a part of our love, and these traditions are important to her. If it had been up to me and Drew, we probably would have eloped."

Eloping would have been Drew's first choice, Shayla suspected. Her brother wasn't that excited to be part of big family events, especially when he was the star attraction. He didn't like all the attention. But he would do whatever Ria wanted, because he was madly in love with her. Shayla had never seen her brother as happy as he'd been the last year, and it was such a nice change. Drew had spent a lot of years away from the family when he'd been serving in the Navy, and she knew he'd been through some hard times. Not that he ever talked about those times. Like Reid, he was close-mouthed when it came to his service.

"You should get changed," Ria said. "I don't want to keep your mom waiting."

"What about Grandma?" Shayla asked. "Is she coming to lunch?"

Ria shook her head, a sad gleam in her eyes. "Your mom said your grandmother isn't having a good day, although I guess she started on a new medication a few days ago, and they're hoping it will kick in soon. I know Drew would really like her to be at the ceremony."

"What was the medication?" Shayla asked.

"Sorry I forget the name; it was really long," Ria said.

"No worries. I'll ask Mom about it."

"What's going on with that new drug you were working on in Colombia?" Nicole asked.

"I don't know now. The trial will have to be completely redone." She wished she could say they were closer to finding a drug that would save her grandmother. She'd gone to Colombia with high hopes, but those had been crushed. "But we don't need to talk about that. We're welcoming Ria to the family. That's all that matters."

* * *

After talking to Matt, Reid felt confident that his friend would at least be able to tell him what interest the FBI and State Department had in his brother. For more personal information, he was going to have to do his own digging, and he knew where that digging had to start—at home, the home of his parents, Gregory and Elyse Becker.

He hadn't spoken to them since the day his wedding

was supposed to take place almost eight years ago. He could still remember in vivid, ugly detail the scene between the three of them.

They'd arrived at his apartment just after eight o'clock in the morning, the apartment he'd shared with Lisa for the past six months. He'd been drunk, having spent half the night nursing a bottle of vodka while Matt and Jared tried to talk him off the edge of doing something even more stupid.

When his parents came in, he'd been happy at first, but that had quickly changed.

"It's good you found out now that Lisa can't be trusted," his dad said as his mom gave him a quick hug.

The words went around in his head. He was drunk but not too drunk to realize that his father had pinned everything that had happened on Lisa. He was pissed as hell at her, hated her, in fact, but she hadn't been alone in the coat room at the restaurant where they were having the rehearsal dinner, she'd been with his brother. His twin brother! And that betrayal had hurt just as bad.

"Robert," he bit out. *"He's not blameless. He destroyed my relationship. Don't you get that?"*

"She seduced him," his mother interjected. *"Robert is not experienced with girls the way you are. He got taken in. She used him."*

He stared at her in astonishment. "Are you serious? That's how you see it?"

"Robert was lonely. He's been having a rough time. He was drinking at the rehearsal dinner, and he made a terrible mistake," she said.

"Is that what he told you?"

"It's terrible what happened," his mother said.

"But at least you now know what kind of woman Lisa is," his father added. *"Better to know now."*

"What would have been better is for this not to have happened at all," he replied.

His mom put her hand on his shoulder. *"I know you're hurting, Reid. I'm sorry."*

At last, an apology from someone; it had seemed to take forever for either of them to get to that point.

"Lisa's parents are canceling the wedding," his father said briskly. *"If you need us to make some calls, we will."*

He stared at his father. *"How about you call Robert and tell him how disappointed you are in him, how he betrayed his own brother, how you don't think you can stand to have him in the house ever again? How about making that call? How about letting Robert know that just because he's smart doesn't mean he gets a free pass to do whatever the hell he wants to do."*

His father's jaw tightened. *"This is between you and Robert."*

"You're both our sons," his mom continued. *"We don't want to take sides."*

He stared at them in amazement. Even after what Robert had done, they still couldn't let go of their idealized version of the golden boy. *"You just did,"* he said. *"You can go now."*

"Reid," his mom protested. *"Don't be like that."*

"Like what? Myself? We all know that it's the three of you on one side and me on the other. We've been pretending we're a family for a very long time. But we're not. We never have been, and we never will be."

"Reid, that's not true," she said.

"Come on, Elyse, let him be," his dad said briskly. *"When you want to talk, Reid, come by the house. Our door is always open."*

Their door might have been open, but he'd never stepped through it, never spoken to them since that day.

They'd emailed him over the years. And every once in a while when his mom had begged for him to just let them know he was okay, he'd written a few lines in return. As the years passed, those pleas got less frequent. They'd all gotten used to the distance between them. They'd accepted that that was the way things were going to be.

So why was he considering changing things now?

Because Robert was in trouble, and if there was anyone Robert had confided in, it was probably the two people who had been Robert's biggest cheerleaders since the day he was born. And there was only one person who could get his parents to talk about his brother, and that was him.

So he left San Francisco and headed south on the freeway. It took him almost forty minutes to get to the two-story Spanish-style house in Menlo Park that his parents had called home for thirty-five years. As he drove down the streets of his childhood, Robert's sketches played through his mind.

His brother had certainly captured the essence of their neighborhood, which was middle class suburbia. While Robert's sketches contained demons and monsters, the real town was a lot quieter, even a little dull, but that suited his parents who were also quiet and a little dull.

As he pulled up in front of the house, his stomach began to churn, and he had more than a few second thoughts about what he was about to do.

He glanced up at the front window, the one in which he'd so often seen his brother, including last night in the sketch in Robert's notebook. But there was no familiar face staring through those panes of glass. He wasn't going to find Robert in this house, but hopefully he would find some answers.

He turned off the engine and got out of the truck. He'd

just hit the sidewalk when his father came out the front door. His steps slowed. When he reached the bottom of the steps, his father towered above him.

Gregory Becker was six-foot-five, a long drink of water as his grandmother used to say. At sixty-two, his black hair had peppered with gray, and his skin pulled taut against the strong bones in his face. His father had never been a man to smile much. In fact, he couldn't remember ever seeing his dad laugh at one of his jokes. His mother and Robert had been able to bring a smile to his face. But somehow Reid had never managed to make that happen, and he doubted today would be any different.

He climbed the steps, ignoring the painful cramp in his hamstring as he did so. His leg always felt worse after a long drive, but he was not going to limp in front of his father, no matter what it cost him. The one thing he did have in common with his dad was an excessive amount of stubborn pride.

"Reid," his father said warily as they faced each other. "I'm surprised to see you here."

"I'm surprised to be here. I need to talk to you about Robert."

A glimmer of something passed through his father's eyes. "Really? I didn't think you spoke to your brother anymore."

"I don't. But you do. That's why I'm here."

"What's going on?"

Before he could answer, his mother came through the door. Elyse Becker was also tall and thin, her brown hair and light green eyes matching his own. She was an attractive woman, and he found her long summer dress and sparkly sandals familiar and a little endearing. She'd never been a woman to wear jeans or slacks. It was always about colorful dresses and unique jewelry. The turquoise pendant around her neck reminded him of her Native American heritage. Her father, his grandfather, had made jewelry, and every Christmas he'd given his daughter a new piece.

It was funny the things he remembered now. He'd thought when he saw his parents that all he'd feel was pain and anger, but oddly enough he didn't feel much of anything. The monsters in his head were just two aging human beings.

"Reid," his mother said, a note of wonder in her voice. "I can't believe you're here. Is something wrong?"

"He came to talk about Robert," his father interjected.

The two of them exchanged a quick look, and Reid knew his instincts had been right on the money. His parents knew something.

"Has something happened to Robert?" his mom asked. "I've left several messages for him, and he hasn't returned any of my calls. Have you spoken to him?"

"No, but one of his colleagues is very concerned about him. She asked me to help her find him."

"Are you talking about Shayla Callaway?" his mother asked.

"Yes. Do you know her?"

"We only met once, but Robert has always spoken of her with great fondness. Why don't you come inside, Reid?"

He hesitated, but he'd come this far, he might as well go all the way. "All right."

"Do you want something to drink?" his mother asked as she ushered him into the house. "Or maybe some food?"

"No, thanks."

As he walked into the living room with his parents, he realized nothing much had changed, except that the furniture seemed more worn. In fact, the whole room looked kind of tired. He sat down on the couch next to his mom while his dad took his usual seat on the leather recliner.

For a moment there was nothing but silence in the room.

It wasn't even that awkward, because it seemed like every other conversation he'd had with his parents. Communication had always been difficult.

Clearing his throat, he said, "When is the last time you spoke to Robert?"

Another look passed between his parents, then his mother said, "It was about three weeks ago."

"Anything stand out about that call?"

"Robert was concerned about his research," she replied. "He said he'd found some anomalies that bothered him."

"What kind of anomalies?"

"He didn't get into details, but I could tell that he was upset about something. It was a change from our previous conversations. The past few months he'd been very excited about the new drug he was working on." She paused. "Robert said he was getting close to a breakthrough, a medication that could change people's lives. But the company he was working for wanted results fast, and if they didn't get them, his research grants were going to go away. He felt like he was racing a speeding train."

That was interesting. "Did he call you from Colombia?"

"No, he was back in town for a few days when we spoke," his mom said. "I asked him to come by, but he said he didn't have time. He was meeting with Karl Straitt, one of Abbott's attorneys."

"What about?"

"I don't know. He didn't give me any details." She paused. "I could hear the tension in his voice. And it was worse than it had ever been, even when he was going through his divorce." She stopped abruptly. "I don't know if you know—"

"Yeah, I heard they divorced," he said. "I don't care about that. I'm only interested in Robert's professional relationships."

"Then you need to know something," his father cut in. "Lisa left Robert for Hal Collins, the senior vice president of Abbott Pharmaceuticals, the man who has been responsible for funding most of Robert's research for the last seven years."

"Lisa and Hal moved in together a few months ago," his mom continued. "They're planning a wedding in the fall."

"Is that why Robert's funding is being cut?"

"He did say he thought Hal wanted him out of the company," his mother replied. "But there were other factors."

"The company Robert works for is being courted for a buyout," his father added. "Branson Biotech is interested in acquiring Abbott Pharmaceuticals, and it will make a lot of people very rich if the deal goes through."

"So the company might be sold, and Robert's research grant might be cut—I can see why that would stress him out." What he couldn't see was how any of that put Robert in danger. Then again they were talking about millions of dollars changing hands and greed could always put people in danger. "Is there anything else?" he asked.

"No," his mom said. "But I'm worried. Do you know where Robert is?"

"I have an idea," he said.

"Are you going to find him?"

"I'm not sure yet."

His answer angered them both, and he was reminded

of how many times he'd disappointed them. He got to his feet, intending to leave, but his leg cramped from the sudden movement, and pain shot down his thigh to his ankle. He reached for the arm of the couch to steady himself.

His mother got up and put her hand on his arm. "Reid, are you all right?"

"Fine" he gritted out. "I just need a minute." He prayed for the spasm to subside quickly. After a moment, he was able to sit back down, stretching his leg out on the coffee table.

"What happened to your leg?" his father asked.

"I broke it." He didn't add any details. They didn't want to hear more, and he didn't want to say more.

His mother gave him a concerned look. "Are you going to be all right?"

"Eventually."

"What can I get you?"

"Maybe some water and if you have any ibuprofen."

"I'll get it," his father said, getting up from his chair.

"You're not going back into the Army, are you?" his mom asked as his dad left the room.

"No chance of that," he murmured.

"Good. I won't have to worry every time I read about a soldier killed in action." She paused, frowning at his surprised look. "You think I didn't worry about you, Reid? I'm your mother. I know that our relationship hasn't been what it should have been. That was partly my fault. But I never knew how to handle you when you were young. You were stubborn and headstrong and determined to do the opposite of anything we wanted."

"You're right about that. Robert could do no wrong and I did everything wrong."

"Robert wasn't perfect," she said quietly.

He met her gaze with disbelief. "I can't believe *you* would say that."

"I know you think we let him get away with things, and maybe we did, but that didn't mean we were completely blind to his faults."

That was news to him.

"Looking back, I think both your father and I got caught up in the excitement and wonder of Robert's extreme gift of intelligence," she said. "I wanted to give Robert the opportunities I never had. I couldn't afford to go to the best university or pursue a master's degree because I had to go to work. And while your father had more financial backing than I did when it came to education, he didn't have the brains to achieve all he wanted to achieve. When Robert's teachers told us how special and extraordinary he was, we wanted to make sure he reached his full potential. In a way, I think we both saw Robert as our second chance."

"But not me," he said. "I wasn't going to do anything to make you proud."

"You tried not to do anything to make us proud," she reminded him. "You were always testing us, taking chances, and pushing the limits. Every time you left the house, I was afraid of what you'd do. Your father said you just wanted our attention, and we didn't want to encourage your behavior, so we tried to pretend that we didn't see it. But that didn't work out well, either."

"Well," he said, not sure what to make of what she'd told him. "It might have been nice to have had this conversation about twenty years ago."

"I don't think you were ready until now." She paused, her gaze narrowing. "When Lisa and Robert got together, we probably made the biggest mistake of all. I thought by not choosing sides, we'd be able to keep the family together."

"But you did choose. Robert committed the worst betrayal imaginable, and you let him get away with it."

"We told him we weren't happy," she defended. "But you're right, we should have taken more of a stand."

"You didn't want to lose Robert."

"No, we didn't. It felt like you were already gone, and Robert was all we had left. But I can't say it was easy to be nice to Lisa, to accept her into our family. I hated her, and I was never happier than I was the day Robert told me they were divorcing. I'm so glad she's out of both of your lives. Now that she's gone, I hope that one day we can find a way to be a family again."

"Again?" he asked dryly.

"I suppose that's fair," she conceded. "But as your father and I get older, we realize how little time there is to make things right. I'd given up hope that you would ever want to see us again, but now that you're here, I'm wondering if there is any chance we could start over?"

"I don't know," he said. "Perhaps."

"I guess that's better than a definite no."

"It's funny," he said.

"What is?"

"When I walked in the door, I thought to myself that nothing has changed. You and Dad are living in a time warp. But I was wrong. Something has changed." He paused, meeting her gaze. "Me."

"Have you changed enough to put the past aside and help Robert?"

"I don't know. Possibly. He is my brother. On the other hand, I'm fairly sure that he's about to screw up my life for a second time, and I don't know if I want to go down that road again."

"I don't think you'd be here if you weren't at least

considering going down that road."

"You might be right about that."

"Will you stay for a while, have dinner with us?"

"Not today," he said. This visit had gone far better than expected. He didn't want to push his luck.

Disappointment ran through her eyes. "Of course, I understand."

"But maybe another time," he added.

"Really?" she asked hopefully.

"I do miss your lasagna."

She smiled. "I'll make you a big casserole. Hopefully, Robert can come, too. I would like nothing better than to sit down to dinner with both of my sons. Help me make that happen, Reid."

"We'll see," he said, knowing that he could not make that promise yet. But he was getting closer.

Chapter Ten

As Shayla drove back to her apartment Friday afternoon, she felt decidedly calmer. Lunch with the female members of her family had been filled with fun and humor, and for a few hours, she'd been able to forget about Colombia. She was still worried about Robert, but she felt confident that Reid would help him. Although, she was a little concerned that she hadn't heard from Reid since that morning. She'd thought he would update her with his plans, but maybe that had been a foolish thought. She'd sent him on his way, and unless he wasn't planning to meet Robert, he really had no reason to check in with her.

And she had no good reason to want him to call her, except that she did.

A sigh escaped her lips as she stopped at a light. While she was feeling better, she wished Kari hadn't gone out of town. It would have been nice to have someone else in the apartment to talk to, maybe have dinner with. But she was on her own.

It would be fine. Tomorrow would be busy with the wedding, and hopefully on Sunday Reid would find Robert, and by Monday, all would be good.

Buoyed by her optimistic mental pep talk, she drove down her street, and was happy to find a parking spot not too far away. She turned off the engine, grabbed her bridesmaid's dress and headed into the building. She jogged up the stairs, preferring to avoid the small, creaky elevator that had a tendency to stall between floors. Her good mood lasted until she was about six feet away from her apartment and realized her front door was ajar.

She stopped abruptly. She told herself that this wasn't the first time the door hadn't latched properly. They'd had problems with it before. Kari probably hadn't shut it all the way when she left.

Forcing herself to move forward, she paused by the door and pushed it open a few more inches. She didn't see anyone. Nor did she hear anything. She waited another minute and then opened the door all the way. The living room was empty.

"Kari?" she said loudly. "Are you home?"

There was no answer. No movement. No sound whatsoever.

She pulled out her phone as she walked toward the hallway and put in 9-1-1. She was ready to hit connect at the first sign of a problem.

Kari's bedroom door was open. The covers on her bed were on the floor. Her dresser drawers had clearly been searched with piles of clothes spilling out of them.

As Shayla moved down the hall, she found more chaos in her bedroom. The scene was very similar to the one she'd seen in Robert's office last night.

Her chest got so tight she could barely breathe.

Someone had been in her room.

Someone had gone through her drawers, touched her things.

She felt completely violated. Backing out of the room, she walked quickly down the hall, her hand still gripping her phone. She wanted to call the police but she knew this wasn't an ordinary burglary. This was about Robert and

Colombia.

Nausea rolled up from her stomach, sending a bitter taste to her tongue. She ran out of the apartment and didn't stop running until she got into her car. Once inside, she punched in Reid's number, praying he would answer.

"Shayla?" he said quickly. "Everything all right?"

Relief swept through her at the sound of his voice. "Someone broke into my apartment."

"Are you all right?"

"I'm shaken. I wasn't home at the time. They're gone now. But I don't know if they're coming back."

"Where are you?"

"Sitting in my car out front. Should I call the police?"

"Wait for me. I'll be there in fifteen minutes. Don't go back inside until I get there."

"Don't worry, I'm not going anywhere," she said, checking again to make sure her car doors were locked. "Just hurry, okay."

As she hung up the phone, she looked in the rearview mirror. The street was quiet, but there were a bunch of cars parked down the block, and she couldn't tell if any of them were occupied. She drilled her fingers on her thighs and tried to breathe naturally. It was broad daylight. She would be fine. It was just going to be a really long fifteen minutes.

* * *

Reid made it to Shayla's apartment in twelve minutes. As he pulled up behind her car, she got out and ran to him. For a moment he thought she was going to throw herself in his arms, but she skidded to a stop in front of him.

"Thanks for coming," she said, wrapping her arms around her body. "Robert was so insistent that I not call the police, I didn't know what to do."

"Give me your keys. I'll check it out."

"I'll come with you."

"You can stay out here. Just get in the car and lock the doors."

"I'd rather stay with you. I've been jumping every time someone comes down the street. I know whoever searched my place is probably long gone, but I can't seem to stop reacting to every shadow."

"I get it. Come on then."

"The door was open when I came home," Shayla said as they entered the building and walked up the stairs. "It doesn't always latch, so I wasn't that concerned at first. But when I saw the state of the bedrooms, I knew someone had been inside." She slid her key into the lock and opened the door.

Shayla stayed right behind him, her hand on his back, as he entered her roommate's bedroom and then hers.

"What do you think they were looking for?" Shayla asked as they returned to the living room.

"Did you bring home anything from the clinic in Colombia?"

"No. I never went back to the clinic after we were rescued. When we were evacuated, we were given ten minutes to grab our clothes before we were put on a plane."

"So you did leave with a suitcase?"

"With jeans and t-shirts in it."

"Nothing else? No trinkets? Souvenirs? Books? Photos?"

She frowned at his series of questions. "No. There wasn't a shopping mall nearby. We were in a very remote part of the country."

"Then maybe they came here to look for Robert's notebook."

"They wouldn't have seen us take the notebook out of the office. You had it under your shirt when we left. I don't think it would have been visible to the security cameras."

"No, but the cameras picked us up. If someone was watching the traffic to Robert's office, they would have seen us go inside."

"But for someone to watch those security cameras, they'd have to be able to get access, and who would have those credentials? I can't imagine anyone at the hospital doing this, unless the police or the FBI or someone else is involved."

"And we know they are. When will your roommate be home?"

"Not until next Wednesday. She's going out of town."

"Good. I think you need to get out of town, too."

"That's impossible. My brother is getting married tomorrow, and if I don't show up, the Callaways will call out the cavalry."

"I don't think you should stay here, Shayla. Maybe you should go to your parents' house or spend the night with one of your siblings."

"If I go to anyone's house, they'll ask questions, a lot of questions that I can't answer. And won't I be putting them in danger?"

"I don't think you're necessarily in danger," he said quickly. "If someone wanted to get to you, they could have done it before now. The fact that they waited until you were gone to come in and search your apartment is a good thing."

"Is it?" she asked in bewilderment. "That's some pretty positive spin from a cynical man."

She had a point.

"What about your boat?" she asked. "Can I sleep on your couch?"

Her suggestion made his gut clench for an entirely different reason. His boat was even smaller than this apartment, and the idea of her in his bed...

"I don't think that's a good idea," he said.

"Why not?"

"Things already got out of hand this morning, remember?"

She met his gaze head on. "I haven't forgotten, Reid, but that won't happen again. I was half asleep, and so were you."

He couldn't make being half asleep an excuse. He was attracted to Shayla, to her intriguing mix of logic and emotion, brains and beauty. But she wasn't a woman to just mess around with and walk away, and that's the only kind of woman he got close to these days.

"Come on, Reid. You're not going to say no, are you?" Shayla asked, a plea in her pretty blue eyes.

As if he could say no to anything she asked.

Before he could reply, the buzzer to her front door rang. Shayla almost jumped out of her skin. "Who's that?" she whispered.

"You're not expecting anyone?"

She shook her head.

He moved to the window, being careful not to be seen by anyone out on the street. He couldn't see who was standing at the front door, but he could see a dark sedan parked in front of the building. He backed away from the window.

"Did you see someone, Reid?"

"I think the feds have come to question you again, or maybe the local cops. Hard to say."

"Should I let them in?"

He debated that as the buzzer pealed again. "Let's not."

"Someone else might let them into the building if they start buzzing other apartments. It's happened before. People don't care that much about security."

"Let's wait. If they're on the right side of the law, they won't try to enter without a search warrant."

"And if they're not?"

He didn't want to have to answer that question. He really wished he had a weapon with him.

The buzzer rang again.

Shayla moved next to him, and he put his arm around her. They waited another two minutes, but no footsteps came down the hall, no knock came at the door.

"Right side of the law?" she murmured.

He nodded. "Looks that way." He went back to the window. The sedan was pulling away from the curb with two men inside. "They're gone. Get whatever you need for the night, and let's go."

"Okay."

While Shayla grabbed her things, he pulled out his phone and called Matt. "We need to meet."

"Where and when?" Matt asked, without bothering to ask why.

"Twenty minutes, my favorite place."

"Got it."

"Who were you talking to?" Shayla asked as he slipped his phone back into his pocket.

"Someone who might be able to help us."

She stared back at him with concern. "You weren't supposed to tell anyone, Reid. Robert was very emphatic about that."

"No, *you* weren't supposed to tell anyone. My job is to actually find a way to save Robert, and for that I'm going to need a little help."

"Where are we going?"

"You'll see when we get there."

* * *

They took Reid's truck to the meeting. While Reid drove with a lot of speed, Shayla didn't feel at all nervous. There was something about Reid that made her believe he could do anything. That was probably a dangerous feeling to have, and more than likely untrue, but right now she found it a comforting thought.

They ended up north of San Francisco in the Marin Headlands, on a magnificent bluff that overlooked the city of San Francisco. While the area would be crowded on the weekends, on a Friday afternoon, they had the scenic spot to themselves.

She followed Reid down a path to a bench that had an incredible view of the Golden Gate Bridge, and the Pacific Ocean flowing into the bay.

"Nice," she murmured.

"I've always liked this view of the city," he said as they sat down on the bench. "This is one of my favorite places."

"I can see why, but I've actually seen a better view of the city than this one."

His eyebrow shot up in disbelief. "There's a better one?"

"Yes, from a helicopter flying in from the ocean and over the bridge. My brother, Drew, is a helicopter pilot. He took me up a few months ago. It was amazing." She paused. "You and Drew would probably get along. He was in the Navy for eight years."

"And he jumped to the Coast Guard? Why?"

"I'm not sure. He said he wanted to be closer to home, but maybe there were other reasons. He's not a big talker, especially when it comes to his years in the Navy."

Reid nodded. "Understandable."

"Is it?" she questioned. "Why can't you talk about what you went through?"

He met her eyes with a steady gaze. "Do you really need to ask me that after what you went through in Colombia?"

"That wasn't the same thing." But wasn't it close enough? And hadn't she found it impossible to talk to anyone in her family about what had happened? "You're right, maybe it is the same."

"There are a couple of reasons for not talking. You don't want to burden the people you care about. It's difficult enough carrying around your own memories. You also don't want to relive the experience by sharing it. And maybe you want to try to forget it ever happened."

"Is there a lot you're trying to forget, Reid?" She couldn't help wondering how all those years in the Army had impacted him. He had to have a lot more nightmares running around in his head.

"Too much," he said, gazing out at the view.

"Why did you stay in the Army so long? Surely you could have gotten out a long time ago?"

"Sure, I could have left, but I'm a soldier. That's who I am."

"It's who you were," she corrected, then wished she'd kept the comment to herself as Reid's eyes filled with anger. "Sorry, that was thoughtless."

"No, it was accurate," he said harshly. "I'm not a soldier anymore."

"You can't go back when your leg is fully healed?"

"No, I'm done." There was not a speck of doubt in his voice.

"So, what's next?"

He let out a heavy sigh. "That's the question of the

year. I don't know. Maybe private security."

"What does that involve?"

"I'm not sure."

"You might want to find out before you sign up."

"That would probably be a good idea. My friend, Matt Kelton, runs the company. We served together for a few years. He's a good guy. He seems to think I could offer him something, although I'm not sure what."

"I'm sure you could offer him a lot. I know it sucks to not be able to do what you love, Reid. But while you may have lost some mobility in your leg, you still have your head and your heart. You're still you, just a different version of you. Maybe even a better one. Did you ever think about that?"

He turned to look at her, a thoughtful gleam in his eyes. "You don't feel sorry for me at all, do you?"

She shook her head. "Not really. I have empathy for you. I'm sure it's going to take you a while to figure out your next move. But you will, because you're not a quitter. And I don't think you're going to quit on your life."

"Some might say that's what I've been doing the last nine months."

"Let's just call that a break," she said, certain that Reid would never live an idle life forever. He had too much drive. He cared too much. Not that he'd ever admit it. "But the break is over," she added. "It's time to get back in the game. You already know that."

"I do," he agreed. "But you might need to take your own advice, Doc, and get back in your own game."

She sighed as she glanced out at the ocean, her thoughts turning to her own problems, her own doubts.

"When did you know you wanted to be a doctor?" Reid asked.

"When I was seven years old."

"Very early achiever."

She smiled as she looked back at him. "I had a reason. I was playing in the backyard with my cousin, Allison. We had a big play structure with slides and tunnels. My parents put it in so that they wouldn't have to take eight kids to the park every day. The boys usually hogged the fort, but that day it was just Allison and I. Allison was climbing on to the slide, and her foot slipped. She tumbled off the side and onto the ground. She was holding her wrist and screaming with pain, and her knee was all bloody. I wanted to help her, but I didn't know what to do. Luckily, my mom did. She took Allison and me to the E.R. While Allison was getting her broken arm set in a cast and the gash in her leg stitched up, I was watching the nurses and doctors rushing around. I decided right then that was what I wanted to do."

"I guess the sight of blood didn't bother you."

"Not then," she said. "Now…I'm afraid I'll never be able to go into an examining room without worrying about the door blowing open and someone coming in with a gun."

"It's going to get better, Shayla."

"I want to believe that. I thought I was a strong person, that I was brave and fearless. When I was younger, I was never afraid to try something new, to risk failure, but I think that's because I never really thought I would fail. Now I can't imagine any other scenario. In Colombia, I realized I wasn't invincible or unbreakable."

He nodded, an understanding gleam in his eyes. "I know that shocking feeling. But you didn't break, Shayla. You're just a little bent."

"I'm practically doubled over."

"But not broken," he said. "You have to stop punishing yourself for what you perceive as your failure to save your patient, Shayla."

"It was my failure. I should have found a way to get to him."

"You need to stop focusing on what you didn't do then and what you can do now, because you're still alive. You couldn't save that man, but you can save other people, lots of other people."

"If my hand stops shaking."

He reached out and covered her hand with his. A jolt of heat ran through her. "It will, as soon as you decide you've punished yourself enough."

"I hope that's true. I've spent the last ten years of my life in pursuit of this goal. I don't want it to be all for nothing."

"Then don't let it be for nothing. You've been knocked down. It's time to get back up. The only way you'll ever banish the fears is to face them." He let go of her hand and cupped her face, holding her gaze to his. "You're stronger than you think, Shayla. My grandfather always told me that steel is forged in fire, and he was right." He smiled as his thumb ran across her mouth. "Sometimes I can see the steel in your eyes, the prettiest blue steel I've ever seen."

She caught her breath at his words, at the intense look on his face.

Desire crackled the air between them.

Reid lowered his head. She leaned in. They met in the middle. It was the most perfect kiss. Tender, passionate, and filled with promise. The warm summer breeze blew around them, and for just a moment she let all of her troubles slip away.

Then a black Porsche sped into the parking lot, kicking up a whirlwind of dust. They broke apart.

Reid jumped to his feet, and she quickly followed.

"Tell me that's your friend," she said. With the cliff

behind them, there was nowhere to run.

Chapter Eleven

"That's Matt," Reid said, as a man stepped out of the car. "He always did like showy cars."

Shayla blew out a breath as Matt walked towards them with a confident step. Like Reid, Matt Kelton was a very attractive man in his early thirties. If she hadn't known he was a security consultant, she might have picked him for a musician. His dark brown hair was long and fell into his face as he walked. As he got closer, he gave them both a friendly and curious smile.

"Matt Kelton, Shayla Callaway," Reid said, making the introductions.

Matt gave her hand a shake. "Nice to meet you."

"You, too," she murmured.

"Thanks for meeting us out here," Reid said.

"No problem. What's this about?"

"Shayla worked with my brother in Colombia. He contacted her on Thursday morning asking for my help."

"She was your source," Matt said with a nod. "I'm not surprised. And I already knew who she was."

"You did?" Shayla asked, surprised by his words.

Matt nodded. "Reid asked me to look into Robert's

activities over the last few months. You were part of his team, therefore you were part of the research."

She wasn't sure she liked the idea of someone digging into her life, but these days privacy seemed to be the least of her problems.

"There seem to be eyes and ears on Shayla," Reid said. "Someone tossed her apartment, and she got a visit from law enforcement. We didn't answer the door, and apparently they didn't have a warrant, because they took off after a few minutes. I'm hoping you can tell me what we're dealing with."

"I'm a miracle worker, but I usually need more than a few hours," Matt said.

"Really. I thought a few minutes would be enough with all your advanced technology."

Matt tipped his head. "Fair point. Here's what I can tell you so far."

"Robert's company, Abbott Pharmaceutical, has drawn the interest of a suitor, Branson Biotech. The owner of Branson has a sister suffering from Alzheimer's, making his interest in Abbott's new wonder drug both personal and professional. If the buyout goes through, the executives at Abbott will be very, very rich. However, Branson is also interested in a rival company, Hanover Chemical. They're in direct competition with Abbott and are working on a similar drug."

"But Hanover is behind Abbott in their development," Shayla cut in. "Or at least they were before the clinical trial in Colombia was wiped out."

"Exactly," Matt said. "Now Hanover may have the edge over Abbott."

Shayla frowned. "Are you saying that what happened at the clinic in Colombia was the result of some sort of pharmaceutical company war? I thought it was random. I thought it was local. That's what everyone said."

"It was certainly made to look that way," Matt replied. "But that's just one scenario I'm considering."

"What else?" Reid asked, his voice grim. "Why are federal agencies involved in this?"

"Abbott Pharmaceuticals apparently asked the FBI for help in locating your brother. They're concerned that he might have been killed in Colombia, or that he's been kidnapped. The State Department is also investigating, using some of their agents in South America."

"That doesn't explain why anyone would search Shayla's apartment," Reid said. "Or Robert's office for that matter. Neither of those searches looked like they were authorized by anyone."

"I don't know anything about that yet, however..." Matt paused. "I'm not sure I should tell you the rest. It has to do with Lisa."

Shayla saw the two men exchange a pained look. Matt obviously knew about Reid's past.

"Say whatever it is," Reid instructed.

"Lisa moved in with Hal Collins, a senior executive at Abbott right after Christmas. Shortly thereafter, Robert's research grant was cut in half. It looks like Robert was going to be on his way out once the trial was over," Matt said. "Clearly, Hal wasn't interested in keeping his new girlfriend's ex-husband on the payroll. But he couldn't get rid of Robert without jeopardizing the trial and the buyout." Matt paused, giving Reid a puzzled look. "You don't seem surprised."

"My parents already told me about Lisa and the new guy."

Shayla was surprised to hear that Reid had spoken to his parents. "When did you speak to them?"

"Earlier today."

"I thought you didn't talk to them."

"I made an exception."

"Had they heard from Robert?"

"Not for a few weeks. They were concerned. They basically told me everything Matt just said."

"Did you tell them Robert called me?" she asked.

Reid shook his head. "No. I was only there to get information, not provide it."

"How did your meeting with them go?" Matt asked. "It's been a long time, hasn't it?"

"Since the wedding that never happened," he said tersely.

"Have they changed?"

"No. But maybe I have." Reid blew out a breath. "Is there anything else you can tell me, Matt?"

"Not yet. I'll keep you posted. In the meantime, be careful."

"I always am," Reid said.

Matt laughed. "You're almost never careful, Becker."

Reid tipped his head. "Fine, I'll be careful."

Matt turned to Shayla. "You're in good hands. This guy is one of the best."

"I'm beginning to realize that," she murmured.

Matt strode briskly back to his car and took off with the same whirlwind of dust that he'd created when he pulled in. As the dirt settled, they walked back to Reid's truck.

"What are you thinking?" she asked, seeing a frown on his face.

"That I need to do something I don't want to do."

"What's that?"

"Talk to Lisa."

She was a little shocked by his words. "Seriously? I can't believe you'd consider that after what she did to you."

"Believe me, she's the last person I want to see. But she's probably the only one who knows the relationship between Robert and Abbott Pharmaceuticals."

"And you think she'd talk to you about it now that she's involved with this other guy?"

"She might. If I give her what she wants."

"Which is what?"

"A chance to say she's sorry."

"Are you sure that's what she wants to say to you?" she asked doubtfully.

"Well, she did at one time."

"A long time ago," Shayla said. "Do you really want to stir up those old feelings?"

"I'm not worried about feelings. But let's table this for the moment. I'm hungry. What about you?"

"I could eat."

"Then let's eat."

"I feel like we should be doing something more important."

"Staying strong is important. And I always think more clearly when I'm not hungry."

"All right," she said. A meal would be a nice way to postpone going back to Reid's cozy houseboat.

It had been her idea to stay with him, but as the night loomed ahead, she was beginning to think that might have been her worst idea yet.

* * *

"You love the water, don't you?" Shayla asked, as they sat a table on the patio deck of Paulie's Pizza in downtown Sausalito, sharing a pitcher of beer, and waiting for their pizza to arrive. "You're never too far away from it. You even sleep on it."

"It's very peaceful, like a rocking chair," he said with a smile. "I missed the water when I was in the Middle East. That hot desert made me long for water. The sand was everywhere, in my eyes, in my hair. Sometimes I'd wake up with sand in my mouth. You could shower for days and still feel dirty."

"Sounds horrible."

"It certainly was a different landscape," he said.

"So tell me something, Reid."

"What's that, Shayla?" he asked with a smile.

She liked his lighthearted mood. It was a nice change. "Does the Army recruit out of GQ Magazine, because you, Matt and your buddy Jared from the bar are all very attractive."

"That is a pre-requisite," he said with a nod.

"And no one is married?"

"Of the three of us, no, but some of our other buddies, yes."

"And some of those other buddies work for Matt?"

"They do."

"Maybe you should seriously consider joining them. Matt seems like a smart, capable guy. And a small, private organization can probably move a lot faster than the Army, not to mention their ability to bend the rules and blur the lines, something you'd probably enjoy."

"You are a smart girl," he said, tapping her beer mug with his.

"That's what my IQ scores say."

"I wasn't talking about your IQ but about your ability to read people, assess situations."

"That's part of my training as a doctor. Patients can't always tell you what's wrong, so you have to read their body language. You have to try to figure out where the real pain is coming from. For example, you think your pain is coming from your leg."

"I don't think that. I know it. I can show you the scar."

"Actually, the pain is coming from your heart."

"That's not the right diagnosis, Doc."

She ignored him, knowing that she was stepping into sensitive territory, but she couldn't stop herself. "You're not drinking every night because your leg hurts, Reid. You're mourning the loss of your career, your sense of self. You don't like to accept failure, and your body has failed you."

"Well, that's true. I do need to find a way to move on," he conceded.

"You're already moving on. And it's because of me," she said, giving him a smug smile.

He smiled back. "Really? You're taking all the credit?"

"I got you out of the bar, didn't I?"

"And almost got me killed."

"But I got you thinking about something besides yourself."

"And almost got me interrogated by the FBI."

"I'm sure it wouldn't have been your first time. You should be thanking me for interrupting your pity party."

"It was not that bad."

"It looked pretty bad to me. When I first saw you in the bar, I couldn't believe that your brother had sent me to you, that you were supposed to save the day. You did not look like a hero at that moment."

"What does a hero look like?"

"I don't know exactly; but I think they shave more than once a week."

He rubbed his grizzly jaw. "Some women find this sexy."

She refused to admit that she was one of those

women. Thankfully, their pizza arrived, and their focus turned to food.

"You eat fast," Reid commented as she finished off her second slice.

She wiped her mouth with her napkin. "I'm the youngest of eight kids. I learned early on to get in fast and stake my claim."

"I wondered about the three pieces you put on your plate."

"I figured you for a fast eater, too. I wanted to make sure I had enough."

"I used to be faster," he said. "I'm trying to take more time with everything in my life, including food. The leg injury has forced me to slow down, and I'm starting to appreciate the new pace of my life."

"Really?" she asked doubtfully, picking up her next slice. "If I'd been living your life and ended up where you are now, I'd be bored out of my mind."

He smiled. "I can't get anything by you, can I?"

"Maybe it's time to stop trying. I understand men with bigger-than-life ambitions and drive. I grew up with a lot of them."

"The Callaways do sound impressive. So tell me again why you can't ask one of your bigger-than-life brothers to watch over you tonight?"

"I already told you—too many questions, followed by worry, then interference. That's not going to help Robert."

"You really want to help him, don't you? Are you sure you're not a little in love with my brother?"

The question was light, but there was a serious note behind his words. "Not even the tiniest bit," she said firmly. "I respect him. I admire him. But I am not in love with him, and I have never ever wanted to kiss him, not when he was married, and not after he got divorced."

"I wonder if Robert feels the same way about you. He obviously trusts you. You were the only person he called for help."

"I'm pretty sure he thinks of me as a little sister, and sometimes an annoying one. I asked him a lot of questions when we were in Colombia, and he was irritated with me. He told me to just do the work I was assigned and stop asking questions." Her words brought an odd gleam into Reid's eyes. "What are you thinking?"

"Just considering whether it was simple annoyance or if Robert didn't want you asking questions for another reason."

"Maybe." She hadn't considered that before, but in view of what had happened, she did wonder if Robert had been secretive for some other reason. She set down her pizza. "Do you think I'm in danger, Reid?"

He met her gaze. "I hope not."

"That's not very reassuring."

"You've been back in San Francisco for a week. You've been on your own, and nothing has happened. That's a good sign."

"You're forgetting about the car that almost ran us down. Unless, you think now that was a drunk driver?"

"The jury is out on that, but until we know for sure, I think we should stick together, at least until I can meet up with Robert."

"So you've decided to go."

"Still under consideration."

"You are so frustrating," she said with a groan. "Why can't you just commit?"

"Because I don't know what Robert is involved in. You may think he's some innocent victim, but I'm not so sure."

"I don't think that's why you're hesitating. But I can't

force you to make a promise you don't want to make."

"Like I said before, I only make promises I'm sure I can keep. And I have until Sunday to decide." He paused. "Which means you're stuck with me for at least another twenty-four hours. If you don't want to stay with your family, then you and I are going to be spending a lot of time together."

"Then I hope you have a tux."

He raised an eyebrow. "Why is that?"

"Because tomorrow we're going to my brother's wedding."

Chapter Twelve

On the way back to his houseboat, Reid tried to think of a reason why he couldn't take Shayla to her brother's wedding, but he still hadn't come up with a good one by the time they arrived. While he didn't want to believe that Shayla was in danger, he didn't like what he'd seen at her apartment, and until he knew for sure she was safe, he was going to stay close.

Unfortunately, staying close was also a problem.

As Shayla sat down on his couch, he was reminded of another couch, of how he'd felt earlier that day when they'd woken up in each other's arms. But that wasn't going to happen again. He would put Shayla in his bed tonight and leave her alone.

But the idea of Shayla in his bed, her long blonde hair flowing over his pillows, was an unsettling thought. How the hell was he going to keep his hands off of her?

Especially when Shayla wasn't that good about keeping her hands off of him. He knew it wouldn't take much persuasion to get her into bed with him, because they'd already lit the sparks. But he knew better than anyone what the aftermath of a bad fire looked like, and he didn't want to put Shayla through that. Or maybe he didn't want to put himself through that.

"Do you want something to drink?" he asked, opening the fridge. "I've got two beers left."

"No thanks. I'm full from the pizza. I haven't felt like eating much since I got back from Colombia, but tonight I was suddenly starving."

"I noticed. You ate more than half the pizza," he said, grabbing a bottle of beer.

"Are you complaining that you didn't get enough to eat?"

"Just stating a fact. I actually like a woman who eats."

"Well, I do eat."

He sat down across from her, realizing how small his boat was when there were two people on it. He'd had a few women on board, but they'd spent all their time in his bed, and he hadn't been looking for things to talk about.

"What do you do at night?" Shayla asked, as if she were reading his mind. "I don't see a television."

"I go on the computer. I read. I have sex," he said with a grin.

"Only one of those activities surprises me. You read? I thought you prided yourself on being the brawn in your family."

"Well, I'm not reading encyclopedias."

"Too bad. They can be very interesting." She leaned over and pulled a paperback novel off the table by the couch. "So you're a science fiction buff?"

"I like different genres."

She flipped the book over and read the blurb. "From the dark shadow of potential destruction comes an unexpected savior." She looked over at him with a smile. "I thought you said that you and Robert didn't have anything in common."

"We don't."

"He draws graphic novels, and you read them."

Reid frowned. "I think old Walt left that behind when he sold me the boat."

"Are you going to blame everything interesting I find in this place on old Walt?" she teased.

"Maybe. Let's talk about you and your twin for a change. Do you have a lot in common with—what was his name?"

"Colton. And, no, not that much in common. We're a little like you and Robert in reverse. I was the brainy one. Colton liked the action. We were four years younger than our nearest sibling, so we were always a little isolated from the rest of the group and we were always called out together as the twins. Sometimes I wasn't sure everyone in the family knew my name."

Her words were light, but he could hear the emotion behind them. "That must have bothered you a little."

"I wouldn't say bother. It was just the way it was. It made Colton and I even closer. We played together all the time. Colton could always make me laugh. He has a wicked sense of humor. He worries about nothing and I worry about everything. This probably won't surprise you, but I'm kind of a serious girl."

"Yeah, I got that."

"What kind of women do you like? Wait, let me guess. You like women who are looking for a good time, no strings attached."

"Bingo." He raised his beer to her.

"Are you sure that's what the women are looking for?" she challenged. "Or what you're looking for?"

"It's a mutual thing, Doc, a meeting of similar minds. I haven't broken anyone's heart."

"Is that because you haven't gotten close enough to

anyone to break their heart?"

He took a long swig of his beer, her questions getting a little too personal. "Love is overrated."

She gave him a thoughtful look. "I don't think so."

"Well, you wouldn't. You're a romance and flowers kind of girl."

"No one has ever given me flowers."

"That can't be true."

"It is true."

"Then you've been picking the wrong boyfriends."

"I've only had two guys that I could call boyfriends, and neither of those relationships lasted longer than a few months. I guess we never got to the flowers part."

"Did they break your heart?"

She slowly shook her head. "One of them put a dent in it."

"Sorry."

She shrugged. "That's what life is about, right?" She paused. "I know you fell in love at least once. You asked a girl to marry you. The man of no commitment was willing to promise forever."

"Yeah, that guy is gone."

"You didn't deserve what Lisa and Robert did to you."

"No, I did not," he agreed.

"How did you meet Lisa in the first place?"

He groaned. "I don't really want to talk about her."

"Well, you're the one who doesn't have a television," she pointed out. "And I'm not a fan of science fiction. So just talk to me."

"I met her at a birthday party when I was home on leave. Her best friend was involved with one of my friends. Lisa was attractive, and she liked me, which I was happy about." He'd also enjoyed her crazy passion. They'd gone to bed that first night and didn't spend a night apart for the next three weeks.

"How long were you together before you got engaged?" Shayla asked.

"About a month."

She raised an eyebrow. "No way. A month? That's impulsive. And that doesn't seem at all like you."

"Looking back I can see where I might have given it more thought. But I was going to deploy, and I didn't want to leave her behind without putting a ring on her finger. I wanted to seal the deal, so to speak. Lisa seemed to want the same thing."

"What do you think changed? There had to be a reason why she hooked up with your brother right before the wedding. And to do it in such a public way—it almost seems like one of them wanted you to find them."

He blew out a breath, wishing Shayla wasn't so perceptive. "I think Lisa wanted out, but she was afraid to tell me."

"Or," Shayla began. "She might have wanted to make sure she had your brother before she said goodbye to you, hedge her bets. I think she did the same thing to Robert. She wasn't divorced five minutes before she was moving in with her new man. She'd obviously gotten involved with him before she left Robert. I don't think she likes to be alone."

"She doesn't. Her father died when she was a little girl. And her mother remarried a couple of times. Lisa told me that every time her mother moved on to a new man, she felt like she was being left behind."

Shayla's brows drew together. "That's a little sad."

"I think as my deployment drew near, Lisa got scared. The reality of my being a soldier sank in. She started to worry about moving to the post, leaving her friends behind, waiting for me to come home."

Shayla nodded. "And being afraid you wouldn't come home, that you'd die and leave her alone like her father did."

"It seems so clear now," he said, settling back in his chair. "It took me a lot longer to figure it out than you just did."

"Well, I wasn't involved with her in the same way. I've seen her from a distance. I've heard Robert talk about her. Actually, I understand her a little better now that you've told me her story." She paused. "But Lisa should have broken up with you. She was a coward for doing what she did. It was inexcusable."

"What about Robert?" he challenged.

"Same thing," she said, meeting his gaze, not a hint of indecision in her blue eyes. "I care a lot about Robert, but what he did was wrong." She shook her head. "I just wish I could figure out what his motive was. It does seem out of character for him. Not only the fact that he hooked up with your fiancée but because he did it in the coatroom. I mean, that is not Robert. He's not that impetuous, that passionate."

"He was that night."

"Did you ever ask him why he did it?"

"No. I haven't talked to him since that day. I didn't care why, Shayla. Because his reasons didn't matter."

"I understand. But maybe when this is all over, you should try to talk to him. Maybe things will be different now, like they were when you saw your parents earlier."

He didn't think that was possible. "I'd rather leave the past alone. It was all a long time ago."

"True. But it's not over."

"It is over. I'm not holding some torch for Lisa. I have moved on with my life many times."

"Oh, I'm sure you have moved on many times, if only

to prove to yourself that you were done with Lisa."

"I was not proving anything to anyone," he argued. "You don't know everything, Shayla."

"Okay, fine." She waved her hand in the air. "I don't know everything, but I do know one thing for sure."

"What's that?"

"You're going to have to talk to Lisa again. Not about the past, but about what's happening now."

He wished he could say she was wrong, but she wasn't. "Yeah, I know."

"You should do it tomorrow, first thing, get it out of the way. But you cannot tell her that Robert has been in contact with me. You just have to be the concerned brother."

"You think she's going to believe that?"

Shayla shrugged. "I'm betting she'll be so rattled by your sudden appearance at her door that she won't have time to consider your motives."

"Probably true. I'll go in the morning, and you're coming with me."

"Oh, no, I do not need to be present for that. And I promised Robert I wouldn't talk to her."

"Don't worry, we're not going to tell her you talked to Robert, but you are his friend, and I think your presence will keep us off the personal track." He smiled at her frustrated look. "Now who's right?"

"You are," she said grumpily.

He smiled. "It's only fair. You're going to make me dance at a wedding, you're going to have to sit through what will undoubtedly be a very uncomfortable conversation with my ex-fiancée."

"All right, it's a deal. But you actually have to dance with me, you know. No hanging out at the bar drinking whiskey shots and picking up the single ladies."

"Well, now you're just getting mean," he drawled.

"I call it like I see it." She paused, looking around for her bag. "Speaking of calling, I need to tell Ria that I'm bringing a date. I hope it won't throw off the numbers."

"You go ahead. I'm going to sit outside for a while. Make yourself at home."

* * *

Shayla blew out a breath when Reid left. She was happy he'd decided to get some air. Things had gotten pretty personal the last few minutes. While she'd liked getting to know him better, the interior of the boat was very small, warm, cozy, and she was way too aware of Reid. It was one of the reasons she'd kept talking. She'd been trying to distract herself from throwing herself at him.

Wasn't she the one who'd told him it could never happen between them?

She didn't want to be a liar.

She also needed to remember that Reid was only with her because she'd asked for his help. He was a natural born protector. He would protect anyone the way he was protecting her. It wasn't special. He was just that kind of guy.

The kind of guy she could really, really like.

With a sigh, she pulled out her cell phone and called Ria. She hated to bother her the night before the wedding, but she didn't want to show up with Reid without telling anyone first. That would only raise more questions.

"Hi, it's Shayla," she said when Ria answered the phone. "I'm sorry to bother you."

"You're not bothering me at all. Megan and I are having a girls' night before the big day."

"Well, I won't keep you from it. I was wondering if

it's at all possible for me to bring a date tomorrow to the wedding. I know it's last minute, but I wasn't sure he'd be able to come, and now he is. I don't need to eat if we're short on food or anything."

"Don't be silly, Shayla. Of course, you can bring someone. It's a casual buffet. One more won't make a difference."

"That's great."

"I didn't know you were seeing anyone."

"It's kind of new. I don't want to make a big deal out of it."

"If you're bringing him to the wedding, it's going to be a big deal," Ria said. "Not with me but with your family. They like to vet all potential newcomers to the Callaway clan."

"Reid isn't going to be part of the clan. He's just going to be my date tomorrow. That's it."

"Well, you never know where one date will lead."

Judging by the dreamy tone in Ria's voice, she was thinking about Drew. "I'm really happy for you and my brother," she said.

"I'm happy, too. You never know when you're going to meet the right person, Shayla. The first night I met Drew I knew I liked him, but I didn't think we would ever see each other again. Yet somehow, months later, on an entirely different continent, we found each other."

"It must have been fate," she said.

"Maybe. Although, Drew likes to tell me that I picked San Francisco because he'd told me he was stationed there."

"Perhaps you did," she said.

"It's possible, but I thought the odds of us meeting in such a big city were a million to one. Turns out I was wrong, and I'm so glad about that, because your brother is amazing."

"I know, but don't keep telling him that. His head is big enough already. I'll see you tomorrow, Ria."

"Yes, and I can't wait to meet your new man. If you're bringing him around the family, then he must be something special."

"He's something all right," she murmured, as she ended the call.

She put her phone into her bag and pulled out her laptop computer. She was happy she'd had the computer in her bag when she was at lunch. It might have gotten taken if she'd left it in her apartment.

Reid's Internet was locked, so she used the personal hotspot on her phone to go online. She checked her emails first. They were piling up fast. She hadn't written anyone back since she'd come home. She skimmed the list to see if there was anything out of the ordinary but there was nothing.

Tapping her fingers lightly on the keys, she debated her next move. On impulse she typed Reid's name into the search engine. He didn't come up on Facebook and Twitter. Apparently, he wasn't on social media. But he was named in several news articles, the most recent from eight months ago. She clicked on the link and was shocked to see a photograph of the President of the United States placing a medal around Reid's neck.

She read through the article with amazement.

On behalf of congress, Army Specialist Reid Becker is awarded the Medal of Honor for distinguishing himself by acts of gallantry and bravery at the risk of his life above and beyond the call of duty during combat operations against an armed enemy in Nuristan Province, Afghanistan. While under attack from an estimated two hundred enemy fighters employing concentrated fire from rifles, rocket propelled grenades, anti-aircraft machine guns, and small arms fire, Specialist Becker ran twice through a gauntlet of enemy fire to rescue two members of his unit and defend an isolated position, singlehandedly beating back an assault force for over two hours, even after being hit twice in the leg and suffering massive blood loss.

"Holy crap." She'd already realized that her first impression of Reid had been wrong, but she'd never imagined it was *this* wrong. The Medal of Honor was awarded by the President and only given to the best of the best.

No wonder Reid didn't know what to do now. He'd been at the top of his game, saving lives, making a difference, and now he was living on a houseboat and getting drunk at the Cadillac Lounge every night.

She turned her head as Reid came back into the room, whistling under his breath. His whistle ended abruptly when his gaze met hers.

"What's happened? What's wrong?" he asked.

"I want to see it."

"See what?" he asked warily.

She turned the computer around so he could see the screen. "The Medal of Honor."

His lips tightened. "So it's not enough to ask me a million questions, you have to go on the Internet and dig into my life?"

She felt a twinge of guilt at his words, but she quickly dismissed it, knowing he was just trying to change the subject. "Where's the medal?"

"It's in a safety deposit box."

"Really?"

"Yeah, I'm not planning on wearing it, and I didn't feel like having it around."

"But you also didn't feel like throwing it away."

"You don't throw away the Medal of Honor."

"I read about what you did."

"I did what I was trained to do," he said sharply. "I did what any man in my unit would have done if they'd been in my position."

"Weren't they in your position?"

"I had the most experience. I was in charge. It was up to me to protect the team, and I did. We were lucky. We didn't lose anyone that day."

"It doesn't sound like it was luck. It was you."

"No, there's always an element of luck. Some days it's in your favor and other days it's not. You can't control life, no matter how much you want to, no matter how smart you are, no matter how far in advance you plan. There's always that moment when things can go wrong. Sometimes they do. Sometimes they don't."

She frowned, having the feeling he'd somehow turned the tables on her. "You're talking about Colombia now aren't you?"

"I'm talking about life. We all want to control what happens to us, but we can't. The sooner you realize that the better." He paused. "What else do you want to know about me? Maybe I can save you some Internet research."

"I'm not sorry for snooping. You wouldn't have told me about the medal if I hadn't seen the article."

"It's not that big of a deal."

"You met the President, Reid. That's a pretty big deal." She thought for a moment. "Your family wasn't there, were they?"

"I didn't tell them about it."

"So you were alone at the ceremony?"

"No, Jared and Matt went with me, and a couple of other buddies showed up afterwards. We had a party."

She smiled. "I'm glad they were there for you."

"They've always been there for me. The Army has been my family since I was eighteen years old."

And it all made perfect sense. "So you didn't just lose your job, you lost your family."

He frowned. "I guess it feels a little like that, but I know they're still around, Shayla."

"They are around. One of them wants you to work for him. The bonds you made in the service are going to last a lifetime no matter what you do."

He stared back at her. "It's not just the idea of family; I liked who I was in the Army. It was the first time in my life I felt like I had found my place."

She got up and walked over to him, taking his hands in hers. "I like who you are now."

Desire sparked in his eyes. "You are playing with fire."

"Arc you going to put it out?"

He drew in a long, shaky breath. "Yes."

Disappointment ran through her. "Why?"

"Because you told me this morning you didn't want me."

"That was this morning."

"And tomorrow you might feel differently again. I don't take advantage of women who don't know what they want. So tonight you're going to take the bedroom, and I'm going to sleep on the couch."

"What if I said I know what I want?" she asked.

"I'd say you were lying. You don't know what you want, Shayla. And you don't know who I am. You think because I got some medal that I'm some white knight come to save the day for you and Robert, but that's not who I am."

Anger ran through her. "I don't think I'm the one

who's confused about who you are, Reid. That would be you. And don't try to tell me what I know or don't know. I make my own decisions."

"Then decide to take the bedroom now," he said tersely.

She stared back at him, the tension sizzling between them. She wanted to be with him, but she didn't want it like this. "All right." She grabbed her bag and her computer and moved toward the bedroom. "Good night."

"Sweet dreams, Doc."

She closed the door on his sarcastic words and sat down on the bed that took up most of the space in the bedroom. The mattress was comfortable, and it was such a warm night she doubted she'd need the blankets.

As she stretched out on the bed and pressed her face into the pillow, she could smell Reid's musky scent. He was so close and yet so far away. A part of her wanted to breach the distance and the other part of her knew that would not be the smart thing to do. She'd always been the smart girl, so why was she considering doing something so dumb?

Because it was Reid.

Because the man made her heart race and her palms sweat, and she had the insane feeling that they could really be something together.

But he didn't want to be anything with her, she reminded herself, at least not anything serious.

With a frustrated groan, she closed her eyes knowing it was going to be another long night.

Chapter Thirteen

Reid tossed and turned for hours. Every time he closed his eyes, images of Shayla flashed through his head. He could see her curled up in his head, her beautiful blonde hair trailing across his pillows, her soft skin warmed by his blankets. He could see her slender legs kicking off the covers when it got too hot. And he could imagine himself covering her body with his, kissing her mouth, her breasts…

He'd been crazy to send her off to bed alone.

But he knew deep down it had been the right thing to do.

Sweating and frustrated, he finally gave up on trying to sleep and made his way onto the deck as the sun was beginning to rise. He'd always liked dawn. The air was still, and the day was filled with potential. There was only beauty surrounding him, no drama, no war, no pain. He could make anything of this day. He had a clean slate.

Unfortunately, today's slate already included two events: a meeting with Lisa and a Callaway wedding. He didn't know which one he disliked more.

Seeing Lisa, probably. Although weddings were not at

the top of his list either. Which brought him back to Lisa.

It seemed unbelievable to him now that he had almost gotten married. What the hell had he been thinking? That was the problem; he hadn't been thinking. He'd been caught up in passion, the sex, and the idea of having someone waiting for him to come home.

If he hadn't seen Lisa and his brother together that night, would she have married him? And if she had, what would his life have been like now? He couldn't even imagine. Although, he doubted that he and Lisa would still be together. They probably wouldn't have made it through the first year. If Lisa hadn't hooked up with Robert, she would have found someone else.

He wondered how long this new guy would last. From everything he'd heard, it sounded like Lisa had traded up to a man with more money. The same man who seemed to now want to cut Robert's research grants. Was that just out of spite? Or was there another reason? If anyone should be pissed, it should be Robert. In this latest chapter of the Lisa show, Robert had been the innocent party, the one left behind, kicked to the curb. There was a bit of poetic justice to that.

So why would Hal want to make Robert's life more difficult? Unless, Hal wanted Robert out of the company so that he wouldn't have to work with him, see him at the company party, wonder if Lisa had any lingering feelings for her ex-husband.

Frowning, he realized he didn't have enough information to come up with a good theory. Which was why he needed to talk to Lisa. It went against the grain. But he couldn't ignore the fact that she was probably the one who knew Robert the best of anyone. And she knew the situation at Abbott Pharmaceuticals. Hopefully, she could tell him something he didn't already know.

Until then…

Stretching his arms over his head, he let out a sigh and then settled into a deck chair with Robert's notebook.

An hour later, the sun was higher in the sky and the air was beginning to warm, another hot day in San Francisco.

He was no closer to deciphering the comic book pages, but he was closer to wanting breakfast. He went inside and started the coffee maker. Then he searched through the refrigerator for food. Along with early mornings, he liked big breakfasts.

He grabbed eggs, bacon, and as many vegetables as he could find. He'd scramble everything together—a Becker special, he thought with a smile. As he cooked, he tried to be quiet, not wanting to wake Shayla up. Although, he'd be really happy when she was out of his bed, then he could stop thinking about turning off the stove, going into the bedroom and leaving breakfast to later—a lot later.

As if on cue, the bedroom door opened. Shayla walked into the room, dressed in leggings and a tank top. Her golden hair was tangled, her eyes heavy with sleep, a beautiful rosy pink in her cheeks.

"I smell bacon," she said with a sniff.

"Breakfast is almost ready."

She blinked at him. "You cooked breakfast?"

"I did. Do you want some coffee? I have to warn you I make it strong."

"Just the way I like it. I've basically had a caffeine drip in my arm the last few years."

He smiled, grabbing a mug out of the cabinet and handing it to her. "Help yourself."

She poured the coffee, took a long sip, and sighed with so much pleasure he couldn't help but wonder how she'd sound after a really good night of sex. Surely he could make her happier than the coffee she was drinking.

"This is the best," she said.

"I am good," he replied with a grin. "And not just with coffee."

She made a face at him. "It's too early to talk about sex." She snagged a piece of bacon off the plate and held it up. "This looks different."

"It's turkey bacon. It doesn't get as crisp, but it's better for you."

"Turkey bacon?" She took a wary bite, chewed, and then nodded. "Not bad. I'm a little surprised though. You don't seem the type to be worried about cholesterol."

"I take care of all my weapons."

"And your body is a weapon?"

"It has been on occasion."

She stared back at him, a question in her eyes. "Have you..."

"What?" he asked, sure he already knew where she was going, but he'd see if she got there.

"Nothing."

"Have I ever killed someone?"

"I was going to ask you that, but I already know the answer."

"Let's eat," he said, taking a seat at the small table.

Shayla sat down across from him, and dug into her eggs with enthusiasm. "This is great. I've always liked breakfast. One of my favorite places to go in the world is Mabel's Pancake House down by the beach. It's where my family goes to celebrate something important. Mabel's blueberry pancakes are the best. And whoever is being honored gets extra whipped cream and blueberries on the top."

He smiled. "Sounds great. Sorry I didn't make you pancakes."

"No, this is good. Aside from special occasions at Mabel's, I don't usually eat a big breakfast. I often just grab a pastry at the coffee cart outside the hospital."

"Doctor heal thyself. Breakfast is the most important meal of the day."

She grinned. "Doctors rarely take their own advice. But if I had someone to whip up a meal like this every morning, I might reconsider." She paused. "I heard you moving around last night. I hope the couch wasn't too uncomfortable."

"I've slept in worse places. How did you sleep?"

"Surprisingly well. No nightmares, which was great. I thought I wouldn't like the rocking, but it was very soothing. I'm not sure I'd want to make a boat my permanent address, but I can see some of the appeal. Do you know any of your neighbors?"

"They're a reclusive bunch."

"Go figure."

He smiled. "There's an older guy about four boats down that I've talked to a bit. He's a widower and a veteran. Good man. Likes to talk a lot about fish."

"Do you fish?"

"I haven't in a long time. I used to do it more when I was a kid. Robert and I spent summer vacations with my grandfather. He was an outdoors man. He taught us a lot about surviving in the wilderness."

She gave him a doubtful look. "I can't really see Robert camping out in the wild."

"He usually had a book with him," Reid admitted. "Or he was drawing pictures. It used to drive my grandfather crazy, but Robert was determined to do what he wanted to do."

"A family trait."

He tipped his head. "True."

"Speaking of Robert's illustrations, we should probably look at the notebook again," Shayla said.

"I've been studying the drawings all morning." He retrieved the notebook and opened it on the table between them. "Something has been bothering me."

"What's that?"

"See the number on the house?"

"One-forty-six. Is that your address?"

"That's the thing. It's not the address. We lived at four-twenty-three. Robert drew all the other details exactly right, almost as if he had a camera, and there's no way he forgot our address, so why change the number?"

She stared at the sketch with a puzzled frown. "It doesn't seem like an idle mistake," she said slowly. "Unless Robert was trying to elevate the story from the real world into the fantasy world. Is there anything else that's off?"

He flipped through the pages. "Here's Razor on a football field with the number eighteen on his back. If we go with your theory that Razor is me, then why not put number sixteen on his back which was my number?"

She looked up at him. "You're fixating on the numbers. Why?"

"Because I don't remember the numbers being there before, and because I don't think Robert would put numbers into the drawings unless they meant something." He turned to another page. A futuristic car was taking flight over a cityscape of tall buildings. There was a man in the car, but only the back of his head could be seen. "The license plate here seems to jump out of the sketch."

"XKJ413," she said. "That doesn't mean anything to you?"

"No."

"What if you put all the numbers in the book

together?" she suggested. "Do you have
a pen?"

He handed her a pen and watched as she jotted down
all the numbers in the notebook.

"We get 1, 40, 6, 16, 4, 1, 3. A sequence of seven
numbers," she said. "That could mean anything."

"Or nothing."

"It could also be nine numbers if we turned 40 into a 4
and a zero." She bit down on her bottom lip as she thought.
"Or the letters could also stand for numbers."

It was a great idea. He shouldn't have been surprised
at her quick mind, but he was.

"X would be 24, K would be 11 and J would be 10,"
she said. "Now you have a sequence of ten numbers." She
frowned. "But I still don't know what that would mean.
Are there any other letters in the sketches?"

"I wasn't looking for letters, but that's a good idea."

As she flipped through the notebook, he said, "You're
pretty good at this, Shayla."

"We'll see. I used to like to make up secret codes. It
was a game Colton and I played, sometimes to bug our
older siblings. We'd write messages to each other in code
so no one would know what we were talking about. It used
to bug the crap out of my oldest sister, Nicole, especially
when she was babysitting."

"Maybe your code cracking skills will come in handy
now."

"I suspect your skills are far more developed than
mine."

"I know something about cryptography, but it wasn't
my specialty. One of my friends is a genius at it. He's
working on Matt's team now. Maybe I should have him
look at the sketches."

She set the notebook down. "We can talk to him after

we talk to Lisa. You haven't forgotten that you're going to see your ex, have you?"

"No, I haven't forgotten. And it's not me, it's we."

She frowned. "You don't think it would be better to go alone? You might have personal things to discuss."

It might be more productive, he thought. It was possible Lisa would be more forthcoming if it were just him. On the other hand, she might fall into hysterics, start to cry, and want to talk about the past, and he didn't want to go there, so he'd take his chances with Shayla.

"We're going together," he said decisively. "Lisa and I have nothing personal to talk about. She might not even remember me. She's obviously fallen for two other guys since we were together."

Shayla shook her head. "Lisa might have cheated on you, but there's no way in hell she ever forgot you."

* * *

"Lisa finally found a man wealthy enough to give her the house of her dreams," Reid said, as he parked his beat-up truck in front of the three-story house in San Francisco's exclusive neighborhood of Presidio Heights a few minutes after eleven o'clock in the morning. He couldn't believe he was about to see the woman who had stabbed a knife in his heart, then twisted it a little. He could still remember the look in her eyes when he'd stumbled upon her and Robert. There had been no shame, only anger, defiance, as if he'd somehow driven her to do what she did. He'd never been able to make sense of that look.

"It's a nice house," Shayla said quietly.

"What am I doing here?" he murmured.

"You're trying to help your brother."

"Is that really why I'm here?"

"I thought it was." She gave him a thoughtful look. "If you don't want to talk to her, Reid, I'll do it. She called me a few days ago. It would make sense that I'd come here out of concern, that I'd have questions."

Shayla was throwing him a lifeline, and he almost grabbed on to it. But he'd never been a coward in his life, and he wasn't going to start now, not with Lisa. She'd been in the wrong, not him. "No, I'll do it. I know which buttons to push."

"Do you want to do it alone? Just in case things get personal, and you don't want me to hear what she has to say?"

"There's nothing you haven't heard already." He shot her a quick smile. "We're a team, Doc."

"Okay, I've got your back."

"Appreciate that."

They walked up the meticulously landscaped drive to the front door. Reid rang the doorbell, holding his finger down for an extra second.

A moment later, the door opened, and the woman he'd almost married stood right in front of him. It was the closest he'd been to her in almost eight years, and it felt strange, almost like a dream. She hadn't changed much. She was still attractive, although her brown hair was mostly blonde now, setting off her dark brown eyes. She was thin, and judging by the yoga pants and tank top she wore, she still liked to work out.

Lisa's jaw dropped when she saw him, her eyes widening with disbelief, followed by wariness. "Oh, my God! Reid! What are you doing here?"

"I want to talk to you," he said.

"Has something happened to Robert?"

"Why would you ask that?" he countered.

"Because I can't think of any other reason why you'd

come to see me after all these years."

He couldn't either. "Yes, it's about Robert."

"He's not..."

"Not what?"

"I don't know. I just have the feeling something terrible has happened to him." Lisa's gaze moved to Shayla. More surprise registered in her eyes. "Shayla. You're with Reid? I didn't know you two knew each other."

"It's a recent acquaintance," Shayla said. "Can we come in?"

Lisa hesitated and then stepped back. "Of course."

"Is your new boyfriend here?" Reid asked as he walked into her beautiful home.

"No, he's golfing," she said, an edge to her voice.

Reid was happy to hear that. He wanted to talk to Lisa away from Hal. In fact, he'd like to keep their conversation private, but he doubted Lisa would do him any favors.

"Your house is beautiful," Shayla murmured, as they followed Lisa through the entry into the large living room, the windows of which looked out on the San Francisco bay. The room was so big there were actually two seating areas. Lisa took them to the one closest to the window, a trio of couches that faced the amazing view.

"I recently redecorated," Lisa said as they sat down. "Hal was living like a bachelor. Everything was dark and heavy and completely wrong for the room." She stopped abruptly. "But you don't want to hear about that."

"Not really," he said.

Lisa clasped her hands together, her fingers playing nervously with what appeared to be at least a three or four carat diamond ring. When she saw his gaze move to her hand, she said, "We got engaged two weeks ago."

"It's certainly bigger than the one I gave you."

She stared back at him, and for a split second he thought he saw a flash of regret, but maybe he was imagining things.

"Do you want to talk about the past?" she asked. "Because you never have before. I tried a long time to set things straight with you, but you would never talk to me. You wouldn't answer my letters, my emails, my phone calls."

"You make it sound like there were thousands," he said with a frown. "You called twice. You sent me two emails. And then you married my brother. What the hell was there to talk about?"

She paled at his harsh words. "Fine, then let's leave it alone."

"That works for me."

"Great," she said, a hint of the old defiant Lisa in her expression now.

"What do you know about Robert's disappearance?" he asked.

"I know that no one has heard from him since the trouble in Colombia." Lisa's gaze moved to Shayla. "You haven't heard anything, have you?"

Shayla shook her head. "No. Can I use your restroom?"

"It's down the hall, second door on the left."

"Thanks, I'll be right back," Shayla said.

So much for having his back, Reid thought, but it was just as well. Shayla couldn't lie very well, and if Lisa started grilling her, she'd probably fold within two seconds.

"What's wrong with Shayla?" Lisa asked.

"She's worried."

"I think she's in love with Robert. She was just waiting for us to get divorced so she could get him for herself."

"She's not in love with Robert," he said, ignoring the little sting Lisa's words had created.

Lisa shrugged. "It sure seemed that way to me."

"It's not." If he had to choose someone to believe, it was going to be Shayla, not Lisa, who'd already proved herself to be a liar. "I understand that Robert and Hal have been fighting the last few months," he said, trying to get the conversation back on target. "Hal wants to cut Robert's funding."

"That's not personal," she said. "Hal is in charge of keeping the company in the black, especially with a possible merger in the works. Robert's research has had good results, but lately there have been problems. Hal thinks that Robert has lost it a little bit, that he's been distracted and disorganized and things are falling through the cracks. He's been making mistakes, costly ones." She paused. "I think Robert was really upset by our divorce, and maybe he hasn't been paying attention to his job the way he should have been."

It all sounded so logical and reasonable and yet completely implausible. "Robert is a lot of things, but he's not disorganized, and he doesn't make mistakes, not when it comes to his job."

"How would you know that, Reid? You haven't seen him in almost a decade. And the fact that you're defending him actually sounds kind of ludicrous to me." Lisa gave him a speculative look. "It's Shayla, isn't it? She's convinced you that Robert is somehow being maligned by the very company that has made his research possible for so many years."

"Shayla hasn't said that at all," he replied. "She's just concerned about Robert's welfare. She was in Colombia when the clinic was attacked. She didn't see Robert get on the plane. She's worried he didn't make it out. She thought you were worried, too, when you came to see her."

"I was worried. I still am. I don't care what Robert has done or not done, I don't wish bad things for him. The whole company is concerned for his welfare. Hal asked me to check in with Shayla, to see if she had any information that would be helpful to finding him. I thought if he would contact anyone, it would be her. She's been his friend for a long time, and Robert doesn't have that many friends. You know how he is, he gets tunnel vision, and he forgets about people, which doesn't make him a great friend or a great husband."

"You knew that before you married him."

She stared back at him. "I did."

"Why did you do it, Lisa?"

She drew in a shaky breath. "So we are going back there."

He hadn't wanted to, but somehow that's where they'd ended up.

"I panicked," Lisa said. "The week before the wedding you were gone a lot. You were getting ready for your deployment. Robert was around. We spent some time together. He listened to my concerns. He seemed like the only person who understood how scared I was."

"That you'd end up a poor soldier's wife?" he asked harshly.

"That," she admitted. "But mostly that I'd end up a widow like my mom."

"Mostly?" he challenged. "I think the money had more to do with it than anything else."

"It had something to do with it, of course. I like money. I like living well. And as our wedding got closer, the idea of living on an Army base in some small shack with people I didn't know started to feel a little too real. I couldn't be that girl who just waited for her man to come back. I was in love with you, but you were going to be gone."

"Why didn't you tell me that?"

"I was afraid you'd talk me into marrying you anyway. I was in love with you, Reid. I was caught in the romance of us. I knew I had to do something that would make you hate me. That's the only way you'd walk away from me. It had to be something unforgiveable."

"And Robert was happy to go along."

"Robert was drunk," she said. "I got him drunk and then I took him in the coat room and started kissing him."

He held up his hand. "That's enough. I don't need to hear more."

"Robert was really sorry," she said. "So was I."

"You didn't look like it. You were so defiant, so in my face about it. I think it was the first time I saw the real you." He paused. "When did Robert figure out who you really were?"

"I was a good wife to Robert."

"Until you met someone better, someone richer."

"And someone who's around. I thought when I married Robert that I'd be the doctor's wife, that I'd be part of the country club, that we'd have beautiful parties and a wonderful life. But Robert started traveling, too. He would go to the other side of the world for months at a time. He was always in pursuit of new plant compounds to use in his research. He didn't want to go to the club or play tennis or have parties. I was alone, just the way I would have been with you. But Hal is at home. He likes the things I like. We're very compatible. And we're going to be happy. This one is going to stick." She blew out a breath, then said, "Don't ruin this for me, Reid."

He arched an eyebrow. "How could I do that?"

She met his gaze. "By telling Hal about us."

"He doesn't know?"

"Not about that part of my life, no. I'd prefer to keep it that way."

She'd just handed him the power to hurt her the way she'd hurt him, but he would never do that, because then he'd be like her. "Your secret is safe with me."

Relief registered in her eyes. "Thank you."

"But I need to know a few more things. Is there anyone at Abbott, besides your husband, who didn't like Robert?"

She thought for a moment. "I saw Robert a month or so ago. I was visiting Hal, and I ran into Robert in the lobby. He was really angry. He said he'd had a bad meeting with one of the attorneys, Karl Straitt."

"Did he say what the meeting was about?"

"No, but he was furious. He said he wasn't going to let them destroy what he'd worked so long to achieve. I had no idea what he was talking about."

"Did you ask Hal about it?"

"I did mention it. That's when he told me that Robert was screwing up, and that they might have to terminate his grants. I told Hal that would destroy Robert, that his work was his life. Hal said it wasn't up to him. That they might not have a choice."

"It seems to me that Hal would have loved to get rid of Robert. What man wants to have his fiancée's ex working in his company?"

"We were all friends, Reid. Before Hal and I got together."

He shook his head in amazement. "Next time you pick someone to hook up with, try choosing someone who isn't a friend or a relative. It might be less messy."

She stiffened. "There's not going to be a next time.

Hal and I are forever."

"Sure, whatever you say."

"I think you should go, Reid."

"I think I should, too."

As he stood up, Shayla returned to the room, giving them both a wary look.

"Everything all right?" she asked, obviously sensing the tension between them.

"Perfect," he said.

"Are you done?"

"Yeah, Lisa and I are done," he said, knowing that was finally true. He gave Lisa one last look. "Goodbye."

She stared back at him, a mix of emotion in her eyes. "You won't forget what you promised?"

"I never forget a promise, and I never break one." He turned back to Shayla. "Let's go."

* * *

"So what did you promise Lisa?" Shayla asked as they got back into Reid's truck. She was a little irritated by the fact that he'd promised Lisa anything. Hadn't the woman broken his heart, destroyed his life, messed up his family?

Reid shot her a look as he started the engine. "Are you pissed about something?"

"Yeah. I'm pissed you made her a promise when you can't do the same for me."

"I promised her I wouldn't tell her boyfriend about our past."

"Oh." She settled back in her seat and folded her arms across her chest. "I guess that makes sense. She doesn't deserve it though."

"I didn't do it for her. I just have no interest in being involved in her life in any way."

"Good. Because seeing her again today reminded me

that she's a bitch."

"She doesn't seem to like you too much either," he drawled.

She glanced over at him. "What did she say?"

"That you're in love with Robert and that you had been waiting for his marriage to end in order to make your move."

"That is ridiculous. I told you before I have no romantic interest in your brother. I don't understand why no one believes that," she said in frustration.

"I believe it. He turned his head to look at her. "Because you don't lie."

Her heart was touched by his words. "No, I don't. Thank you."

He shrugged. "Just calling it like I see it, Doc."

"So did Lisa give you any information that might be helpful?"

"She told me that Robert's job was in real jeopardy, that he was screwing up, making mistakes. Hal said they might have to fire him. Apparently, he also had some argument with one of the attorneys, Karl Straitt. Do you know him?"

"No, but I didn't really know anyone at Abbott."

"Robert was definitely in some sort of battle with his company. And I have to believe that his disappearance has something to do with that battle."

"But why would he go into hiding? Why would he feel he was in danger?"

"That I don't know." He paused. "One other thing I thought was interesting. Lisa told me that Hal asked her to get in touch with you. He thought Robert would contact you, which leads me to wonder if the people at Abbott think Robert might have shared some information with you."

"Information that they thought might be at my apartment?"

"When they couldn't find it in his office—maybe."

"You think Robert's employer conducted the break-in?" The idea was mind-boggling. Why would a multimillion dollar pharmaceutical company want to search my apartment?"

"Because of whatever they think you might have."

"And you think they would break the law to do that?"

"Oh, I don't think any executive participated directly," he said. "But at someone's orders, yes, I think that's a possibility."

Her stomach turned over. She was sickened by the idea of some stranger being in her apartment, going through her things. "I thought the trouble was over when I left Colombia. I thought everything would be normal here."

He gave her a look of empathy. "Sorry."

"Me, too. What do we do now?"

"I'll call Matt, ask him to look more closely at Hal Collins and anyone else Robert worked with at Abbott. Maybe he can link them to something."

"Do you think there were any fingerprints left behind? I worry now that we didn't call the police."

"They wouldn't have found anything," he said. "Whoever searched Robert's office and your apartment knew what they were doing. Although, I am curious if the security cameras in Robert's building captured anyone going into his office."

"I should call them back, see if they found out anything," she said. "It wouldn't look strange, right? Since I found the office in disarray, it would only make sense that I would be interested in who did it."

"Sounds logical to me. But before you do that, let me

talk to Matt. He might be able to get that security footage on his own."

"Really?" she asked in surprise. "He can do that?"

Reid smiled at her. "He can do a lot more than you want to know."

"Then maybe I won't ask," she said. "Because I don't think I can take anything more right now. I feel a little overwhelmed."

"Well, you can dance it off later," he said lightly.

"That's right. We still have our dance ahead of us." She was relieved by the change of subject, but she was feeling a little close to the end of her rope.

"What time do we have to be at the wedding?"

"Around three-thirty, we have a few hours." As she finished speaking, her phone rang. "It's my sister, Nicole. Hey, Nic, what's up? Whoa! Slow down." She listened for a moment. "Okay, it's not a problem. I can be there in fifteen minutes. Don't worry about it. Everything will be fine."

"Something wrong?" Reid asked when she put her phone away.

"Remember how you said we were going to stick together today?"

"Where are we going now?"

"My sister, Nicole, is getting her hair done for the wedding, and her husband, Ryan, was supposed to be back by now, but his plane got delayed. He's a commercial pilot, and she wants me to watch the kids for an hour. If you want to drop me off, I can meet you at the wedding later."

"I'll go with you."

She sent him a doubtful look. "Really? You want to babysit?"

"Unless you're not allowed to have your boyfriend

over?"

She grinned. "That used to be the rule, but hopefully Nicole will make an exception this time."

"Hopefully, she will. When you used to have your boyfriends over while you babysat, did you ever make out after the kids went to bed?"

She laughed. "Not even once."

"Damn."

"I told you I wasn't a fun girl."

"Oh, I think you have some fun in you," he said with a sly smile. "You just need someone to bring it out."

And she had a feeling she wasn't going to have to go far to find a volunteer.

Chapter Fourteen

He couldn't believe he'd just volunteered to help Shayla babysit her sister's kids. He hadn't really been around kids since he was a kid. But what else was he going to do in the few hours he had in between now and the wedding?

A half dozen ideas immediately sprang to mind, all of which provided better options of what to do with his day, but none that included Shayla, and he had promised to stay close to her today. He also felt he owed her for going with him to Lisa's house. Even though she'd managed to bail on most of the conversation, he'd liked having her by his side. He couldn't remember when he'd spent so much time with a woman that didn't include sex. Although to be honest, he'd been thinking a lot about having sex with Shayla.

"Are you having second thoughts?" Shayla asked. "Because you can still just drop me off."

"No, we're a team, Doc. We stick together. Tell me about the kids we're babysitting."

"My nephew, Brandon, and his twin brother, Kyle. They're seven years old."

"These are the twins that were separated at birth and then reunited through a kidnapping?"

"Yes. You remembered."

"It's not that easy to keep your family straight, but that

one stuck in my head. Tell me again what happened."

"Brandon and Kyle were kidnapped. Fortunately, they weren't hurt. Now the boys are together again, and Brandon, who is autistic, is benefitting greatly from having his brother in his life. Kyle has somehow given Brandon a link to the world. It's quite amazing to see. We're really lucky that Jessica, Kyle's mother, was willing to move to San Francisco so the kids could grow up together. If she hadn't, it could have been really difficult to make it all work out."

"You guys should have your own reality TV show."

She groaned. "Not in a million years would I want to do that. I just want to live my life, the life I've been working towards for more than a decade."

She was talking about medicine now, and he could hear the strain in her voice. "You'll get back to it."

"Do you really believe that, Reid? Or are you saying it to make me feel better?"

It was a question that deserved an honest answer. "I do believe it. But it doesn't matter what I think. You're the one who has to find a way to believe."

She nodded in understanding. "I know. But how do I get there?"

"First you walk through the door, then you take it one step at a time."

"I was a basket case just going into Robert's office last night."

"Well, I do think once Robert is safe, you'll feel differently about things."

"I hope so. I do feel like things can't go back to normal until I know he's okay. He's the missing piece. Without him, the puzzle goes unsolved." She paused for a moment, then said, "I know you must have gone through some terrible experiences. Did you ever question whether you could continue to be a soldier? I'm sure you saw far worse things than I did."

"I've had a lot of sleepless nights," he said. "But I never questioned whether or not I should be a soldier."

"Why not?"

"Because it was my duty. If I couldn't save a hundred people, maybe I could save one. And one life was worth the sacrifice."

"You're right."

"I usually am," he said lightly, wanting to lighten the shadows in her eyes.

She gave him a half-hearted smile. "I need to toughen up. I've been too idealistic, too soft."

"No, you're fine the way you are."

"How can you say that? I'm a mess right now."

"You're in the middle of a battle, but you'll come out the other side. I think being a good doctor requires a certain sense of optimism, a belief that you can win, no matter the odds."

"That's true. Thanks."

"For what?"

"For being you."

He smiled. "Well, that is the first time anyone has ever thanked me for that, Doc."

She smiled back at him. "Maybe you don't stick around long enough to hear it."

"Maybe I don't," he conceded, knowing that he had a tendency to cut and run. But with Shayla he didn't even want to think about saying goodbye.

"Turn right at the next street," Shayla said. "Nicole's house is the third one on the left."

"With the nervous woman pacing up and down the sidewalk? I figured."

"Thank you, thank you, thank you," Nicole said, as

they got out of the truck. "You are saving my life, or at least my hair."

"It's fine. I'm happy to help," Shayla said.

Nicole shot Reid a curious look. "I'm sorry, have we met?"

"Reid Becker," he said, shaking her hand.

"Robert's brother," Shayla added. "This is my sister, Nicole."

"I hope I didn't interrupt something," Nicole said, a curious gleam in her eyes.

"You didn't," Shayla said shortly. "You should go, Nicole. You're already late."

"I should. Nice to meet you Mr. Becker."

"Reid, please, and we'll talk more at the wedding."

"Really?" Nicole said in surprise. She gave Shayla a very curious look. "I didn't realize you were bringing someone to the wedding, Shayla."

"It was a recent decision," Shayla replied. "Where are the boys?"

"They're in the living room. They shouldn't need anything for a while. I just fed them lunch. But if they're still hungry—"

"I will feed them," Shayla finished. "Not my first babysitting gig. Go."

"Call me if you have any problems." Nicole paused, giving Reid an apologetic look. "If my son ignores you or screams in horror at the sight of you, try not to take it personally. I don't know if Shayla told you—"

"She did, and I'm good," Reid said. "Don't worry about it."

As Nicole got into her car, Shayla turned to him and said, "So you do know that Nicole is going to have questions for you when you see her later tonight, right?"

"She couldn't possibly ask as many questions as you

do," he said dryly.

"Ha-ha. Let's go inside." As they walked up the steps, she added, "And if you think I ask a lot of questions, wait until you meet Kyle. Brandon may not speak at all, but his brother makes up for it."

"I think I can handle a seven-year-old."

She smiled. "We'll see."

* * *

While Reid had assured both Nicole and Shayla he could handle whatever reaction Brandon had to him, he was relieved when Brandon barely glanced in his direction and instead focused on building a castle in the middle of the living room. He wasn't sure how he would have handled a screaming, agitated child.

Kyle, on the other hand, gave him a cheerful, friendly smile and immediately looked up from the plane he was playing with to ask him if he was Shayla's boyfriend.

Shayla quickly said, "No, he's not my boyfriend, Kyle. He's just a friend."

"Do you really think he knows the difference?" Reid murmured.

"Maybe not, but he asked, and I answered."

"We're going to a wedding later," Kyle said, as he got up from the floor. He walked over to the couch as Shayla and Reid sat down. "We're going to carry the rings like we were supposed to do for Aunt Emma, but we couldn't, because someone bad hurt Uncle Max. Do you think something bad is going to happen to Uncle Drew?"

"Not a chance," Shayla replied. "Everything is going to be great, and you and Brandon will do a wonderful job."

"Do you want to see my book on snakes?" Kyle asked Reid, quickly moving on to the next subject. "It's really cool."

"Uh, sure."

"I'll get it," Kyle said with a sparkle in his blue eyes. "I'll be right back."

"Cute kid," Reid said. Kyle and Brandon both had blond hair, blue eyes and a smattering of freckles across their faces. "But what was Kyle talking about? What happened to Uncle Max at Aunt Emma's wedding? Is Max one of your brothers?"

"No, Max is my brother-in-law. He's the cop I was telling you about. He's married to my sister, Emma. She's the fire investigator. The day of their wedding, Max went into a bank with his brother to get some foreign currency, and they ended up in the middle of a bank robbery."

"Seriously?"

"Yes. I guess it wouldn't have been a Callaway wedding without a little drama. It's easy to talk about it now, but it was terrifying when it was happening. The second time around, they opted for the courthouse and that's why Kyle and Brandon didn't carry the rings. It was a small, simple ceremony." She paused, her gaze reflective. "I feel bad that Emma didn't have her perfect day, but she always said it wasn't about the wedding; it was about the marriage."

"Sounds like your sister is smart, too."

"Well, she doesn't have my IQ, but she's okay."

"You sound like Robert. He loved to tell everyone how many IQ points he had on me. Maybe with twins, only one gets the brain power."

Shayla frowned. "You're oversimplifying and generalizing."

"Two big words," he murmured. "Showing off again?"

"Those are not big words."

"They have a lot of letters in them."

She rolled her eyes. "And you like to pretend to be

dumb—how's that for a short word—when we both know you're a very bright individual. So give it up, Becker."

He held up his hands in surrender. "Okay, you win."

"I'm glad you see it that way."

He glanced over at Brandon, still thinking about the twin connection. "Is it weird though that only one twin is autistic?"

Shayla sighed. "Yes. We've all wondered about that. Nicole and Ryan have tried to blame themselves for it, thinking they did something wrong, or that there was something in the environment that hurt Brandon. They want there to be a reason, and so do I. I prefer it when things add up, when science makes sense, but there are still things that go on in the body that we don't understand."

She stopped talking as Kyle returned to the room with a skip and a smile, bringing his book over to Reid.

"Did you know that snakes smell with their tongue?" he asked with a giggle.

Reid couldn't help but grin back at such delightful innocence. "I did not know that."

"Did you know that snakes have ears on the inside of their body?" Kyle asked, doing a little spin at the end of his question.

He smiled at the kid's energy. "I don't know if I believe that."

"It's true," Kyle said with earnest blue eyes. He opened the book and handed it to Reid. "Look it says so."

"You're right, it does say that." He stopped abruptly, a little taken aback to find Kyle climbing on to his lap.

"You can read it to me," Kyle instructed, as if there was no possibility he'd say no.

"Uh, I guess I can."

"While you read to Kyle, I'm going to make a call,"

Shayla said.

"To who?" he asked quickly.

"To Kari. I need to tell her what happened at the apartment."

"I don't think that's a good idea."

"I have to let her know, Reid. She's my roommate."

"You said she wasn't coming back until next week."

"She's not, but—"

"So, wait. Let me find Robert tomorrow, figure out what's going on, then you can talk to her. The fewer people who know about any of this the better."

She sat back down. "All right. I'll wait."

"Read the book," Kyle ordered. He put his hand on Reid's face and literally pulled it toward him.

Reid smiled at the impatient gesture and couldn't help thinking that his life had really changed since Shayla had gotten him out of that bar. "Okay," he said, flipping back to the first page. "Fun facts about snakes. Snakes don't have eyelids." He looked at Shayla. "I did not know that."

"You're learning a lot today," she teased.

"More than I ever thought I would."

As he read, Kyle would occasionally interrupt to point something out on the page. It was quite obvious he'd read the book dozens of times. When Reid finished the last page, he looked up, surprised to see that Brandon had left his blocks and was now standing a few feet away, his gaze on his brother.

Kyle got off of Reid's lap and grabbed Brandon's hand and together they sat down on the floor in front of them.

"Brandon wants to hear the story, too," Kyle said. "Can you read it again to both of us?"

Reid looked over at Shayla as she wiped her eye. Apparently, whatever was happening was unusual enough to make her cry.

"Go on," she urged. "If you don't mind."

"I don't mind." He read the book again, this time adding more embellishments, wanting to make the story come alive for the silent little boy who seemed to be listening, although his gaze never quite connected with anyone but his brother.

When he was done, Kyle announced that he and Brandon needed some juice.

"I'll get it for you," Shayla said.

"We can do it ourselves," Kyle said. Together, the boys took off for the kitchen.

"That was really nice of you," Shayla said, giving him a thankful smile as he closed the book.

"Why did you look like you were going to cry?"

"When Brandon sat down in front of you on the floor, it reminded me of when he wasn't autistic. He was totally normal until he was two. I used to read to him when I babysat. He was such a happy, loving boy. And then the lights went out in his head, but now they seem to be coming back on. Even though I know he'll probably never be that little boy I remember, I hope someday he'll be able to connect with us. Anyway, you were a good sport. I particularly liked the voice you gave the python. Very impressive."

"I wanted to keep my audience entertained."

"You're good with kids."

"I don't know that I am. I can read a book, and I can probably keep them alive, but beyond that, I have no idea how to take care of children."

She smiled back at him. "Well, keeping them alive is the first priority. Do you want to have children?"

"I've never thought about it."

"Never?" she challenged. "What about when you were engaged to Lisa?"

"We didn't talk about it, or if we did it was some distant day in the future. She wasn't interested in having kids right away, and I was caught up in my career."

"What about now?"

"Now?" he echoed, running a hand through his hair. "I have to admit it hasn't crossed my mind."

"It could be part of your next chapter."

"Yeah, whatever that's going to be."

She smiled. "It's going to be amazing."

"There's that optimism again."

"Hey, you just told me I should never lose it. Maybe you should think about getting it back."

"I'm too far gone for that."

"No, you're not." Her expression turned serious. "You couldn't have done what you did for the last sixteen years without believing you could make a difference."

"But I can't make that difference anymore."

"Maybe not in the same way. But there's always another way." She got to her feet. "I'm going to check on the boys. Whenever it's too quiet, I get worried."

Shayla had barely left the room when the front door opened. A man walked into the entry, setting a small black roller suitcase by the staircase. He had dark brown hair and wore a pilot's uniform. He had to be Brandon's father, the pilot.

Reid got to his feet as Ryan entered into the living room.

"Hello," the man said, surprise in his eyes. "You are…"

"Reid Becker. I'm a friend of Shayla's. She was called in for an emergency babysitting gig. You must be Ryan."

"Right, yes. I'm late. My flight got delayed in Dallas by some massive thunderstorms." He walked around the couch to shake Reid's hand. "Nice to meet you. Where is

Shayla?"

"Getting the kids something to drink."

"Okay, good." Ryan let out a breath. "I'm glad you guys could help us out. I know Nicole had a lot to do today with the wedding."

"Not a big deal. We haven't been here that long, and we spent most of the time reading about snakes."

Ryan nodded, understanding in his gaze. "Kyle's latest fascination. A few months ago it was sharks. The kid gets on a topic and he doesn't let go."

"Well, it was very educational."

"So, are you and Shayla…" Ryan began with a speculative look.

"Just friends."

"Interesting. Are you going to the wedding?"

"I'll be there," he said, beginning to see what Shayla had meant when she'd told him he'd be the subject of a lot of attention.

"Brave man," Ryan said lightly.

"Why do you say that?"

"The Callaways can be very protective, especially where the women are concerned, and Shayla is the youngest, so she has always had a lot of siblings looking out for her."

"Shayla and I aren't together."

"Her family won't believe that any more than I do. No man willingly babysits someone else's kids unless there's an end game."

Reid met Ryan's gaze and had to admit the man had a point. "Ordinarily I'd agree with you, but this is different."

"What's different?" Shayla asked as she came back into the room. "Hi, Ryan."

"Hey Shayla. Thanks for helping out." Ryan gave her a quick hug. "You're a lifesaver."

"No problem. What were you two talking about?"

"Just getting acquainted. You can go now. I'm sure you have better things to do. I'll see you both at the wedding."

As Ryan left the room, Shayla gave Reid a speculative look. "You two got friendly really fast."

"Your brother-in-law is a friendly guy."

"What did he say to you?"

"He thinks we should come up with a better cover story before we hit the wedding."

Her brows knit together in a frown. "What did you tell him?"

"What you told Nicole, that we were just friends. He didn't believe me."

"Why not?"

"Maybe because you're gorgeous and I have eyes," he drawled.

His words seem to leave her speechless.

"You really need to learn how to take a compliment," he added, realizing that she wasn't faking her surprise. She really had no idea how pretty she was. She saw herself as a nerdy brain, but that's not what the outside package said.

"I—I can take a compliment," she said slowly. "Maybe I should talk to Ryan before we leave, set him straight."

"You'll be wasting your breath. And does it really matter what anyone thinks about us?" he challenged.

"No, you're right. It's no one's business what our relationship is or isn't." A sparkle entered her eyes. "If they want a story, maybe we should give them a good one."

"Oh, yeah? Like what?"

"We'll tell them we're incredibly hot for each other, that all we can think about day and night is getting naked together. That should give them something to talk about."

His throat went dry and his body tensed. Shayla was joking, but she had no idea how close she was to the truth—at least on his side.

Chapter Fifteen

Shayla regretted her teasing words as soon as they came out of her mouth. She had never been good at sexual repartee and apparently that hadn't changed. Since getting back into the truck, Reid had changed from the warm and generous man who had been reading stories to Kyle and Brandon to a stone cold statue. Obviously, she'd crossed some line.

The silence continued on their drive back to the boat, and with every passing mile, Shayla's tension increased. Part of her wanted to know what he was thinking, and the other part of her told her to leave bad enough alone and not say anything else. But it was going to be a long night if Reid wasn't talking to her anymore.

As Reid pulled into the lot by the harbor, she couldn't take it anymore. "Should I apologize?" she asked as he stopped the car.

"For what?"

"You know what. You haven't talked to me since we left Nicole's house. I was just joking. Apparently not very well, but—"

"I know what you were doing. I'm thinking, that's all. Unlike you, I don't have to talk every second."

"What are you thinking about?"

"I don't know—stuff," he said with annoyance. "Look I've agreed to take you to your sister's wedding and watch out for you. Let's leave it at that. I'm going to drop you off at the boat so you can get dressed. I need to run to the store."

She didn't dare ask what he needed at the store. "All right."

He pulled a key off the ring and handed it to her. "I'll be back in twenty minutes. Try not to get into any trouble while I'm gone."

She had a feeling she was more likely to get into trouble when he was there. But all she said was, "Fine."

She got out of the truck and headed down the docks to his boat. She was actually grateful to have a few minutes alone. She needed to pull herself together, and she was happy for the privacy. She and Reid had been attached at the hip all day. It was no wonder they were both driving each other a little crazy.

She went into the small bathroom to wash her face and hands, then quickly stripped off her jeans and tank top and put on her bridesmaid's dress. She was just applying her makeup when a knock came at the door. She stiffened for a moment, realizing she hadn't locked the door behind her. How stupid was that?

Fortunately, it was only Matt Kelton who came through the door.

"Hello," he said, surprise widening his eyes as he saw her. "Shayla. I didn't expect to find you here. You look—great."

She liked the male appreciation in his eyes. After Reid's icy behavior, her self-esteem needed a little boost. "Thanks. I'm going to my brother's wedding."

"With Reid?"

"Yes. He ran out to the store, but he should be back

soon. Do you have some information?"

"I do. Do you mind if I wait?"

"Of course not. This is Reid's home after all."

"You look like you're pretty comfortable here." He sat down on the couch and propped one leg up on the other, giving her a thoughtful look.

"Don't get the wrong idea. I'm only staying here because of the break-in at my apartment. Reid didn't want me to stay there alone, and my family is caught up in wedding mania, so I can't get any help there. Plus, I didn't want to worry them."

"You don't have to explain anything to me. I'm happy to see a woman here. Reid has been a hermit the last six months."

"A hermit?" she asked doubtfully. "When I first met him in the bar he seemed to have plenty of female companionship."

"Yeah, that's true, but most of those girls never made it out of the bar with him. And his friends didn't have much better luck. I know I couldn't get him off that barstool for any amount of money." He smiled. "But you did."

"Actually, I think it was Robert who did that. I came to Reid with a message from his brother."

"I know that's what happened, but I don't think Reid would have followed Robert out of that bar. There's a lot of bad blood between them. Somehow you made Reid not care about that. And I find that interesting."

"I wouldn't say I made him care. I just made him curious." She perched on the edge of the chair. "I didn't know the whole history of Reid, Robert and Lisa until this weekend. Robert and I have been friends for a long time, and I respect him greatly, but what he did to his brother was really bad. I can understand why Reid holds a grudge."

"I can, too. I was there that night. I lived through the aftermath. I'd never seen him so angry, so bitter, so destroyed."

"I can't even imagine."

"So tell me why Reid wants to help his brother now?"

She stared back at him. "Weren't you and Reid in the Army together?"

"Yes, we were. Why?"

"Then you already know why he's helping Robert. Reid is an intensely loyal person. And he'll help anyone who needs help."

A gleam entered Matt's eyes. "You're right. He'll save anyone, no matter the cost to himself, but he's already lost a lot. I don't want this save to cost him anything else."

She thought about that for a moment. She hadn't considered that it might not be fair to Reid to bring him into the middle of a dangerous situation. She'd just done what Robert asked her to do. "I hope this will end quickly and easily. I don't want Reid to get hurt either."

"Then let's work together to make sure that doesn't happen."

She didn't understand his tone. "What exactly do you mean?"

"If Robert has been doing some shady things, you'd be doing all of us a favor by coming clean. Then we'll know what we're getting into."

"I don't know that Robert has done anything wrong. Do you?"

He shrugged. "The picture isn't entirely clear yet. I don't like to make assumptions based on minimal evidence."

"Well, when you get some evidence, let me know."

He nodded. "I'll do that. We're on the same side you

know."

"It isn't really feeling like that right now."

"Okay, maybe I'm more on Reid's side than Robert's. I won't protect Robert at Reid's expense. I won't do that to the best friend I ever had."

"I understand," she said, hearing the passion in his voice. "I hope it won't come down to that choice."

"Me, too."

"I should finish getting ready." She got up, then paused. "Reid told me that you want him to work for you."

"I do, but I haven't convinced him yet."

"Why do you think that is?" It seemed to her that Matt was offering Reid the perfect job.

He sighed. "When you win the gold medal, when you climb the highest mountain, when you're the best of the best, it's hard to figure out what to do next when it's over. Everything pales in comparison."

"I suppose it does."

"Reid needs to reinvent himself."

"He will," she said confidently. "He'll find his feet again."

"I hope so. I'd love him to join my team. He'd be a tremendous asset. So anything you can say in that regard—"

She immediately cut him off with a shake of her head. "I have absolutely no ability to persuade Reid to do anything."

Matt grinned. "Oh, I wouldn't go that far. I have a feeling you could persuade him to do a lot of things."

She flushed a little at the innuendo. "I told you it's not like that. We only met a couple of days ago."

"Things usually happen fast around Reid. He's the kind of man who goes after what he wants—once he figures out what he wants."

"Well, he doesn't want me. I'm just a link to his brother."

Matt frowned. "Yeah, that actually might be a strike against you. After what happened with Lisa and Robert, I can't see Reid wanting to hook up with someone involved with his brother."

"I'm not involved with his brother. I'm not involved with anyone. I'm single. I'm a doctor. That's it."

"What's going on?" Reid asked, his voice interrupting what had become a heated conversation, at least on her part.

"Nothing," she said. He didn't want to answer her personal questions. She didn't have to answer his. "I'm going to do my hair."

She went into the tiny bathroom and pulled the door closed. She heard Reid ask Matt what they were talking about, but she didn't hear Matt's answer. She opened the door a few inches and realized they'd gone out to the deck. Was that because they didn't want her to hear the conversation or because they were giving her some privacy?

It didn't matter, she told herself, shutting the door again. She needed to finish getting ready, and for the rest of the evening she was going to focus on her family and the wedding and not give Reid and his annoying sexy moodiness another thought.

* * *

"I like Shayla. She's got fire," Matt told Reid as they walked out to the deck.

"What did you say to piss her off?"

"I think it was more than one thing," Matt said with an unrepentant smile. "You know how good I am with women."

"Why are you here?"

"I have some information for you."

"Tell me."

Matt's expression turned serious. "A body was pulled out of the bay yesterday. The deceased was a man by the name of Karl Straitt. He was an attorney at Abbott Pharmaceutical."

"What?" His gut clenched in shock. Matt certainly had his attention now.

"According to the initial investigation, Straitt was an avid boater and had been on vacation for the past two weeks. His boat has not been located. And his apartment was in good shape, no signs of foul play. However, one of the senior executives at Abbott told the police that Karl and Robert had had some heated arguments in the last few months."

"Was the executive's name Hal Collins?"

Matt nodded. "Yes. He gave the police quite an earful about Robert, saying the guy had gone off the rails since his divorce, that he was making mistakes and some of his grant money seemed to be missing."

"I never heard that before. The deceased—Straitt—he was an attorney at the company?"

"Yeah. You've heard his name before?"

"A few hours ago. Lisa told me that Robert had had an argument with Straitt about a month ago."

Matt's jaw dropped. "What did you just say?"

"Yes, I saw Lisa. I went to her house to ask her about Robert."

"I cannot believe you did that."

"It had to be done."

Matt nodded, concern in his eyes. "How was it?"

"It sucked," he admitted. "I had to listen to her rehash our whole fraud of an engagement."

"She's a materialistic bitch."

"Yeah, she is," he agreed. "And probably the worst punishment Robert could have received for his betrayal was getting stuck with her for seven years."

Matt gave him a doubtful look. "You're not forgiving your brother, are you?"

"You know what? I'm done with the whole thing. It's not about forgiving or forgetting. It's just over."

"Well, good."

"Good," he echoed. "So what do the police think happened to Straitt?"

"Right now it looks like an accidental drowning. But if it turns into more than that, your brother is probably going to be a suspect."

He wondered if that was why Robert had gone into hiding. Had he killed Straitt? Or had he realized he was being set up? "We need to find out more about the relationship between Straitt and my brother."

"My team is looking into it. I also got your text earlier about the hospital security video, and I happen to have a friend who knows a friend—"

"And?"

"The security video from the last three days seems to be missing," Matt replied.

"Well, that's convenient. So we don't know who searched Robert's office."

"No, but there's one good thing; there's no evidence of you and Shayla visiting Robert's office either."

"Not to the general world, but to whoever has the tape…"

"Right."

Reid thought for a moment. "You need to check on all the executives at Abbott starting with Hal Collins. See if you can find a money trail of any sort. I think someone at

Abbott paid for a search of Robert's office and Shayla's apartment. Maybe they even paid off a security guard to lose the video coverage."

"Already on it," Matt said with a smile. "But I like how your mind is working. You're getting back in the game, Becker."

"Well, you want me in your company, prove to me how good you are."

"Done. I like a challenge. But while I'm doing that, what are you going to do?"

"I'm going to find my brother."

"Do you need backup?"

He hesitated. "I don't know yet."

"All you have to do is call."

"I'll keep that in mind. For now I'm flying solo."

"Not exactly solo." Matt tipped his head toward the interior of the boat. "Are you taking Shayla with you?"

"No. I might need you to watch out for her when I leave."

"Say the word."

"Thanks."

Shayla popped her head out of the doorway. "I'm sorry to interrupt, but the wedding starts in an hour, and I'm supposed to be there in twenty minutes."

"I'll get dressed," he told her.

As Shayla went back inside, Reid couldn't help but notice the knowing smile on his friend's face. "What?"

"You know what happens at weddings don't you? The champagne is flowing. Everyone is looking good. Love is in the air…"

"I know what's *not* going to happen at this wedding," he retorted. "Shayla is a friend."

"A friend you want to have sex with. But hey if you're not interested, I'm single, and she's—"

"Not for you," Reid cut in sharply.

Matt laughed, taking no offense. "I thought it was like that. Why are you fighting it? She's beautiful and smart."

"Go home, Kelton."

"Fine, I'm going. But a word of advice?"

"Why would I take advice from a man who has a terrible track record with women?"

"Good point, but you're no better."

"I don't need your advice. I know what I'm doing."

"I hope so. Or the next wedding you go to might be your own."

* * *

Matt's words ran around in Reid's head as he took a quick shower, shaved and put on dress slacks and a button-down shirt. Shayla said the wedding wasn't formal, which he hoped was true, since he didn't own a tie or a suit. He'd made a quick trip into town to buy a better razor so at least he was clean-shaven. As he took a quick look into the mirror, he almost didn't recognize himself.

He hadn't thought about dressing for anyone in a very long time. The women he met at the bar saw him in shadows and through a haze of alcohol, which made everyone look better. But Shayla was seeing him as he really was, which was a disturbing thought. He didn't like how good she was at reading between the lines. He didn't like how she'd gotten under his skin. He didn't like how comfortable it felt to have her around in his space, space he usually kept only to himself.

Unfortunately, he did like *her*—too much. Which was the real problem.

"Reid," she called. "Are you almost ready? We need to go. I can't be late. My family will kill me."

"I'm ready," he said, wishing it were true. But ready or

not, the Callaways were waiting.

Chapter Sixteen

"What did Matt have to say?" Shayla asked as they drove to the church.

He really didn't want to tell her about the death of Robert's coworker, but she was involved, and she had a right to know what was going on. "An attorney for Abbott Pharmaceuticals, Karl Straitt, was found dead in the bay yesterday."

Her eyes widened with shock. "Are you serious? That's the guy Lisa told you about, isn't it?" she asked, shock in her eyes.

"Yes."

"How did he die?"

"He drowned. Apparently, he was a boater."

"So it was an accident?"

He heard the hopeful note in her voice and didn't want to disappoint her, but he also didn't want to lie to her. "I doubt it, Shayla."

"Then—someone killed him?"

He glanced over at her, seeing the fear back in her eyes. He hated that he'd been the one to put it there. "They don't know what happened. It's probably better if we don't jump to conclusions."

"What else did Matt tell you?"

"He said that Hal Collins told the police that Robert

and Karl had been fighting the last few months. Karl thought that Robert had made some mistakes, that his work was getting sloppy."

"How would a lawyer know that?" she challenged. "I worked directly with Robert, and I can tell you with complete certainty that he was never sloppy."

"It's possible that Hal is trying to make Robert look like the bad guy. Whether that's related to the love triangle that was going on between Hal, Robert and Lisa or something else I couldn't say."

"This is getting worse and worse," she murmured. "Did the man have a family? A wife? Kids?"

"I don't know anything about him." What he did know was that Karl Straitt's death had raised the stakes and made him realize that Robert was in real danger. He needed to find his brother before someone else did. And with the way things were going, it wouldn't be just the bad guys looking for Robert, it might be the police as well. Because he had a feeling that Hal Collins was setting up Robert for murder.

He wondered when Karl had been killed. He should have asked Matt that. If the body had been in the bay for a while, that would have made it impossible for Robert to be the killer. Not that he believed for a second his brother could kill anyone, but the cops might not feel the same way.

Maybe Karl's death was the reason Robert had gone into hiding. But what did Karl's death and the attack in Colombia have to do with each other? He was still missing too many important answers.

"What time are you leaving to meet Robert tomorrow?" Shayla asked.

"Did I say I was going?" he countered.

"You know you are. Don't waste my time, Reid."

He sighed, knowing she was right. "Nine."

"Are you going to tell me where you're meeting him?"

He shook his head. "No."

"Why not?"

"Because the less you know the better." Even as he said the words, he wondered if she already knew too much. "You should go to your parents' house tomorrow. The wedding will be over. Make up an excuse as to why you have to stay there." He couldn't stand the thought of her being alone in her apartment.

"Like what?"

"Tell them your apartment has a gas leak."

"Oh, sure, that's a great idea. My father and two of my brothers are in the fire department. You don't think they'd be over there in a split second?"

"Well, tell 'em you have rats. I don't know. Come up with something."

"I'll think about it."

"You shouldn't stay at your apartment alone."

"I was alone there all week."

"Before someone broke in," he reminded her. "And I can't believe you're arguing with me on this. You don't want to be there alone. The other night you begged me to stay with you."

"That was the other night."

"And what's changed?"

She frowned. "Nothing, but I'm not thrilled about involving my family in this situation. I can get someone to change the locks on my apartment. Or maybe I'll go to a hotel."

"God, you're stubborn," he muttered.

"Like you aren't?" she retorted. "All the Callaways are stubborn. It's a family trait, and the one thing I actually have in common with everyone else." She settled back in her seat and folded her arms across her chest. "Let's just drop it. You're going to do what you have to do, and I will do the same."

"Fine. It's your life."

"Exactly, it's my life. Take the next turn. We're almost there."

His annoyance grew as he drove into the Presidio, a former Army base. Not only did he have to go to a wedding, he had to do it on a damned Army base, reminding him of the life he no longer had.

"The church is over there," Shayla said.

"I see it," he ground out. He parked in the lot across from the beautiful church and wondered if he could find any excuse not to go inside. It wasn't like Shayla was going to be in danger while she was surrounded by her family and friends. He could watch over her from here, couldn't he?

But as much as he wanted to find an excuse, he couldn't do it, not because he couldn't find one, but because he didn't make excuses. When he was on a mission, he finished it. He didn't stop when things got uncomfortable.

He shut off the engine and gave her a scowl. "What are you waiting for?"

She stared back at him. "I don't want to go into the wedding like this. I know you're angry that I don't want to stay at my parents' house, but that's my decision. I will find a safe place to stay. I'm not stupid."

"I know that."

"Then what's the matter?"

"Look around you," he said. "Look where we are."

She gave him a confused look, then glanced out the window. "Oh," she said. "We're on an old Army base." She turned back to him. "I'm sorry. I didn't even think about the location of the wedding. If you want to leave, you should go. I'll be fine here. We can meet later."

"No, we made a plan, and I'm sticking to it."

"Then you have to find a way to be happy about it, because I don't want to ruin Drew and Ria's day with any of my own drama."

"We won't ruin anything. I've got this." He drew in a deep breath and let it out. "All good. Let's go."

"Okay."

They walked across the parking lot, pausing at the street to let a car go by. As they crossed to the other side, a dark-haired man in a charcoal gray suit came jogging down the front steps.

"That's my brother, Colton," Shayla said, giving him a wave. "My twin."

Great, Reid thought. The interrogation was about to begin. He forced a smile on to his face and went to shake hands with Shayla's brother.

* * *

Shayla was relieved to see Reid's smile. It was going to be a long day of questions and she didn't want the first one to be: Why is your boyfriend so angry?

But there was no sign of Reid's earlier irritation as he shook hands with Colton. He was keeping his promise to her. She shouldn't be surprised. He'd told her numerous times that if he made a promise, he kept it.

"Shay," Colton said, giving her a hug. "I haven't seen you since you got back from Colombia. How are you? Mom told me a little about it, but no one seems to know the details."

Which was exactly the way she wanted it. "I'm doing great."

"What happened?"

"I'll tell you later. Today it's all about the wedding."

"So you said your name is Becker," Colton asked Reid.

"Yes."

"Isn't Becker the name of that doctor you work for?" Colton asked, turning back to her, a question in his eyes.

"Yes, Reid is Robert's brother."

"Are you a doctor, too?" Colton asked Reid.

"No."

"He just got out of the Army," Shayla put in, knowing her brother wasn't going to be satisfied with Reid's abrupt answer.

"What did you do in the Army?" Colton asked.

"A little bit of everything," Reid replied.

"Not much of a talker, are you?"

"Colton," she protested. "That was rude."

Her brother laughed. "I think your friend has heard worse."

"I've heard a lot worse," Reid agreed with an easy smile. "But what I was doing is classified. I can't talk about it."

Colton nodded. "Got it. But don't be surprised if you have to answer that question at least eight more times today."

"I've already prepared him for the Callaway inquisition," Shayla said dryly. "I just didn't think it was going to start with you."

"Hey, you're my little sister, I have to watch out for you."

"Little by two minutes."

"Every minute counts."

"Is everyone else here?" she asked.

"Everyone but Grandma and Grandpa and Burke. Drew is getting a little nervous that his best man is going to miss the wedding."

"Where's Burke?"

"His shift ran long. He's been on a hotel fire since six a.m. He was supposed to be off a few hours ago."

She frowned. She'd grown up in the shadow of fire and danger to her loved ones, but she still hated to hear about it. She preferred to know after the fact rather than during the event when she could drive herself crazy with worry. "Maybe we can delay the ceremony for a while," she suggested.

"Hopefully, it won't come to that. Aiden is ready to step in and be the best man if he has to." Colton grinned. "He's always happy to take Burke's place."

Her two oldest brothers had always been in competition. "Very true."

Colton checked his watch. "We have fifteen minutes, so hopefully that won't be necessary." He paused as a car pulled up at the curb, relief sparking in his eyes. "At least Grandma made it."

Shayla turned her head to see her grandmother being helped out of the car by her grandfather. Yesterday they hadn't been sure she would be able to come to the wedding, but she looked good today wearing a light blue dress that matched the color of her eyes.

"That's my grandmother, Eleanor," Shayla told Reid. "Let me introduce you."

She grabbed Reid's hand and led him over her to grandmother, feeling a strong need to have her grandmother meet him. It was a silly wish, because after today she probably wouldn't see Reid again. But she still wanted the two of them to meet. Being the youngest in the family, she'd spent a great deal of time with her grandmother, who had often watched her and Colton while her parents were at work or driving the older kids around.

"Shayla," Eleanor said, a bright smile on her face, her eyes clear of the haze that often shadowed them. Eleanor's hair was white, and she'd shrunk a couple of inches since her youth, but she was still a very attractive woman.

"Grandma." She gave her a hug and a kiss on the cheek. "You look amazing."

"I think this is a new dress," Eleanor said, a twinkle in her eye. "But who can say what's new or what's not? Lord knows I certainly can't remember."

Shayla felt even better at her grandmother's teasing words. Today was definitely one of her better days. In the last year, weeks had gone by where Eleanor barely recognized anyone or spoke in cryptic, mysterious sentences. "Well, it's the first time I've seen the dress, so I'm going to call it new," she said.

"Who's this handsome man?" Eleanor asked.

"Reid Becker," he said extending his hand to her grandmother. "It's nice to meet you. Shayla talks about you with the highest regard."

"Well, isn't that sweet." Her grandmother squeezed Reid's hand. "You have callouses on your palms. A working man, are you?"

"On occasion."

"I always liked a man with a strong handshake." She turned to Shayla. "Your grandfather almost broke my fingers the first time he took my hand. But I never felt safer or more loved."

"My grandparents have been together for more than fifty years," Shayla told Reid.

"Impressive," he said.

Eleanor smiled. "It hasn't always been easy, but I've never regretted the day I said *I do*. And I can't wait to see Drew make the same vows today."

"Shall I walk you in?" Colton asked.

"Not yet. It's nice to be outside. It's a lovely summer day, isn't it? And I get to talk to my two favorite grandchildren."

Colton laughed. "You say that to everyone, Grandma."

"You're both very special. How could you not be, being twins? I remember when you used to play that game where you tried to read each other's minds."

"Shayla was better at that," Colton said.

"Only because I always guessed you were hungry," Shayla said with a self-deprecating smile. "It's funny that you remember that, Grandma."

"Some days I remember everything, and I try to hang on to those memories as tightly as I can, but then they go. I've been thinking about trying to write some of them down," she said. "There's a woman at the support center where I go who has volunteered to write down my story. I'm thinking about taking her up on it, but Patrick isn't sure it's a good idea."

"It sounds like a great idea," Shayla said, wondering why her grandfather didn't like it. "Unless Grandpa thinks it will be frustrating for you in some way."

"He always has my best interests at heart." She sighed. "I feel so badly for your grandfather and your father. My disease is not as hard on me as it is on them. They've always been the kind of men who could fix any problem. They hate that they can't fix me."

Shayla wished she could fix her grandmother's problem, too, but after what had happened in Colombia, she felt like she was even further away from being able to do anything more than hope for the best, and she hadn't gone to medical school so she could hope for the best.

"How was your trip, Shayla?" Eleanor asked. "No one will tell me what you were doing down in South America, but I'm sure it was important. You're such a smart girl."

"It was important, but I didn't get to do everything I wanted to do."

"You're young. There's plenty of time to do it all."

Maybe she had time, but her grandmother didn't.

What's wrong?" Eleanor asked. "You look suddenly sad."

"Sorry. I was just thinking. Nothing to worry about."

Eleanor's gaze moved to Reid. "You need to make her talk to you. Shayla likes to keep everything inside, and it isn't healthy."

"I agree," Reid said. "But quite frankly I've had more trouble shutting her up than getting her to talk."

Shayla's jaw dropped at his comment. "Reid, that's not true."

He smiled at her. "We both know it is, Doc."

Eleanor laughed. "I think I like you young man."

"Well, I know I like you," he replied with a charming smile.

Whatever mood Reid had been in earlier had completely disappeared. Shayla was both happy and a little wary at his complete turnaround.

"Why don't you walk me into the church, Reid?" Eleanor suggested. "We'll get better acquainted."

"I'd be honored."

"Tell your grandfather I'm in capable hands and not to worry," Eleanor said, as Reid took her arm and ushered her to the steps.

"Well, well," Colton drawled.

"What?" she asked.

"I never pictured you with a soldier. I thought you'd end up with an engineer or a rocket scientist, maybe an astronaut."

"He's just a friend. I didn't want to be the only single

one at the wedding."

"Hey, I'm single, and I'm on my own."

"Really? You didn't bring a date? You always have a date." Colton had been popular with the girls since they were in middle school. But while he had a lot of dates, he didn't have many relationships. She had a feeling he had a hard time finding a woman who could keep up with him.

"Not today. I'm on my own."

"I'm sure not for long. I think Ria has some single friends coming today."

"We'll see. I guess we should go inside."

"One second," she said, putting a hand on his arm. "There's something I've been wanting to ask you, Colton."

"That sounds serious. What's up?"

"Did it bother you when I skipped ahead of you in school?"

His eyes widened in surprise. "That's what you wanted to ask me? Why?"

"Reid and Robert are twins."

"Soldier boy and Doogie Howser are twins? I never would have guessed that."

"Robert skipped way ahead of Reid in school. And Reid mentioned that his genius brother got a lot of attention from his parents and the rest of his family, and it made me think about us."

"You think you took all the glory?" Colton asked with a teasing smile.

"I'm serious, Colt. Did it bother you?"

"That you were smarter than me? Sometimes it annoyed me that you could do your homework so fast, but frankly when you jumped ahead in school, I was happy to get rid of you. Having my sister in my grade was cramping my style."

"Gee, thanks."

He grinned. "You asked. And, frankly, I'm thrilled that you're such a brain and that you wanted to be a doctor. I can go to you instead of the E.R."

"That should save you a lot of money. You've broken more bones than the rest of us combined."

"No pain, no gain."

"True."

"We're good, Shayla. I have no festering feelings of anger toward you."

"I'm glad. I thought we were okay, but I started to wonder if I'd been too self-absorbed and maybe missed some things. I can get tunnel vision sometimes."

"That's what makes you good at what you do."

"Where's your grandmother?" her grandfather, Patrick Callaway, interrupted with a sharp tone.

Shayla didn't take offense to the gruff note in her grandfather's voice, because he'd always had a big bark, but rarely did he bite, and that was only when he was feeling protective. And Patrick Callaway had always protected his wife. It was killing him now to know that there was nothing he could do to make her better.

"She's inside," Colton said.

"She seems to be feeling well today," Shayla added.

He nodded. "I hope it lasts until the ceremony is over. I need to get to her."

"We'll go in with you," Shayla said. It was time for her to be a bridesmaid.

* * *

"You haven't told me how you met Shayla," Eleanor said to Reid as they sat together in the first pew at the front of the church.

"Through my brother." He looked around for Shayla, thinking he did not need to be sitting with the family, but she was nowhere to be seen.

Since escorting Eleanor into the church, he'd been introduced to several other Callaways, including Shayla's parents, Lynda and Jack, who thankfully had been too busy to question Eleanor's declaration that he was Shayla's boyfriend.

"Shayla always liked Robert," Eleanor mused. "He was kind to her when she first started college. She was so young, so out of her depth, not with her studies, of course, but with the other students. She used to tell me how she didn't fit in. I felt so badly for her, but I knew she would find her way eventually. She's a strong woman. She reminds me a lot of her father, my son, Jack. He was a smart kid, too, not like Shayla, but very quick. And very determined to be the best." She paused, smiling. "Actually, I just described most everyone in the family."

"Shayla has told me a little about her family. They sound amazing."

"And Shayla needs an amazing man." Eleanor gave him a pointed look. "Are you up to the challenge?"

"I think you have the wrong idea about us."

"Oh, I don't think so, and I'm too old and too wise for you to argue with, young man."

He tipped his head, liking Eleanor more and more. "You remind me of my grandfather. He was not one to be disagreed with."

"Do you take after him?"

He thought about that for a moment. "Maybe I do. My grandfather was his own man. He didn't march to anyone else's beat. Some people didn't like that about him, but I always respected how comfortable he was in his own skin."

"Is he still alive?"

"No, he passed away."

"I'm sorry. But it sounds like you had a good relationship." Her gaze turned reflective. "I was always close to the grandchildren, but my husband, Patrick, never had enough time to really get to know them. I think it was his loss as much as theirs. But he was a busy man. He was very focused on his career."

"Shayla told me the family business is firefighting?"

"It is. Sometimes I wish it wasn't." Her eyes filled with shadows. "The fire stole too much from us."

He frowned, her words not making much sense. He suddenly had the feeling that Eleanor was slipping away, and he couldn't let that happen. He knew how important it was to Shayla and her family to have their grandmother present and lucid for the wedding.

"Tell me about Shayla," he said in a commanding voice.

And like all the men and women he had led into battle with that tone, Eleanor straightened up and her gaze became more focused. "Shayla?"

"What was she like as a child?"

Eleanor's smile came back. "Shayla was very controlled, organized, and determined. I used to pick her and Colton up from school when they were little. When we got home, Shayla would immediately start on her homework while Colton would go outside and play."

"Sounds like my brother and I. He hated anything that took him away from his books."

"Well, Shayla did like her books, but she was also good at sports. She could kick a soccer ball halfway across the football field. Surprised just about everyone she played against. They didn't think so much power could come from such a small package."

"She never told me she played soccer."

"She was a good swimmer, too. She won all kinds of

medals on the swim team. She thrived on competition, and she hated to lose."

Something he had in common with her. "She didn't tell me about the swimming medals either."

"Well, I'm sure you two have more interesting things to talk about, or maybe you don't talk much at all," she added with a gleam in her eyes. "When I remember my life, which isn't all that often these days, I do remember what it felt like to be young and in love. It gives me so much pleasure to see my grandchildren experiencing the same joy."

"Shayla and I are not in love."

She put her hand on his arm. "Sometimes you can't see what's right in front of you. Or maybe you don't want to see it. But take a little advice from an old woman. The greatest thing that can ever happen in your life is love. It's not that easy to find the right person, but when you do, you don't run away from it."

Her words stirred him on a deep and emotional level. He tried to tell himself that he wasn't in love with Shayla. How could he be? They barely knew each other. And yet he felt like he knew her better than some people he'd known for years. "Thanks for the tip," he said. "I'm going to sit in the back. I think we're about ready to start."

"Don't be silly. You won't be able to see Shayla from there."

Eleanor had a point, but as her husband, Patrick approached, Reid decided to make a run for it. He could handle Eleanor, but he had a feeling Shayla's grandfather would be a little tougher.

"Patrick, this is Reid, Shayla's boyfriend," Eleanor said as her husband reached the end of the pew.

Reid stood up and shook Patrick's hand. "I'll let you sit by your wife."

"Thanks for keeping her company," Patrick said. "Sorry Ellie, I got waylaid by the relatives."

"I wasn't worried."

"I'll see you later," Reid said, giving Eleanor a smile. He nodded to Patrick as he left the pew and hustled down the aisle.

He took a seat in the back of the church. From his vantage point, he could see the bridesmaids lining up in the vestibule. His heart sped up when Shayla caught his eye and gave him a smile.

Even in a sea of beautiful women, she stood out. In fact, he couldn't really see anyone else, and a knot grew in his throat as their gazes clung to each other.

Maybe it was the wedding. Maybe it was because he hadn't been in a church since the night of his rehearsal. Maybe it was because Shayla was so goddamned gorgeous. Whatever the reason, he couldn't seem to get his pulse to slow down, and he'd always been a master at calming himself down. He'd had to hone those skills in the service. His jobs in special ops had required him to remain silent and still, sometimes for hours at a time, and he'd never ever *not* had complete control over himself. But tonight he felt like he was hovering on the edge of a cliff.

He didn't have to fall or to jump, he reminded himself. He could slowly back away. And the first step was breaking eye contact with the hot blonde in the short silky gold dress.

He forced himself to turn his head, to look at the church, to listen to the music, to see the groomsmen filing out to the front of the altar. There seemed to be some discussion going on among the ushers. He wondered if Shayla's older brother had made it to the church.

The music began to play, the crowd hushed, and Kyle and Brandon started their walk down the aisle. They wore matching black pants, white shirts and gold ties, their blond hair slicked back. Kyle held on to a pillow with one hand and Brandon's hand with the other as they made their way down the aisle. Reid could see Ryan sitting in the second row at the front of the church, watching the boys with an eagle eye, obviously ready to swoop in at the first sign of a problem.

Brandon didn't look at anyone in the church. His gaze was on the floor, but he did keep walking. When they got to the front, the twins slid into the pew next to Ryan.

Reid turned his head back to the entrance. Shayla was about to start down the aisle but paused as a loud siren echoed through the church.

The crowd shifted in their seats as the siren got louder. From his vantage point, he could see the edge of a red fire engine pulling up outside. Then he heard a man shouting at them to wait.

Shayla walked back into the vestibule as a man came running into the church, shrugging his way into a suit coat, a gold tie in his hand.

Shayla said, "Burke, you made it."

Nicole stopped her brother, fixed his tic, and then sent him on his way down the aisle.

When Burke got to the groom, he said, "Sorry, I'm late."

Drew slapped his brother on the shoulder. "First time in your life that you're late, and it has to be today?"

"I'm here now."

As Burke joined the other groomsmen, Reid was struck by the similarity of their features. They all had brown hair of varying shades. They were all about the same height, within a few inches, and they had a presence about them.

Shayla was right. The Callaways were a formidable

group.

And yet she hadn't turned to any of them for help; she'd turned to him.

He liked that a little too much.

The music began to play. Shayla started down the aisle again, giving him a big smile as she passed by. When the wedding party was settled in at the front of the church, the bride made her entrance.

Ria walked alone, her head held high, her gaze on the man waiting for her.

Reid liked that she was on her own, that she was giving herself to her husband. And it was obvious that her groom adored her. The look of love that passed between them made his heart turn over in his chest.

After his botched wedding attempt, he'd given up on love. He'd thought it was an illusion, but he couldn't deny what was right in front of him. He rationalized that everyone looked like this at the beginning. It was the middle and end that changed things. But as his gaze moved back to the first pew, to Eleanor and Patrick, he had yet another shining example of a long-term union. And then there was Lynda and Jack, Shayla's parents, watching the ceremony with pride and love.

His gaze returned to Shayla, and he felt the knot in his throat get bigger. Shayla would want all this—the love, the marriage, the kids. Well, maybe not the marriage and kids right away. She was a doctor, and she wanted to work. But he knew in the end she would want the same kind of family she'd grown up in.

But he didn't want that…did he?

He felt suddenly uncomfortable, like his tie was choking him, like he didn't have enough air, like he didn't belong here.

The real problem wasn't that he didn't belong—but

that he wanted to.

As the ceremony continued, he fought to stay in his seat. When Drew and Ria finally sealed their vows with a kiss, he slipped out the back door as the crowd burst into applause. He walked across the parking lot to a patch of trees and drew in several deep breaths.

He didn't know what the hell was wrong with him. He'd faced down a barrage of automatic gunfire without even flinching, but a wedding ceremony had left him with his heart pounding against his chest. He couldn't even blame the emotion on what had happened to him before. It would be easy to try to make it about Lisa, but it wasn't about her at all.

It was Shayla. She was the one who had him so rattled.

Shayla would be out of his life tomorrow, he reminded himself. She'd go back to her world, and once he found his brother, he'd go back to his.

But they still had tonight to get through.

Chapter Seventeen

Shayla saw Reid leave the church right before the wedding party made their way down the aisle. She was a little disappointed by his hasty exit, but then again he'd probably lasted longer than she should have expected. He didn't know the people getting married, and no doubt the whole wedding experience was one he preferred to avoid. She wondered if he'd ever be able to make that trip down the aisle.

But maybe she wasn't giving him enough credit. Judging by all the medals he'd won, the man had more guts than most. However, that was physical and mental bravery, not emotional. And it would take a lot for a man with his level of pride to put his heart on the line again.

Not that it should matter to her. They were two ships passing in the night. By morning, all evidence that they'd ever been in the same hemisphere would probably be gone.

She found that thought a little disappointing, but she forced a smile on her face. She'd brought Reid to the wedding so everyone would believe she was okay and happy. She couldn't defeat that purpose by looking glum or worried.

Her smile continued through a flurry of photos taken on the steps of the church with the bridal party and various family shots. Finally, she was done. She walked over to Reid, who was chatting with her cousin Lauren, an attractive twenty-nine-year-old news reporter.

Shayla had never been particularly close to Lauren, who was five years older than her, but she'd always admired her ambition and work ethic. Lauren had spent most of her twenties doing on-air reporting from small towns, to medium towns, and finally to San Francisco. She'd always enjoyed Lauren's stories of adventure and dating. Now, however, she felt a little jealous at the fact that Lauren had gotten Reid to smile. She shouldn't be surprised. Lauren had always had a way with men.

"Sorry to leave you on your own so long, Reid," she said as she joined them.

"No problem. Lauren was keeping me company," Reid told her.

"We were talking about my favorite bar, the Cadillac Lounge," Lauren added. "I thought Reid looked familiar, and it turns out we've both been in the bar a lot in the last few months. My friend, Kelly, is a waitress there, and Reid's friend, Jared, is the owner."

"Yes, I know." She wondered if they'd made a date to meet up at the bar later or next week or whenever. "We should probably go to the reception," she said, unable to keep the sharp edge out of her voice.

"We'll talk again soon, Reid," Lauren said with a flirtatious smile. "Maybe I'll see you at the bar."

"Good chance of that," he replied.

"Looks like you made a friend," Shayla said, unable to keep the edge out of her voice.

"A very pretty friend."

She shot him an irritated look. "You're supposed to be my date, you know."

He raised an eyebrow. "Jealous?"

"Don't be ridiculous. But if you're flirting with my cousin, my family isn't going to believe you're with me."

"I don't think you have to worry about your family. Your grandmother told everyone I was your boyfriend. I think she's convinced your parents we're close to making our own walk down the aisle."

She stopped walking. "Seriously? Why didn't you stop her?"

"She's a sweet old lady, and I didn't want to upset her."

She supposed she should be happy about that, but now she was going to have to answer a lot more questions. "Fine, I'll deal with all that later."

"Good idea. Next week you can tell everyone I'm a jerk, and you dumped me."

"Right. That's what I'll do. It won't be that difficult to say actually."

The scowl returned to his face. "What's the problem, Shayla?"

"Nothing."

"If you say what you want, you might get it."

She thought about his suggestion and decided to take him up on it. "Fine. I don't want you to flirt with Lauren tonight or anyone else for that matter."

He stared back at her, a serious gleam in his eyes. "Then I won't. I'm all yours, Doc."

She licked her lips, wishing that were actually true. On the other hand, if he were all hers, would she be able to handle him? She was used to being in control, but with Reid there was no chance of that happening. And that was both a terrifying and exciting thought.

"Let's go to the reception," she said, turning away from his gaze. She had the feeling he could read her mind, and if he really wanted to give her what she wanted, how would she be able to say no?

* * *

Despite Reid having told her he was all hers, Shayla found herself watching him from a distance on more than one occasion. Every time she left him to do some bridesmaid's task, someone from her family came over to talk to him. Now, it was Aiden, who had slid into her empty chair and engaged Reid in conversation. The two men were joking and laughing, and why wouldn't they get along? Reid was a lot like the men in her family.

She stopped at the bar to grab a glass of champagne, even though the last thing she needed to be doing was drinking.

"Your boyfriend is hot," Emma said, joining her. "Why have I not heard about this guy before tonight? It seems strange, since Reid and Robert are brothers."

She wasn't surprised that Emma would be the first to interrogate her. Her sister loved putting puzzles together, and clearly she was not buying their story.

"It's a new thing," she said, sipping her champagne.

"He's not at all like the nerds you usually date."

She would have liked to argue that point, but she couldn't. "Not at all," she agreed with a little sigh.

Emma gave her a sharp look. "Okay, now I think I'm wrong, which is unusual, since I am rarely wrong. I thought he was just a cover so you wouldn't have to answer questions about Colombia, but you like him. You actually like him, don't you?"

She couldn't say he was just a cover, since that would defeat the purpose of him being a cover. And she couldn't say she didn't like him, because Emma wouldn't believe her.

"I'm going to take your silence as a yes," Emma said.

"Take it any way you want," she said, draining her glass. "I'm going to rescue Reid."

"Are you sure it isn't the other way around?"

She set down her empty glass on the bar. "What does that mean?"

"It means I'm still not buying your story. Robert is missing. You show up with his sexy brother, who also happens to be ex-military, and from what I could Google on my phone, quite the hero."

"You looked him up? When?"

"When I went to the ladies room ten minutes ago."

"It's my business, Em. I don't need you in it."

"You're my little sister. Of course I'm in your business."

"I'm a grown woman and a doctor, I can take care of myself." She started to walk away, but Emma put a hand on her arm.

"Shayla, where's Robert?" Emma asked abruptly.

She stared back at her sister. "I don't know."

"He's in trouble though, isn't he?"

"Maybe," she admitted. "Will you let go of my arm, please?"

"In a minute. You're in trouble as well, am I right?"

"I'm fine. I'm handling things."

"Reid is helping you," Emma said, making it more of a statement than a question.

"Yes," she answered, deciding to tell at least that little bit of truth.

Emma nodded. "Good. He looks like someone who can handle a problem. But if you need more help, you know we're all here for you."

"I don't want to involve the family in this. Please don't tell anyone what I said."

"Only if you promise to call me if things get out of

control."

Things had been out of control for a while, but she didn't want to get Emma worked up. "I promise. It's really all about Robert, Emma. He's the one I'm worried about, not myself."

"Okay. I hope he's all right."

"So do I. May I go now?"

"Can I give you some advice first?"

"Can I stop you?" she asked with a sigh.

"Be careful."

"I'm being very careful."

"I'm not talking about whatever is going on with Robert; I'm talking about your heart. I have a feeling that guy over there has broken a lot of hearts."

"You don't have to worry. It's not like that with us. I'm not going to give him my heart."

Emma didn't look like she believed her. "For all you act like you're all brains and no emotion, we both know that's not true Shayla."

"I know what I'm doing," she said, hoping that was true. "And right now all I'm going to do is rescue Reid from Dad," she added, seeing her father sitting down at the table with Aiden and Reid. "God only knows what he'll say."

"Let Reid handle it."

"Why?"

"Because you need to know if he can."

She looked into Emma's eyes and knew exactly what her sister meant. "I would only need to know that if we were really dating."

"Still…"

"What are we talking about?" Nicole interrupted.

"Nothing," Shayla said hastily, sending Emma a pointed look.

"Good," Nicole said. "Because Megan wants one more photo of all the bridesmaids in front of the cake. She promises this is the last photo."

"Okay," Shayla agreed, giving Reid one last look. He was laughing at something her father had said.

"He's fine," Emma said, sliding her arm around Shayla's waist. "And you're the worst liar in the family."

"I already knew that," she said.

"You do like him, don't you?"

"I really wish I didn't."

"I know that feeling. Falling in love is scary stuff."

"I'm not going to fall."

Emma smiled. "I have a feeling that's already happened."

"Let's go take that picture," she said. "Today is about Ria and Drew, not about me."

* * *

Shayla didn't catch up to Reid for another twenty minutes as one photo turned into two. Then there were toasts followed by the traditional toss of the bouquet and the garter.

As Shayla lined up with the other single women, she saw Reid talking to her sister-in-law, Sara. Sara had baby Chloe in her arms, and Reid was smiling at the happy child.

He tried to act like a loner and a hard-ass, but there was a whole lot of love inside Reid. He just kept it bottled up most of the time. His relationship with his family had probably started the cycle of self-protection. He couldn't care too much in case someone didn't care back. And Lisa had finished that cycle, destroying his love with the worst kind of betrayal. It was no wonder that Reid trusted only a few people, people that had already proved they would die for him, just as he would die for them.

But he needed to be able to trust beyond his band of brothers. She wondered what it would take to make that happen.

Probably more time than she had. Tomorrow Reid would be off to save Robert. They might never see each other again.

The thought made her feel a little sick.

"Ladies," Ria said, grabbing the microphone from the band. "Are you ready?"

Shayla was pushed to the side as Lauren joined the crowd.

"Gotta get a good spot," Lauren said with a wide smile.

"Have at it. I am not interested in catching the bouquet."

"Still all work and no play, Shayla?"

She shrugged.

"I like your guy," Lauren said. "Is it serious?"

She started to say no, but for some reason the word would not come out of her mouth. "It might be," she said instead, knowing it was a little green-eyed monster who had made her say that.

"Well, good for you," Lauren said, but there was a gleam of disappointment in her eyes. "Let me know if you decide to throw him back into the pool. I haven't met a single guy like that in a while."

"What do you mean?"

"He's a man's man and a woman's man. You're lucky, Shay."

"Yeah," she said, her gaze drifting back to Reid. He was watching her now. She wondered if he was worried that she might actually catch the bouquet. Then there would be even more questions.

She turned back to the stage as the drumroll began. A moment later, the bouquet sailed straight towards her. The beautiful flowers would have landed in her hands if Lauren hadn't snatched them away from her at the last moment.

"Sorry, Shay," Lauren said, with absolutely no apology in her eyes. "I'm older than you. I need this more than you do."

"It's fine. I hope it brings you luck." As long as that luck didn't include Reid, she was good.

Shayla walked toward Reid, but he was being hustled onto the dance floor by her brother, Colton. Joining them was her oldest brother, Burke, several of her cousins, and a bunch of Drew's friends from the Coast Guard.

After peeling the garter off Ria's leg, Drew gave a happy grin and used the garter like a sling shot to fling it into the crowd. A couple of the guys jumped up to catch it, but Colton came down with it. He promptly put it around his bicep and announced to the ladies that he was available.

Amid the laughter, Reid came over to her. "Your brother went for that like a hungry dog after some meat. Is he that interested in getting married?"

"No, but Colton likes to win."

"I think you could say that about a lot of your family members," he said dryly.

"You've been a really good sport tonight, Reid."

"And you've been gone a lot," he said pointedly. "You missed your father's interrogation, although I saw you out of the corner of my eye having some champagne at the bar. Why didn't you rescue me?"

"I thought you could handle my father."

"He's an interesting guy. Loves to tell a story."

She smiled. "He does. I actually didn't rescue you, because I have trouble lying to my father. I start with the best intentions, a resolute spine, a stiff jaw, and then he looks at me and I crumble. It's terrible. Do you know how many times I took the fall for Colton? Who, by the way, could make any lie sound like the truth."

Reid smiled at her. "You do tend to show your emotions in your eyes."

"I do? No one has ever told me that before."

"Maybe no one looked closely enough."

She caught her breath as her heart began to beat faster the longer he looked at her. "So, anyway…" She searched for a subject change that would direct his gaze somewhere else, but she couldn't quite find it.

"Anyway," he repeated. "You owe me, Shayla."

"What do you want?"

"I'll have to think about it. I had to go through seven siblings plus grandparents plus significant others, all with questions about us. You've run up a good-sized debt, Doc."

"What did you tell them about us?"

"I stopped trying to tell them we were just friends after the third time someone laughed in my face. They all seem to think I'm special because you apparently do not bring many men around the family."

"That's true. But we both know why I brought you, and we shouldn't forget the real reason you're here." Her words took the humor out of his eyes.

"Oh, I haven't forgotten, Shayla. I know exactly why I'm here. But you still owe me." He leaned forward and pulled her hair aside to whisper in her ear. "And I am going to collect."

She shivered at the sensual promise in his voice. He was a little too close.

Then he got even closer, running one hand through her hair while the other slid on to her hip.

"Dance with me," he said.

She would not have been more surprised if he'd told her to jump off a cliff with him. "Really? I thought you'd find a way to get out of that."

"Not a chance. I promised you I'd dance with you, and like I said before, I never make a promise I can't keep."

"That's true. Do you actually know how to dance?"

He gave her a cocky smile that charmed her right down to the tips of her toes. "No one has complained yet."

She doubted anyone ever complained about being in his arms, held against his broad, masculine chest. Butterflies danced through her stomach at the thought.

He gave her a speculative look. "What are you thinking about?"

"Nothing," she said quickly. "We're getting some attention." She could see Burke staring at them from the next table.

"We're supposed to be a couple, so that's a good thing. Let's dance, babe."

"I'm not your babe."

"Tonight you are." He grabbed her hand and led her out to the dance floor, which was filling up with couples as the band played a slow song.

Reid pulled her into his arms, and as she slid her arms around his neck, she couldn't help thinking how perfectly they fit together. She liked the fact that her head could rest on his shoulder. She'd been part of a big family her entire life, but she'd always felt like she had to stand on her own, prove herself, and she was a little tired of being so independent. It felt good to lean on Reid, to feel his arms around her. And he had a natural rhythm.

Some men thought dancing was simply walking her around in a circle, and an awkward circle at that. But Reid moved with the beat and with her body, and they seemed so in sync that she couldn't help wondering what it would feel like to make love with him, to strip away the barrier of clothes, and create their own music.

As the heat rose within her, she closed her eyes so Reid wouldn't be able to see what she was thinking, what she was wanting…

Chapter Eighteen

Shayla felt like an angel in his arms with her warm, womanly curves and golden blonde hair that smelled like a garden of flowers. Reid told himself not to get too worked up. It was just a dance, nothing more.

But it felt like something more, like he'd woken up from a long sleep, like his cold body was thawing under a warm sun, like the pain he'd been carrying around was slipping away.

He could still feel the twinge in the muscles of his leg when he moved too quickly, but it was the pain of losing his career and his sense of who he was that was disappearing. Being with Shayla had reminded him that there was a world outside the Army. He'd thought he would hate being at the wedding, but he'd enjoyed himself. He'd liked talking to her family far more than he'd ever imagined he would. He'd even enjoyed the sharp interrogation by her father, because he'd seen the protective love in Jack's eyes, and he'd instantly respected the man for caring so much about his daughter. A part of him had wanted to be the man worthy of Shayla, but he didn't think he was that man.

Jack's questions had only echoed the questions in his own head. Jack hadn't come right out and said, 'you're too old, too jaded, too dark for my beautiful daughter', but he'd come close, asking him questions about his service, about what he was doing now, and his plans for the future. Since he had no idea what he was doing next, his answers had not been that good, and he knew that Jack had not been impressed with him.

But he also knew that Jack's worry about Shayla extended far beyond her wedding date. Jack had asked him whether Shayla had confided in him about what happened to her in Colombia. It was obvious her father was worried about her. And there was nothing Reid could say that could alleviate that worry. So he'd tried to be evasive and had been thrilled when the wedding bouquet and garter toss had distracted Jack and given Reid a chance to break away from their conversation.

Shayla needed to talk to her parents, and he hoped that would be sooner rather than later. He was still concerned about leaving her alone when he went to meet Robert. Maybe he could find a way to persuade her to go to her parents' house in the morning.

In the morning...

His body tightened as he thought about all the hours until then. Would he really have enough willpower to send Shayla to his bed alone? Especially if she didn't want to go?

Their slow dance had brought them so close together he could practically hear her heart beating, and she seemed to like being wrapped up in his arms. In fact, she was holding him like she never wanted to let him go. Which was fine, because he didn't want to let her go either.

She lifted her head and gave him a dreamy sensual smile. The sparks of fire in her blue eyes reflected the passion brewing between them. They were an explosion waiting to happen. The match was already lit. It wouldn't take much to set off the fireworks.

But the fallout could be really bad.

That's what he needed to focus on. That's what would give him the strength to stay away from her.

Dancing with her had been a really bad idea, but he'd wanted to get her into his arms all night. Unfortunately, it wasn't enough. There were too many clothes between them, too many people surrounding them, too many curious eyes watching. Maybe that was a good thing. The fact that her family was being so attentive would stop them from doing something stupid. Maybe...

The song finally ended, and as the other couples began to clap, he knew he needed to let her go. But he couldn't seem to move. She couldn't either. As everyone started walking past them, she finally stepped back. She ran her hands down his arms, her fingers touching his. She lingered, held on, and the fire crackled again.

"Reid," she murmured. "I think we should get out of here."

Her words hit him like an electric jolt. "But—but the wedding isn't over."

"No one will notice."

"Are you kidding? Everyone will notice. But why the hell am I saying no?"

"Are you saying no?"

There was a question in her eyes now and a hint of insecurity, reminding him that Shayla had an innocence about her that he didn't want to crush.

"I thought," she began. "I misread. Never mind." She let go of his hands. "I'm going to get some champagne."

She ran off the dance floor, and he quickly followed. When she reached the bar, he grabbed her hand and pulled her toward the front door.

"Reid. You were right. We shouldn't leave," she protested. "What will people think?"

"I don't care what they think," he said, hustling her outside. "And you didn't misread anything, Shayla." He wanted to get her to the truck, to the houseboat, but he couldn't wait that long for the kiss he'd been wanting for hours. So he pulled her into the shadows of the trees. His mouth covered hers, and as he tasted the warmth of her lips and the hint of champagne, he knew that he was going to get really drunk tonight. It wasn't going to be on booze but on Shayla.

This kiss wasn't like the other ones, because this one was going somewhere, and they both knew it.

"Truck," Shayla mumbled, pulling away, her golden hair shining in the light of the moon.

"Another good idea. You're full of them tonight."

She laughed as they jogged across the parking lot. "I was actually thinking that they were probably all bad ideas."

He pressed her up against the truck and stole another kiss. "Bad can feel really good." Then he opened the door for her and jogged around the front to his side. As he started the engine, he said, "You've got fifteen minutes to decide if you want this to happen or not."

She stared back at him with those wide blue eyes, but she didn't answer, and that made him nervous.

It was going to be a really long fifteen minutes.

* * *

It didn't seem like fifteen minutes, more like five, Shayla thought as Reid pulled into the harbor parking lot and shut off the engine. But she hadn't needed time to change her mind. She'd made it up a long time ago.

She stepped out of the truck, meeting Reid on the sidewalk, and they walked down the dock to his houseboat in silence. It was a beautiful summer night. The midnight blue sky was filled with bright, twinkling stars, and the air was warm, even here on the bay. The breeze was coming from the east, from the valleys, and not from the ocean as it usually did, and with it came the heady scent of flowers and grapes from the vineyards and farms that were miles away.

It was the perfect night for romance. Not only was she warm and tingly from the champagne and from watching a wedding between two people who adored each other, she was with a man who made her feel more feminine, more needy, and more filled with desire than she could ever remember.

Reid extended his hand to hers, and she took it, the heat between them shoving away any lingering doubts.

"Shayla?" he murmured, his husky voice sending a shiver down her spine. "If you want the bedroom to yourself, you only have to say so."

She shook her head. "I don't want the bedroom to myself. I want to be with you, Reid."

His eyes sparked but despite the glitter of desire, he hesitated. "I don't want to take advantage of you. You're a little drunk."

"I had two glasses of champagne. I'm not drunk."

"Well, you seem a little reckless."

"That's not because of the champagne, that's because of you." She squeezed his hand. "You don't have to worry, Reid. I know what I'm doing. And I'm not expecting any promises. I know we might not see each other after tomorrow."

"We might not," he agreed.

"If tonight is all we have, let's make the most of it."

She leaned forward, put her hands on his shoulders and kissed the corner of his mouth. Then she went for his tie, loosening the knot and pulling it over his head. Next she went to work on the buttons of his shirt, pulling the hem out of his pants as she impatiently undressed him.

As she got him out of his shirt, she caught her breath at his masculine beauty, the broad shoulders, the muscled abs, the light smattering of hair that ran down his chest, and the slash of a white scar that started at his waist and disappeared below his belt line.

She put her fingers on that scar, giving him a questioning look. "How did you get this?"

"We don't have time to count all my scars, Doc." He pulled her to him, his hand sliding through her hair, as he kissed the side of her neck. Then he stepped back and pulled her inside, letting the door clang shut.

He turned her around and slowly pulled the zipper down on her dress. It slid off her body, pooling on the floor, as his fingers trailed down her spine, raising goose bumps along her bare skin. He paused at the clasp of her strapless bra, then flicked it open with one sure move. His tongue then took the same path his hand had already taken, and she shivered.

She'd thought with Reid it would be hard, fast, impatient, but he was taking his time, and with her bare back no less. She could only imagine his tongue on other more needy parts of her body.

Slowly he turned her back around to face him. She let her bra fall off of her arms, so she was standing only in a skimpy lace thong and her high heels. Reid stared at her with an intensity that made her heart beat even faster.

"Beautiful," he murmured, his hands sliding down her shoulders to her breasts.

His fingers stroked the tender peaks, and it was all just

too much delicious torture. She needed to even the score.

She pulled at his belt buckle, then the snap on his slacks, the zipper, finally sliding her hand inside to cup the hot hardness.

Reid moved, obviously no longer interested in being patient. He kicked off his pants and slid down his briefs.

He was a magnificently gorgeous male and she swallowed hard at the sight of him, not knowing where she wanted to touch first. She was more than a little familiar with the human body. She'd seen many, but none that were like this. Reid's body had been a weapon and a shield. It had been well used. And she felt not only passion but also tenderness at the jagged scars that marred his skin. He'd been through tremendous pain, and she wanted to take that pain away.

Reid took her hand, pulling her toward the bedroom. They squeezed through the tiny doorway, tumbling on to the bed together. He pulled her panties down her legs, and she kicked off her shoes as he kissed her long and hard, his tongue sliding into her mouth, his kiss changing from passionate to possessive.

His mouth slid down her jaw, his lips trailing a hot path down the side of her neck and across her breasts. As his tongue swirled around her nipple, his fingers sank into her core, and she let out a moan of pleasure that was echoed by the low growl in his throat as he lifted his head and his eyes met hers. He came in for another kiss as his body covered hers.

She loved the taste of him, the feel of him, the impatient passion of his kiss, echoing the growing need within her.

"Now," she said, shifting beneath him.

He lifted his head and smiled. "So impatient. How about a little foreplay?"

"We've been playing all night. Actually, we've been playing since we met. Don't make we wait, Reid. I want to be with you."

His eyes flared with passion. "All you had to do was ask."

"Now," she repeated, and his lips came down on hers as he slid into her body, taking possession in a way that thrilled every nerve and satisfied all of her senses. They moved together in perfect sync, each anticipating what the other needed, until they collapsed together.

Reid rolled off of her and on to his side, but he brought her with him as he did so. She snuggled against him, her head on his chest as he slung one arm around her as if he didn't want her to leave. She liked that he wanted to keep her near to him, because she wasn't at all ready to go. She wondered if she ever would be.

"You're an angel, Shayla," he murmured, his eyes heavy and a little dazed.

"That was pretty close to heaven," she agreed, stroking his chest with her fingers.

"We should have gone slower. Next time."

She lifted her head to smile at him. "You sound pretty sure there's going to be a next time."

"Well, I might have to kill myself if there's not," he murmured, meeting her gaze. He let his finger drift down the side of her face. "You're special."

"So are you."

He shook his head. "No, I'm as beat up as my truck."

"You do have a lot of scars. I want to know the stories behind them."

"No, you don't," he said.

The seriousness of his tone told her to be careful, but she couldn't be too careful. She wanted him to know how she felt. "I'm not scared of your scars, Reid."

"Maybe you should be."

"Well, I'm not. And maybe I can't appreciate the beauty of your truck, but I can appreciate you." She scooted forward and kissed him on the lips.

"I knew you were going to be trouble the first night we met," he said.

"This kind of trouble?" she asked, raising an eyebrow.

He smiled. "I hoped for this kind of trouble, but…"

"But what?"

His smile faded. "I was more concerned about the what-comes-next kind of trouble."

"I told you I don't have any expectations," she said, knowing that was no longer completely true. Actually, it had probably never been true, but he didn't need to know that.

"You did say that," he agreed. "But you're not the kind of woman who just has sex for fun."

"I haven't been in the past, but maybe I should be, because this was really fun."

Reid brought out the side of her that had always scared her a little, the side that wasn't smart, practical, analytical or logical, the part that was romantic, passionate, daring.

"You told me to ask for what I wanted earlier," she said. "So I did. It was good advice."

He gave her a wry smile. "Happy to help."

She smiled back at him. "So, I promise that come tomorrow I'm not going to cling to your leg or beg for your love or text you a million times. But tonight, I'm going to be a little girlie."

"You've already shown how girlie you are."

"Well, it gets worse."

"How so?" he asked warily.

"I want to cuddle."

That Summer Night   237

He laughed. "That I can handle."

"Good." She put her head back on his chest, closed her eyes and sighed with pleasure. "This is perfect."

* * *

It was perfect, Reid thought. Terrifyingly perfect. He'd never been that interested in spending an entire night with a woman. Sex was great. But afterwards, he liked his own bed, his own space, and usually he cut and run as soon as possible. But tonight he had no interest in going anywhere even if he could leave. He wanted to hold Shayla until the morning, until the sun crept up in the sky, until they both had to face reality.

But now, he just wanted to enjoy.

Her softness, her heat, enveloped him, making him feel like he'd finally come out of the cold. The numbness of the past few months was completely gone. He felt alive, painfully alive. His leg was cramping a little bit under hers, but it was a good ache, and one he wanted to hang on to, just like he wanted to hang on to her.

But he wasn't a fool. Shayla and he were as different as night and day. And once this was all over, which would probably be soon, she would go back to her life, and he would finally have to figure out what his life was going to be. But he knew one thing. He knew now that he wanted to have a life, and that was because of Shayla.

She'd come to him to save Robert, but maybe he was the one who was going to end up being saved.

As she curled up even closer to him, he closed his eyes and wished for the night to go on forever, because in the morning they were both going to have to start thinking again.

Chapter Nineteen

Shayla awoke to a crashing clatter and a male curse. She wrapped the blanket around her body and bolted out of bed.

Reid was in the living area, surrounded by a pile of camping gear that appeared to have come out of an overhead storage unit in a blaze of glory. Reid was rubbing a red spot on his forehead.

"Are you all right?" she asked quickly.

"Fine. Sorry. The box broke. I didn't mean to wake you."

"What time is it?"

"A little after eight. I need to get on the road soon."

"Right," she said, as he reminded her of the task ahead, the reason she'd come to him in the first place, which certainly hadn't been to have sex. But it had been really good sex, especially the interlude in the middle of the night when a delicious dream had turned into an even better reality. She blushed at the memory.

Reid smiled and then crossed the room, leaning in to steal a kiss. "Morning, beautiful."

She smiled back at him, pleased by the tender look in

his eyes, the way he'd dropped everything to give her a kiss. She wished they could have spent the morning in bed together. But Reid was obviously focused on what he had to do. And she needed to focus on that, too. "I should get dressed."

"I wish I could tell you not to, but—"

"But Robert is waiting for you."

He nodded. "Have you decided where you want to go today? I'll drop you off on my way out."

"I have decided. I have to make one call first. Then I'll let you know."

As she turned, her gaze caught on a gun sitting on the counter. Her heart stopped and her breath stalled in her chest. Her mind flashed back to the clinic, the gun in the man's hand, the thundering blasts, the bullets whizzing by her head. She sat down on the couch, her legs suddenly weak. "You're taking a gun?"

Reid frowned but gave a grim nod. "Yes." He paused, giving her a long look. "Are you all right?"

Her blood was roaring so loudly through her veins she could barely hear the question.

Reid was suddenly on the couch next to her, taking his hand in hers, giving her fingers a reassuring squeeze. "Shayla, come back."

She gave him a blank look. "What?"

"You're not in the clinic. You're safe."

"How did you know where I went?"

"You're white as a ghost, and I can practically see the scene you described to me earlier playing out in your eyes."

She licked her lips. "The gun reminded me."

"Sorry. I should have put it away. I wasn't thinking."

"Are you really prepared to—to shoot someone?"

"I am," he said, not the slightest hesitation in his

voice. "But only if I absolutely have to, and there's no other choice."

"Do you think that's going to be a possibility?"

"I don't know. Karl Straitt is dead, and Robert is on the run. I have to be prepared for anything."

Logically, she understood what he was saying. The closer he got to Robert, the more danger Reid would be in, but she couldn't stand the idea of Reid getting hurt because of her. And it would be because of her. She'd gone to him. She'd told him to go to his brother. She'd pushed him to help Robert.

"This is my fault," she said. "I should have insisted Robert go to the police, or I should have gone to the police and told them what I knew."

"You knew nothing. You still don't," he reminded her. "It's going to be okay, Shayla. You did the right thing."

"What if it's not okay? I don't want you to suffer for whatever Robert has done."

Some emotion passed through his eyes at her words. "Well, I appreciate that, but this isn't on you, Shayla. I'm choosing to do what Robert asked me to do. He's my brother."

"A brother who's bringing you into danger."

"Well, I like danger," he said lightly.

"This isn't a joke," she protested.

"I know." He gave her another kiss. "I can take care of myself, Shayla. You don't need to worry, but you do need to get dressed."

She gave him a long look, making a sudden decision. He wasn't going to like it, and she wasn't going to tell him until she absolutely had to.

* * *

While Shayla was getting dressed, Reid put a first-aid

kit, a knife, a sweatshirt, an extra t-shirt, and a sleeping bag into a backpack. As he packed, his movements were swift and sure. He'd prepared for battle a thousand times, and while this battle might turn out to be nothing more than delivering a notebook to Robert, he was going to be ready for anything. Along those lines, he threw some granola bars and apples into the pack along with several bottles of water.

He'd just stashed the pack in the back of the truck when Shayla came out with her overnight bag and her bridesmaid's dress. She'd put on jeans and a t-shirt and had pulled her hair back into a ponytail. He could see a tender red area by her ear, and his body instantly hardened with the memory of that delicious little bite. But he hadn't meant to hurt her. He never wanted to hurt her.

"What are you looking at?" she asked, a self-conscious light in her eyes.

"You. I seem to have trouble taking my eyes off of you." He took her bag and tossed it behind the seat, then laid her dress on top of it.

"Why do you have to be so charming when you're leaving?"

He smiled at the question. "I've always been better on my way out the door."

"I think you're pretty good on both sides of the door." She put her hands on his shoulders and pressed her mouth to his. "One for the road."

He slid his arm around her waist and pulled her back in. "Let's make it two."

The second kiss went on a lot longer than the first, and by the time it ended she was breathless.

"Man, I wish we could go back inside," Reid said. "Robert is always screwing up my life."

She smiled. "I have to admit he's been a thorn in my

side this week, too."

"Then it's time for me to pull out that thorn. Get in. I'm going to lock up."

He headed back to the boat, checked to make sure he had everything, then grabbed Robert's notebook and returned to the truck. He tossed the pad behind the seat as Shayla buckled her seatbelt.

"So where do you want to go?" he asked as he started the engine. She stared back at him with blue steel in her eyes, and his heart sank. "No way. You're not coming with me."

"I have to come with you, Reid. I started this. I need to finish it."

"You almost passed out when you saw my gun on the counter."

"I was surprised, but I'm over it now. I want to go with you. I want to be your backup."

"You won't be my backup, you'll be my liability," he said forcefully. "If I have to worry about you, I won't be concentrating on my job. You're not coming."

She crossed her arms in front of her chest, stubbornness written in every line of her face. "I won't be a liability. I can take care of myself. You don't have to worry about me."

"I may not have to worry about you, but I will. This was the deal all along, Shayla. I go to meet Robert on my own. If you won't give me another address, I'll take you to Nicole's house."

She groaned. "You're so frustrating."

"So are you."

"Fine, take me home then. I'm not going to my sister's house."

"You're better off staying with your family."

"You don't want to take me with you, that's your

choice. But you don't get to dictate what I do while you're gone."

He sighed. "Home it is."

They didn't speak as they drove over the Golden Gate Bridge and back into San Francisco. Reid was happy with the silence. He needed to focus on the trip ahead and not let himself get distracted by a beautiful and now angry angel.

As he came to a stoplight, he glanced in the rearview mirror and saw a sedan moving into his lane three cars back. His nerves tightened. He'd looked around the harbor when he'd been loading up the truck, and he hadn't seen anyone watching the boat, so where had they come from? He mentally cursed himself for missing something.

Two more blocks, and the car was keeping pace but carefully staying almost out of sight. He made a quick turn. By the time he got to the end of the block, the other vehicle was making the same turn. He weaved across three lanes, heading back toward the bridge.

"What's going on?" Shayla asked in surprise.

"We've got company."

She glanced over her shoulder. "I don't see anyone."

"Black sedan."

She didn't say anything for a moment, then said, "I see them. What are we going to do?"

"We're going to lose them."

He wove in and out of traffic and had a bit of a lead by the time he hit the Golden Gate Bridge. When he got over the bridge and onto the wider highway, he sped up, hitting ninety as he put some distance between him and the sedan. When the sedan was out of sight, he made a quick exit, and drove through the parking lot of a crowded mall, then back on to the city streets.

"I don't see them," Shayla said, turning around in her

seat.

"Keep an eye out," he told her.

"I guess this means I'm not going home."

"I guess it does," he said grimly.

"It's the right decision."

"I hope so," he said, not at all sure it wasn't the worst possible decision.

* * *

Shayla's neck began to ache as she scanned the highway behind them. Reid had turned off the main freeway, taking long, winding side roads through farms and vineyards leading into the Napa Valley. She hadn't seen any sign of the sedan in at least thirty minutes.

"I think they're gone," she told him, shifting in her seat as she rolled her neck around on her shoulders. "Do you think they were watching the boat all night?" The thought of that made her feel a little sick to her stomach.

"It's possible," Reid said in a clipped voice. "I should have taken you somewhere else last night. That was stupid."

"We're okay," she said, wanting to take away the guilt that was clearly raging through him.

"Only because they had a reason for watching us and not doing something else."

"Something else like…" Her voice trailed away. She didn't want to voice or even think about what that *something else* could have entailed. "Why would they have been watching us?"

"They probably think one of us will lead them to Robert."

"Are we going to lead them to Robert?"

"Not if I can help it."

"Where are we going now?"

"Robert asked me to meet him in the mountains. We'll need to make a stop on the way in though."

"For what?"

"Hiking boots. Those sandals you're wearing won't last five minutes on the trail."

"The trail?" she echoed. "Robert asked you to meet him somewhere that involves hiking? That doesn't make any sense." She shook her head in confusion. "Robert hates the outdoors. He doesn't even like to take walks. And I can't imagine him climbing a mountain." She paused as the word *mountain* ran around in her head. Robert's words from his cryptic phone call several days ago flashed through her mind, and she found herself saying them aloud. "*It is not the mountain we conquer but ourselves.* What does that mean, Reid?"

"Exactly what it says. Sometimes the mountain is just a metaphor for life."

"I like metaphors. So, you're saying we're not going to climb an actual mountain?" she asked hopefully.

"I'm not saying that at all, Shayla, which is partly why I didn't want to bring you along."

"I can hold my own. I'm a Callaway. I've been camping since I was a kid."

"Really?" he shot her a quick look. "Now you've surprised me. I thought you'd be a girl more comfortable in a library."

"I did that, too, and I have to admit that camping wasn't my favorite activity. But with eight kids, camping was one of the things we could all do together that didn't cost much money. And my father was big on teaching survival skills. Not that there was any chance I was ever going to get lost in the woods. But if I did, I could find water, make a fire with stones and sticks, and maybe even be able to put up a rough shelter."

"Maybe I should be glad you're coming along. You can take care of me."

"I haven't actually done any of those things since I was about twelve years old, so I may have forgotten a little of what I was taught. What about you? Are you a camper?"

"Yes. I can do everything you can do," he said lightly. "My grandfather made sure of that. And what he didn't teach me, the Army did."

"I don't think I've heard anything about your grandfather. Is he still alive?"

"No, he died when I was seventeen."

"What was he like?"

"Hard, tough, and spiritual."

She had been about to say he sounded like Reid until he got to the last word. "Spiritual?"

Reid nodded. "My grandfather was Native American, part of the Northern Paiute tribe that roamed the mountains above Yosemite."

She had to admit she was surprised by his answer. She couldn't really see any Native American in him, although maybe that's where he got his olive skin and strong jaw. "Is this the grandfather on your mother's side or father's side?"

"Mother's side. My grandmother was white, so my mother was half Native American, and I'm a quarter. My grandfather was a carpenter and worked construction for most of his life. But his real love was nature and the outdoors. He built a cabin in the woods, and after my grandmother died he would spend six to nine months a year up there. Robert and I would go in the summers. During the day he'd take us fishing, teach us how to hunt, how to survive off the land. At night he would tell us stories about coyotes who tricked people into doing bad things." He gave Shayla a quick smile. "Every story had a moral, some very thinly disguised. As I got older and more rebellious, I think he made up stories that were just for me."

She smiled back at him. There was affection in his voice when he spoke of his grandfather. Reid hadn't been close to anyone else in the family, but he had had someone in his life who had meant something to him. She was happy about that.

"My grandfather would tell us over and over again to pay attention to what he was saying. He was afraid that after he was gone we wouldn't know anything about our heritage," Reid added. "And he was probably right."

"But now you can pass the stories on." She could totally see Reid taking his son up to the mountains and teaching him the ways of his ancestors, because Reid valued history and tradition and the land. Of course whether or not he'd commit to a woman and have a child was impossible to know. "What about your father's parents? Did you know them?"

"No, they lived back East. And they passed away before I was in my teens. I remember them from a few Christmas visits, but not much else."

"Well, at least you had one grandparent to spend time with, and it sounds like you were close."

"I wouldn't say close. He was a hard man to get close to, but he was someone who taught me a lot about challenging myself, setting high goals, not being afraid to tackle what appears to be impossible. He told me not to let fear ever stop me from doing what I wanted to do."

"It's not the mountain we conquer but ourselves," she said again. "I get it now."

"I took that saying with me into the Army. I enlisted a month after my grandfather passed away. I told him I was thinking about it right before he died. And he told me that whatever I did I should do it well. I should make him proud."

"And you did."

"I tried."

"You didn't just try, you succeeded, Reid. Please, no false modesty now. We both know you have a healthy ego."

He laughed. "Good point."

"So, are we going to your grandfather's house?"

"Yes. Grandfather left me the place in his will. Unfortunately, I haven't been able to spend much time there. The last time I was up there was about three years ago. I have no idea what condition it's in now. But I'm pretty sure it's still standing."

"And no one knows about this house? Isn't it possible that Robert told Lisa about it?"

"Very doubtful. Robert hasn't been up there in twenty years. He hated going to the mountains. It was not his scene at all. It's very remote and hard to get to, which would make it a good place to hide out."

"How far away is it?"

"Three hours of driving, and then we'll have to hike in." He gave her a brief smile. "I know you wanted the metaphor, but we're going to climb an actual mountain, Shayla."

"I was afraid you were going to say that."

Chapter Twenty

Reid kept a close eye on the traffic as he drove toward the mountains of the Sierra-Nevada. There was no sign of the sedan he'd seen in San Francisco. Hopefully, he had lost the tail for good. He mentally kicked himself for not taking better care of Shayla. He'd gotten so caught up in her at the wedding that he hadn't even looked in the rearview mirror on their trip back to the boat. All he'd been able to think about was taking Shayla to bed.

He should have been thinking more about keeping her safe.

He'd had a definite lapse in judgment. He wouldn't have made the same mistake a year ago. Although, a year ago he would have been in the Army, operating under orders and with a professional team behind him, not going out on an unplanned, mysterious mission to save his brother.

He couldn't change what had happened, but he could do better in the future.

"I'm going to call Matt," he said.

"Can you put the call on speaker? I'd like to hear what he says."

"Sure." He punched in Matt's number.

"What's up, Becker?" Matt asked.

"I picked up a tail by my place. Black sedan, two men inside."

"Where are you?"

"I'm out of the city now."

"Do you want to be more specific? I can meet you."

He thought about that. As much as he'd like to involve Matt, he didn't want to go back to San Francisco. "I think I've lost them, so I'm going to keep going."

"Going where?"

"To meet Robert."

"I don't think that's a good idea," Matt said, a serious note in his voice. "I have some new information, Reid. My team has been able to tie the attack on the clinic in Colombia to a bank account in the U.S. It's a dummy corporation, and it's going to take us some time to get a real name, but the assault wasn't random."

"Mercenaries," he said, his stomach tightening. He'd wondered why Shayla had been spared, and now he knew why. But he still couldn't stand the thought of her being that close to men who killed for money and sport.

"Looks that way," Matt said. "My guess is someone wanted to destroy that clinical trial."

Reid glanced over at Shayla. She looked shell-shocked. Her face was pale, and her eyes were way too bright.

"I can't believe it," Shayla said. "Three people died in that attack. They didn't just destroy the clinic and the trial, they killed people."

"The deceased were part of the trial from what I know," Matt said. "That tells me that there's a reason those three were targeted."

"And why I wasn't killed," she murmured. She put a

hand to her mouth as if she might be sick.

"Do you want me to pull over?" Reid asked her.

She shook her head. "No, keep going. I want this to be over."

"Anything else, Matt?" Reid asked.

"My gut tells me that your brother was also a target. But somehow he wasn't there when it all went down. I don't know if he had some advance notice or if it was just luck, but obviously he went into hiding afterwards, so I figure he knew something. If you meet him, you're going to put a target on your back."

"I think it's already there."

"You should at least drop Shayla off somewhere. I'll come and meet her."

"No, I'm going with Reid," Shayla interrupted. "This is my deal, too. I was in Colombia. I saw those people die, and I want to do something now to get justice for them. It's the least I can do."

"We'll be in touch," Reid said, seeing the determination on Shayla's face. He'd see if he could find a way to drop her off later when she wasn't so fired up.

"Tell me where you're going," Matt said.

He wanted to tell Matt, but he didn't want to give the information out over his phone, "I'm not sure yet. I'll let you know. In the meantime, get me a name. I want to know who ordered that hit on the clinic."

"I'll do my best. Be careful."

"I'll do my best," he echoed. He set his phone down and looked at Shayla. "You hanging in there?"

"It doesn't make sense to me that Abbott would destroy their drug trial. Maybe it was Hanover Chemical— the rival firm. If they took out Abbott, then Branson Biotech would be more interested in buying them instead of Abbott."

"That makes sense."

"It would also make sense that Robert was a target, because without his research, his talent, Abbott was going to have a difficult time bringing that drug to market."

"That's not what the people at Abbott seem to think," he reminded her. "Lisa told me that Hal said Robert had been screwing up for months."

"That was a lie." Her brows pulled together in a frown. "Robert was not replaceable, Reid. They needed him."

"Okay, let's go down another road. You said Robert was distracted, that he told you there were problems with the trial. Maybe it was a bust. Maybe the results weren't what Abbott wanted, and they decided to shut it down."

"Isn't it a little drastic to kill people in order to do that? They could have just called it off."

"Not when millions of dollars are at stake. If that drug wasn't going to be the miracle they were hoping for, then their purchase price was going down. Maybe they would be worth nothing at the end. This way, the trial looks like it's been stopped by random violence. By the time they get a new trial going, the merger is already done."

She ran a hand through her hair as she pondered his theory. "I hope that's not true, because it seems really sick. I don't want to believe a company that makes drugs to save people's lives would do something like that."

He wished he could tell her that they wouldn't do that kind of thing and that he was wrong. Then her view of the world could stay intact. But he couldn't honestly say any of that. However, he could provide another theory. "It's possible that it's not Abbott behind the assault. It could be Hanover Chemical as you said. Or it could be a rival researcher, someone who wanted to destroy Robert and his success. It might not have been a corporate maneuver but a very personal attack on my brother, which would make sense since Robert obviously knew he needed to hide out."

She nodded. "I guess all that matters now is that we get to Robert before someone else does."

"That's the plan."

* * *

Two hours later Reid pulled into the parking lot of a camping supply store in a small town in the foothills near Yosemite National Park. After picking up hiking boots for Shayla, they grabbed sandwiches and food from a nearby deli and then got back into the truck. As Reid was about to start the engine, he saw the sign for a motel on the other side of the gas station. He glanced at Shayla, knowing she was going to fight him, but he had to try.

"I think you should stay here," he said. "There's a motel over there. I'll call Matt to come and meet you."

"Don't be ridiculous. I'm going with you."

"Shayla, I don't know what we're heading into."

"We're meeting Robert. That's not going to be dangerous unless we bring trouble with us. And we're not doing that, are we?"

"I hope not. But the truth is I don't really know. And I don't want to put your life on the line."

"You're not doing that, I am." Her blue eyes were determined. "I was there, Reid. I was in Colombia. This is my battle even more than it's yours."

"I can forcibly take you out of this car."

"I suppose you could, but I'll find a way to follow you. I'll call your parents. I'll get them to tell me where the cabin is. You know they will, because they'll be worried about Robert and about you."

He sighed. Her quick mind was no match for his. "Why are you so eager to get into a bad situation? Aren't you the woman who isn't sure she can work in the hospital E.R.?"

She frowned. "Yes, that's me. I've been an anxious, panicked mess since I got back from Colombia. And that needs to change. You told me the only way to get over fear is to face it, to walk past it."

"I was talking about doing your job, not this."

"Right now, this is what's going to get me back to doing my job. I may be afraid, but I'm not going to let fear stop me, just like your grandfather said.

He was both angry and impressed by her resolve. "All right. I'm done arguing."

"Thank goodness. We're wasting valuable time."

He started the engine and took another look through his mirrors, seeing nothing out of the ordinary. As he shifted position behind the wheel, he winced a little at the movement. Sitting for long periods of time always made his leg stiffen up.

Shayla shot him a quick look. "If you're getting tired, I can drive."

"I'm fine."

"Your leg isn't cramping?"

"It's nothing I can't handle."

"You don't have to handle it if you let me drive."

"We don't have that much further to go, and I know the road, you don't."

"Fine, but are you sure you're up to a hike, Reid?"

"I'll make it."

"You don't like to admit weakness, do you?"

"Not a good idea when you're going into battle."

"If you're honest with me, maybe I can help you, if you need it."

"I'll let you know if I do. I can be as stubborn as you, Shayla."

She sighed. "I can see that. So why don't we each just take care of ourselves?"

He nodded, but he knew that he was going to do everything in his power to take care of both of them.

Twenty minutes later, he pulled into a small clearing. "This is where we park," he said. "It's about two miles in."

"Your grandfather didn't have a road to his cabin?"

"He wanted to feel like he was in the wilderness, no cars, no traffic, no people."

"I'm guessing no cell phone coverage."

"You got that right."

"So Robert won't be able to call us."

"No, but he'll know where we are, if he can remember how to get there. It's not the easiest path."

Shayla waved her hand around the open space. "There's no other car here."

"We must be ahead of him." He hoped Robert would show, because if he didn't, Reid had no idea what he would do next.

After grabbing the backpack, Reid slung it over his shoulders, tucked the gun into the waistband of his jeans and they started off on their trek.

For almost thirty minutes, they didn't speak. Reid didn't know what Shayla was thinking about, but he did know she was determined to keep pace with him even if it meant jogging a little every now and then. And he was just as determined to ignore the growing ache in his leg. They were both focused on getting to the end of the road.

A moment later, he heard Shayla stumble and swear. He stopped walking and saw her rubbing her shin. "Are you all right?"

"I didn't see that rock. I was looking up at the mountains. They are magnificent."

"They are," he agreed, realizing how much he'd

missed this part of the world. When this was all over, he was definitely coming back. "Shall we keep going?"

"Sure," she said, then paused. "Do you hear that?"

"It sounds like a helicopter." He gazed up at the sky.

"I don't see anything."

"It's probably too far away."

"Maybe that's Robert helicoptering in, like James Bond."

He grinned. "While I wouldn't put it past Robert to take the easy way out, he is definitely not James Bond."

"That's true. That's more your role."

"You're right, and today I have the requisite beautiful blonde by my side."

She smiled back at him. "Who hopefully will not have to save your ass."

"Hopefully," he agreed.

"Let's keep going."

He started walking again. "There's a beautiful view not too far ahead. You're going to love it."

Fifteen minutes later, they came out of the thick woods into a clearing. Reid looked at Shayla as she took in the scene. A waterfall cascaded off the face of a majestic rock wall, the stream falling a half a mile into a deep gorge.

"Wow!" she muttered.

He led her over to a waist high rock wall. "Not bad, huh?"

"It's spectacular. This was actually worth the walk."

"There's more to come."

"Hang on. I need to retie my shoe."

As she squatted down, a blast echoed through the canyon.

"Shit!" Reid swore as he grabbed her hand, yanked her to her feet and sprinted toward the trees.

* * *

"What's going on?" Shayla asked, stumbling behind him.

Another blast rang out, answering her question.

Someone was shooting at them!

She couldn't believe it.

Reid dove behind a large boulder, pulling her with him. He pulled out his gun and said, "Stay here."

"Wait, where are you going?"

"To create a diversion."

"Reid!"

He wasn't listening to her. He grabbed a large rock and tossed it into the trees twenty-five feet away from them, then he ran, ducking behind trees as he did so. Another shot rang out, followed by a blast from Reid's gun.

She crouched down behind the boulder in terror, not sure how to help. She didn't want them to shoot Reid, but she also didn't know how to help him.

Her heart hammered against her chest. She flashed back to the clinic, to that terrible feeling of paralysis as the shots rang out, as she expected to be hit, killed, at any moment.

The rapid fire continued for thirty more seconds. And then it was silent. She waited another minute and then forced herself to inch towards the edge of the boulder. She couldn't see anyone. Nor could she hear anything.

Her stomach turned over. She felt nauseous at the thought of Reid being shot or even worse. A rustle of leaves and branches sent her heart into her throat. She thought she heard someone moan.

Was it Reid? Was he hurt? Or was it the person who'd been shooting at them?

With fear running through her veins, she forced herself to her knees. She glanced over the boulder. Several feet away she could see a man on the ground.

It was Reid. He was down.

She wanted to throw up. She wanted to run. She wanted to wake up from this horrible new nightmare. But she wasn't dreaming. This was real.

Reid needed her help.

Scrambling to her feet, she forced herself to move, terrified that each step would end with a blast, a shot to the head or the chest. But she kept going, because she could see Reid. He wasn't dead, thank God. But he was having trouble getting up. He'd definitely been hit.

The sight of his courageous struggle to stand made her run. She got to his side and saw blood dripping down his arm, spreading across his t-shirt.

More memories assailed her, the blood on her patient, the blood on the floor, so much blood.

That was then. This was now.

She had to focus.

"I'm okay, Shayla," Reid said, the pallor of his face and the pain in his eyes belying the statement.

"You've been shot."

"It's just a flesh wound. Help me up. We need to get out of here."

She looked around. "Where's the shooter?"

"He's over there. He's dead." Reid tipped his head toward a patch of trees. "I think he was alone, but I don't know for sure."

She didn't want to consider the fact that another shooter might be nearby, maybe reloading his gun. But she couldn't think about that now. Reid was her first concern.

"You need to put pressure on the wound, Reid." She wished she had a scarf or a sweater but neither one of them was wearing any extra clothes.

"I'm putting pressure on it," he said, pressing his fingers against his bicep.

She made a quick decision, slipping her arms out of her shirt, so she could unhook her bra. She peeled it off and said, "I'll tie this around you."

"So all it took for me to get your bra off was to get shot," he muttered, his attempt at a joke falling short as he winced with pain.

She pulled his hand away from his arm and saw a gaping wound. It looked like the bullet had gone right through and not hit any bones or significant arteries. Thank God for that. "This is going to hurt," she said, wrapping her pale pink bra around the wound as tightly as she could. "But it will help until we can get to the car."

"We're not going to the car. It's too far away. We'll go to the cabin."

"You need to get to a hospital, Reid."

"Why? I've got a doctor with me."

"But I don't have anything."

"There's a first aid kit in the backpack. You can help me at the cabin."

"Reid—"

"Shayla, please don't argue," he added, his skin turning another shade of pale.

"Okay. We'll do it your way." She picked up the gun from the ground, feeling the heat of the barrel against her fingers. Then she helped Reid to his feet.

"I'll take that back," he said.

She was fine with returning the gun to him. Just having it in her hand made her nervous. "Where is the man you shot? I need to see him."

"No, you don't." He shook his head, a grim expression in his eyes.

"I do. There are too many faceless ghosts in my dreams."

Reid hesitated and then led her through the trees until she saw the body on the ground. The man appeared to be in his forties, with light brown hair and a thick beard. There was blood all over his chest. It was clear that he'd been shot through the heart. She felt a little nauseous, but she battled through it. "Who is he?"

"No I.D."

"Are you sure?"

"I checked. I was on my way back to you when I started to pass out."

She shot him a worried look. "What should we do with him?"

"Leave him for now. I want to get to the cabin before anyone else shows up."

That made sense, but it still felt strange to walk away.

They retrieved the backpack from behind the boulder, and Shayla threw it over her shoulders as Reid struggled to walk. He was going to need all his strength to make it down the trail.

"How much further do we have to go?" she asked.

"About twenty minutes."

She didn't ask him if he was going to make it, because she knew there was no way he was not going to make it.

As they walked, Shayla kept waiting for another shot to ring out, but they got to the cabin without any more problems.

His grandfather's house was very small and all the windows were boarded up except one. Reid staggered up the three steps to the front door. He pulled a key out of his pocket and unlocked the door.

She followed him across the threshold. There was no electricity and the interior was very dark with only a bit of light coming through the one unblocked window. There was a couch in front of a fireplace and a scarred wood coffee table. A tiny galley kitchen was adjacent to the living room and there was a bathroom and another doorway leading to a bedroom, which appeared to have only a bed with a bare mattress and a box spring. Clearly, no one had been in the cabin in a long time.

As Reid collapsed on the couch, she dug through the backpack for the first aid kit and then walked over to him. She perched on the edge of the sofa and took a closer look at the wound. The bleeding seemed to have slowed down. "I need to clean your wound. I don't want it to get infected."

"Do what you have to do," he replied, his eyes glittering with pain.

She untied the bra and ripped open his sleeve. She cleaned the area where the bullet had gone through and applied an antibiotic ointment. Then she wrapped a gauze bandage around his arm.

Through it all, Reid didn't say a word. He certainly had a high tolerance for pain.

When she was done, she grabbed the bottle of pain relievers and poured three tablets into her hand. "Take these," she said, handing them to him, along with a water bottle.

He downed the medication and took a long swig of water. "Thanks."

She looked at the beads of sweat on his forehead and compared them to the goose bumps on his arms. She got up, grabbed the sleeping bag and unrolled it. Then she covered him with it. "Shock," she said.

"I'm fine. I just need a minute."

While Reid was resting, she explored the small cabin, checking out the kitchen and the closets to see what was there. The answer was basically nothing. There was no electricity, but there did appear to be running water, although it came out a bit yellow from the rust in the pipes. She definitely did not want to drink it. Thankfully, they had water and snacks to get them through the night.

Although, the idea of spending the night at this remote cabin in the woods with God knows who out in the wilderness was not appealing at all. She wanted to get them both back to civilization, but she couldn't navigate the woods without Reid's help, and he needed to rest.

She moved over to the backpack, digging through it to see what else Reid had brought. The sight of the notebook reminded her of why they were here—Robert.

Where the hell was he?

She took the notebook with her as she returned to the couch, sitting down by Reid's feet. His eyes were closed. She didn't know if he was sleeping or breathing through the pain, but she let him be. Hopefully, Robert would be here soon, and they could finally get some answers.

But as she thought about Robert making his way through the mountains, she couldn't quite believe he could do it.

A terrifying thought suddenly occurred to her. What if whoever had shot at them had already taken Robert down? He could be lying in the woods somewhere.

Her pulse began to race as she tried to think logically. If the gunman had gotten Robert, he wouldn't have been shooting at them. Robert was the target, right?

She really wished she knew who the enemy was. Then it would be easier to fight.

She opened the notebook, hoping she'd be able to find a clue that Reid might have missed.

Chapter Twenty-One

Reid awoke to the sound of crackling wood. He looked over to the fireplace to see Shayla attempting to build a fire. She had a few sparks going and was blowing on the small flame, attempting to spur it forward with the heat of her breath. He smiled at the determination on her face.

She was one hell of an amazing woman, he thought. She'd dodged bullets and left the protective cover of the rocks to go and look for him. Then she'd ripped off her bra, applied a tourniquet and carried a heavy backpack through the woods. She'd cleaned his wound without a second thought and now she was attempting to build a fire.

Although, the thought of the smoke curling out of the fireplace was enough to make him say, "Shayla, wait."

She turned her head in surprise. "You're awake."

"The fire," he muttered. "Smoke."

She stared at him, as if trying to decipher his words. "I know there's smoke, but I've almost got it going."

"Someone could see the smoke," he got out, his tongue dry and thick.

Awareness dawned in her eyes. "Oh, I didn't think. I'm

sorry. I thought it might get cold, and it's going to be really dark in here in about a half hour. I'll put it out." She beat the flames into submission until there was nothing left but smoking ash. "That was a stupid mistake."

"I don't think there was any harm done. It's dark outside. No one is going to come after us until the morning."

"You don't think so?"

"No." He glanced at his watch, realizing it was after eight. He'd slept for several hours. During that time, he'd left Shayla to fend for herself. He should have stayed awake. "You should have woken me," he told her, irritated with himself for falling asleep on the job.

"You needed to rest. I would have woken you if I needed to."

He shifted into a sitting position. He still had pain in his arm, but he felt better.

She got up and walked back to the couch, sitting down beside him. "Robert should have been here by now."

"Yeah," he agreed. "He won't make it up here in the dark." He saw the question in her eyes and wished he had an answer. "I don't know what happened to him, Shayla. Maybe he'll be here tomorrow."

"Do you really believe that? After what happened to us?"

"I'm trying to keep a positive attitude."

"And you call me the optimist."

"At this point, there's nothing we can do but wait until the morning and see what the sun brings."

"Hopefully not more shooting."

"Hopefully," he agreed.

"I've been looking through Robert's sketches. And I made some notes." She picked up the piece of paper she'd torn out of the back of the pad. "I started to play around with the numbers but nothing was grabbing me, then I realized that there were also letters. If you put them together, they kind of make sense, especially when the letters are N, S, and W. I think they're GPS coordinates, Reid."

He stared back at her in surprise and amazement. "Oh, my God. You are brilliant."

"I know," she said with a smug smile. "My phone isn't getting a signal, but I'm going to take a wild guess and say that the GPS coordinates are somewhere around this cabin."

"Of course they are."

"I think Robert either wants us to meet him at those coordinates or that he buried something in the woods," she continued. "Have you ever heard of geocache?"

He frowned. "Is that the game where people bury stuff around the world and other people dig it up?"

"It is, and Robert is a big fan. Now I don't know under what circumstances he'd bury something, but I think we should consider the possibility."

"I think we should, too. Whatever he has, someone is willing to kill for."

Shayla's lips tightened. "And to die for."

Reid met her gaze. "I had to kill him, Shayla. It was him or us."

"I know that, Reid. It was completely self-defense. It's not like I haven't seen people pass away. I'm a doctor. I've worked in the morgue. But it's different when it's violent and it's right in front of you, and that's happened twice in the last two weeks, so I'm a little shaken."

"Understandably so."

Her lips tightened. "When you left me behind that rock and the shots kept coming, I didn't know what was going to happen. I was so afraid that you—"

"Sh-sh." He leaned forward, putting his finger across her beautiful mouth. He could feel her lips tremble under his touch. "Don't think about it."

"I've been trying not to, but it keeps coming back. You could have died, Reid. You could have died because I went to you. I got you involved in all this. If I hadn't taken Robert's call, followed his instructions, you'd still be happily drinking in the Cadillac Lounge."

He saw the moisture gather in her eyes and felt his heart turn over. She was so lovely, so full of heart, and the fact that she cared so much about him made him feel incredibly lucky. "I'm fine, Shayla."

"You're not fine. You have a bullet hole in your arm." She wiped a tear off her cheek.

"And you fixed me up. Don't you see now that all your worrying was for nothing? You're a born doctor. You left cover to find me, to save me. You had no idea if someone was going to start shooting again, but that didn't matter. You saw that I was hurt and you went to work. You didn't even think about it. You're not going to be a hell of a doctor, you already are one."

"I feel like I could have moved earlier."

"I didn't want you to do anything but what you did. And what you did was strip off your bra and wrap it around my arm without a second thought."

"It was all I could think of," she said giving him a teary smile.

"It was smart. It stopped the bleeding."

"It did. But you were lucky, Reid. If that bullet had hit an artery or anywhere else on your body—"

"It didn't. I don't deal hypotheticals, Shayla, only reality."

"How does your arm feel?"

"It hurts," he admitted. "But it's better now."

"You look better. There's more color in your cheeks. There's some food. Do you want something?"

"Not right now," he said, settling back on to the couch.

"How do you think that guy found us? No one was on the road behind us, not for miles, and we were a mile into our hike."

He thought about that. "The helicopter. It must have tracked us. We were looking on the road. They were following us from the sky."

"How? Do we have something on us?"

"Maybe one of our phones or the truck, although I did look the truck over before we started driving. All I know for certain is that whoever sent that guy into the woods after us is probably the same guy who bought the mercenaries in Colombia. That someone has a lot of money and maybe even a lot of power."

She raised an eyebrow. "You think someone in the FBI or the State Department..."

He shrugged. "Anything is possible. I'm beginning to understand now why Robert called you, why he was insistent you speak to no one, including Lisa." He stopped abruptly. "Damn."

"What?" she asked with alarm. "What's wrong now?"

"We were at Lisa's house yesterday. She must have told Hal we were there, that we were together. He probably tracked me to the boat." He shook his head. "She screwed me over again."

"I don't know that we gave her any new information," Shayla put in. "She already knew Robert and I were friends. And if anyone was following me, then they saw us together, probably that first night when we left the bar."

"You're right. Well, there's nothing we can do about any of that now."

"So, what's next?"

He picked up the piece of paper and studied the series of numbers that Shayla had pulled out of Robert's illustrations. "We follow the clue you found."

"Even if those are GPS coordinates, we're not going to be able to find the location if your phone doesn't work."

He gave her a smile as the numbers running around in his brain settled into a familiar pattern. "Actually, I don't need a phone to find this location."

"What do you mean?"

"I know where Robert buried his cache. My grandfather taught us all about latitude and longitude and how to use a compass."

"I didn't see a compass in the backpack."

"No, but I know where these numbers lead, because Grandpa used to send Robert and I on treasure hunts. He used it as a way to test our knowledge of the wilderness and use our skills to get the treasure and return home. Funny, I never thought Robert was paying attention during those games. He was always complaining about bugs and having to walk too far. But I guess some of my grandfather's lessons stuck."

"Do you think when we get there, we'll also find Robert?"

He wished he could say yes. "I don't know."

She stared back at him. "If you remember the GPS coordinates, then I'm thinking that Robert knows them, too. So why would he need this notebook to refresh his memory? He wouldn't need the crutch."

"Nope." He could see exactly where she was going, and as usual she got there quickly.

"He was never going to meet you," she said slowly. "He wanted you to find whatever he buried. That's why he wanted you to have the notebook."

"Lucky for me you figured it out. I might still be putting numbers together and looking for a bank account somewhere."

"You would have figured it out eventually." She let out a sigh and shook her head. "You were right to wonder if Robert was luring you into trouble."

"And you were right when you told me that I'd never be able to walk away from Robert, because he's my brother, and blood counts."

"Maybe it shouldn't count when your life is at risk."

"It always counts," he said quietly. "The past few days I've had a chance to reconnect with my parents and even with Robert through these ridiculous drawings. And coming here to these woods reminds me of where I come from. Family is important. I forgot that for a while. I shouldn't have."

"You're a pretty good guy." She looked at him with a love that made his heart skip a beat. "Do you know that?"

"Of course I know that. I've been telling you that all along," he joked.

"Right. I almost forgot that the size of your ego is as big as your heart." She paused. "Actually, I don't believe that's true at all. You just like to joke when things get a little serious or uncomfortable."

She knew him far too well.

"I should take a look at your wound again," she said, changing the subject. "I want to change the bandage, make sure everything is clean."

"It's okay. You don't need to bother."

"You're probably going to have another scar."

He grinned. "But it's sexy, right?"

"You don't need another scar to be sexy, Reid. You've got it all going on."

"So do you." He paused. "You know, we have quite a

few hours until morning."

Pink colored her cheeks. "Reid, you're injured."

"Just my arm. The other parts of my body are feeling pretty good. They'd feel even better with some tender, loving care from my personal physician. What is it that doctors say—you need to treat the whole patient, not just the injury?"

"That does not include sex."

"But if sex is what the patient needs..." He leaned forward until his mouth was a breath away from hers. "Shouldn't the doctor prescribe the right treatment?" He pressed his mouth against hers. "God, you taste good."

"It's the chocolate I had earlier," she murmured.

"No, it's you, babe, sexy and sweet. It's the perfect combination."

"I like sexy. Sweet I'm not sure about. I think I'd rather be hot."

"You're definitely hot, but you are sweet, Shayla. You're kind, compassionate, generous, loyal—maybe even when you shouldn't be." He paused. "I've never met anyone like you."

"Really? I'm not that special."

"You are that special, even more so because you don't know it. You have no idea how beautiful you are."

She tucked a strand of hair behind her ear. "You know how to turn it on to get what you want."

"I mean every word. You need to learn how to take a compliment."

"I've just never been the beautiful one. I was always the smart one."

"You're both."

"I'd like to be both," she said candidly. "But it's funny that you can see dimensions in me but none in yourself. You think you're just the brawn, the physical guy, the man of action, but you're smart, too, Reid. Like I said before, you have it all going on."

"Not all. I'm still a man without a career."

"Once you finally realize that being a soldier is not who you are, just what you did, you'll be able to move on."

Her words resonated deep within him, because he'd finally come to the same realization. He'd been afraid to let go of who he was, but whether he was afraid or not, he had to let go. The past was done and the future was already here.

"I've got a move I want to make right now," he said.

"No way. You need to rest. But..."

"But?" he asked hopefully.

"I do have a treatment in mind that you might like."

"What's that, Doc?"

"Just lay back," she said, a mischievous gleam in her eyes. "And let the doctor take care of you."

He closed his eyes and let her do just that.

Chapter Twenty-Two

"Shayla, wake up," Reid said.

She blinked her eyes open, sleep still heavy on her lids. Reid was standing by the window and she could see the sun coming through the trees.

She sat up, wrapping the sleeping bag around her as she became aware of the cold. "Is it time to go?"

He nodded, a light of determination in his eyes. Reid was back in battle mode, and she was a little sorry to see her charming lover disappear. Their passion during the night had been tender and loving, and they'd fallen asleep in each other's arms. But while their nights together seemed to border on perfection, every morning brought a new challenge.

She got dressed, adding a sweater over her t-shirt and jeans, then used the bathroom. When she returned to the living room, Reid had changed into a clean shirt and thrown on a hooded zipped sweatshirt. "I should check your wound," she said.

"Let's wait until we get back to civilization."

She frowned at his words. "Who's the doctor here?"

He made a face back at her. "You are."

"Then let me take a look at your arm. I want to change the bandage and apply more antibiotic cream. You don't want an infection, Reid."

He sighed, then unzipped his sweatshirt and sat on the couch while she got the first aid kit. She unwrapped her bandage from the night before, relieved to see the bleeding had stopped, and there were no signs of infection in the wound. She put on a new dressing and bandaged him up, trying not to cause him any more pain while she did so.

"What's the prognosis?" he asked.

"You'll live," she said briskly.

"Glad to hear it." He paused. "You have a great touch, Shayla, tender but competent and quick."

"I've been putting on bandages since I was a little girl. First my dolls, then the family dog and the neighborhood kids. Anyone who came near me with a scratch got a bandage. My brothers used to run when they saw me coming with my kid-sized first-aid kit."

He smiled. "I'm betting you chased them down."

"Of course. So what now?" She set the first aid kit on the table.

"Now we go treasure hunting."

"Should we take everything with us?"

"Grab the notebook in case we need it. I'm going to see if there are any shovels in the shed." As he finished speaking, he took the gun off the table and slipped it into his waistband.

She hated to see his hand on the weapon, but after what had happened yesterday, she was happy they had it. She'd never thought of herself as a violent person, someone capable of killing another human being. But if she'd had the gun and Reid's life had been in danger, she was pretty sure she could have pulled the trigger. Luckily, she hadn't had to make that decision, because Reid had drawn the danger away from her. He'd put himself in the line of fire to protect her. That was the kind of man he was.

They walked onto the porch. Reid pulled the door shut and locked it. "Just in case anyone comes by. Hopefully they won't realize we were ever here."

He walked over to the shed and opened a door that was already off of its hinges. He returned a moment later with a shovel. He set it on the steps, then grabbed a long, leafy branch from the ground and swiped it through the dirt, apparently attempting to erase any footsteps.

It was very quiet where they were. She could hear the breeze rustling through the trees, the distant sound of the waterfall and the squawk of a bird overhead, but the rest of the world felt very far away. But that's what she'd thought yesterday, right before someone had taken a shot at her.

Reid tossed the branch into the trees and gave her a nod. She followed him around the cabin, going in the opposite direction from where they'd come the day before. She had no idea where they were anymore, but she trusted Reid to get them to where they were going and hopefully back out again.

They walked for fifteen minutes, the path climbing up the mountain, a little steep in places, but she stuck close to Reid until the trail widened and they were facing a beautiful stream that was probably a raging river when the snow melted. But in July it was little more than a trickle.

"I don't know that Robert would bury anything near a creek where the water might rise and flood the surrounding area," she said.

"I agree. We're going across to the other side."

He eyed the creek, found a spot where three flat rocks provided a nice footbridge, and then they crossed. They walked away from the water to a large outcropping of rocks that overlooked the other side of the canyon.

Reid studied the rocks, then put his shovel into the dirt and began to dig. He'd only made a small indentation when she saw the pain on his face.

"Stop," she ordered.

He didn't pay her any attention. So she grabbed the shovel and made him stop. "Give it to me. You're going to start bleeding again."

"I can handle it."

"So can I. Let go, Reid. When I get tired, you can take over."

He reluctantly let go of the shovel. She tossed the notebook onto the ground and started to dig. After ten minutes of digging, she was a little over a foot down and hadn't seen anything but a few worms. Reid was restlessly pacing behind her, obviously itching to make faster work of the process, but in his condition, he wouldn't be able to do much better than her.

"Are you sure this is the spot?" she asked breathlessly.

"I'm not sure about anything," he muttered. "I'll take over."

"Not yet." She picked up the pace. Three more heaping piles of dirt, and her shovel hit something hard. Her pulse sped up in anticipation. "I've got something."

Reid came over, and they both dug through the dirt with their hands. Finally, Reid pulled out an aluminum capsule about the size of a thermos.

"We found it," she said, feeling a little amazed.

They stood up. Reid broke the seal and pulled out a rolled-up stack of papers.

"What is it?" she asked impatiently, moving next to him.

He unraveled the papers, and together they read the first one. It was a listing of items in the capsule. But the listing wasn't as important as what was apparently coming, details of medical trials, financial reports, and private emails. Shayla tried to make sense of what she was reading.

"Damn," Reid said. He lowered the papers to look at her. "Robert was building a case against Abbott Pharmaceuticals. The drug trials were a bust. Data was being falsified. It's all right here. Robert was going to blow the whistle on the company."

"Let me see those," she said, needing to look at the evidence herself. If the drug trial was a bust, why hadn't Robert told her? Why hadn't he told anyone? Or maybe he had. "Look," she said. "Emails between Robert and Karl Straitt."

Reid took the paper from her hand and skimmed the information. "Robert told Karl that the drug was making people sick, that they needed to stop, and that he needed Karl to help him convince Hal and the others, because they wouldn't listen to Robert. This email was dated one week before the assault on the clinic," Reid said.

"Why didn't Robert just stop the trial? How could he let people continue to get sick?"

"I think he was trying to do that." Reid flipped through more papers. "Here's a transcript of a phone call between Hal and Robert. 'If you try to end this, we'll end you. You're not the only one who knows how to gather evidence.'" He looked at Shayla. "Sounds like a threat to me. We need to get this information to the right people."

"Who would those people be? Robert didn't trust anyone except us."

"Matt will know the right people. And Robert is trusting us to protect this information, which we're going to do. Hopefully, he'll get back in touch with you, and we can get him to safety, but I'm not going to wait here for him." Reid took the emails from her hand and shoved them back into the capsule along with the rest of the papers.

Shayla heard the rustle of bushes and a slippery slide of rocks. "Someone's coming," she said, her heart leaping into her throat.

She whirled around to see a man emerging from the trees, a rifle in his hands. He wore a tan coat over jeans, a baseball cap on his head. She didn't know why he hadn't already shot them, but she didn't think their good fortune was going to last long.

"I've got what you want," Reid said quickly, holding up the aluminum capsule. "It's all here. The information your bosses want. Just take it and go."

"Drop it on the ground," the man said in a clipped, cold voice.

Shayla could see Reid's hesitation. He was trying to think of a way out. But there was no way out. This time she wasn't going to escape with her life. The certainty settled over her like an icy blanket.

"Drop it," the man repeated.

"I'm setting it down," Reid said, both hands in the air in a defensive posture.

She willed him to go as slowly as possible, to put off the moment when they had nothing this man wanted, although, he could just kill them and take the capsule. She didn't really know why he hadn't.

A dozen thoughts ran through her mind as she contemplated what was about to happen, all the things she'd wished she'd said, not only to her family, but also to Reid. But it was too late now.

Reid dropped the capsule on the ground and kicked it toward the gunmen.

The man took a step forward, then staggered to his knees as a large rock hit him square in the back of the head.

Shayla was stunned at the sudden turn of events.

Reid raced forward and grabbed the rifle as the gunman lost consciousness.

Her heart skipped another beat as another man emerged from the woods, obviously the man who had thrown the rock, and she could hardly believe her eyes. It was Robert.

"Is it really you?" she asked. He didn't look anything like he usually did. He wasn't wearing a suit or a white coat. He had on jeans and a t-shirt, and dressed the way he was she could see the similarity between him and Reid, although Robert was thinner and his hair was lighter, his skin more pale.

"It's me. Are you guys all right?" He looked from Shayla, to Reid, then to the man on the ground. "I did it. I knocked him out. I wasn't sure I could take him down with one rock," he said, amazement in his voice. "But I knew I only had one chance."

"Your timing was perfect," she said, her voice still shaking with fear. She looked from Reid to Robert as the two men exchanged a long look filled with complicated emotions.

"Thanks for coming," Robert said. "I was hoping you would."

Reid moved the gun to his left hand and took a step forward.

Shayla thought the two brothers were going to hug it out. But instead, Reid drew back his arm and slugged Robert in the face. Robert stumbled backward, putting his hand to his nose as blood spurted down his face.

"What was that for?" Robert yelled.

"For almost getting us killed," Reid snapped back. "What the hell were you thinking contacting Shayla, getting her involved in all this?"

"She was the only one I could trust. I thought she would give you the message and that would be the end of it. I didn't know she was going to come with you." He sent Shayla an apologetic look, then said, "Why did you come with Reid?"

"Because someone was watching me, following me, and because I wanted to help you."

"I'm sorry, Shayla. I really didn't want you to get involved beyond contacting Reid and giving him the notebook."

"You should have told me what was going on, Robert," she said.

"You looked through the capsule," he said, his lips tightening.

She nodded. "Why didn't you stop the trial?"

"I was going to stop it the next week. I had to taper the patients off of the drug first. I couldn't end it abruptly. That would have done more harm. And I had to be careful how I did it. There were people who wanted to make sure I didn't do anything to stop that trial."

His explanation made her feel marginally better. At least he had been concerned about his patients.

"I'll explain everything to you," Robert promised, wiping the blood from his nose.

"You'll explain later," Reid said. "We need to get out of here now before someone else shows up."

"I know, but I can't just give that evidence to anyone. I need your help, Reid. You must have connections from your days in the Army," Robert said. "Abbott has a lot of power, friends in high places. They already killed the first person I talked to. I have to be smart about this."

"Was that Karl Straitt?" Reid asked.

Robert nodded. "He told me what I needed to do

before I could blow the whistle on Abbott. He called me when I was in Colombia, the day of the attack. He told me that I was in danger. He gave me the name of someone who could help me get out of the country. I was talking to that man when the clinic was raided. I had no idea anything like that would happen. I thought I was the target, only me. You have to believe that." He looked at Shayla. "I was terrified for you, but the man I was with told me that you'd been rescued, that you were fine, that the medical team was at the embassy and that he couldn't guarantee my safety if I went to join you. I was so relieved when I heard you were all right."

"So you didn't know the attack was coming?" she asked. "You have to be honest with me, Robert. I have to know the truth."

"I swear I didn't, Shayla. If I had, I would have made sure you weren't there. I never imagined they'd go after the clinic or the patients. I was shocked beyond belief."

She looked into his eyes and saw nothing but the truth in his eyes. "I want to believe you didn't leave us to fend for ourselves."

"I wouldn't do that."

"Where have you been since then?" Shayla asked.

"It took me four days to get out of South America. Then I had to make my way up from Los Angeles without anyone figuring out where I was. There are a lot of people looking for me." He paused, his lips drawing into a tight angry line. "I was watching the news the other night and I saw that Karl's body had been pulled out of the bay. I couldn't believe they'd killed him. It probably happened right after he warned me. I never should have gone to him in the first place. If I hadn't, he might still be alive. I've made some bad mistakes. I'm just glad I wasn't too late today."

"Did you drive here?" Reid asked.

"No, I took a bus to Helmsley and then I hitched a ride with a trucker to the south entrance. It look me longer to get here, but I thought it would be a safer trip."

"You were smarter than I was," Reid said grimly. "We were followed. Someone tried to take us out yesterday. I had to shoot him."

Robert's expression turned grim. "I am sorry. I honestly didn't think you'd be in danger. I appreciate your help. I know you didn't have to come and you probably didn't want to."

"Well, you sent the right person to ask me," Reid returned. "Now let's get the hell out of here."

* * *

They didn't talk at all on the long hike back to Reid's truck. Shayla had a million questions running around in her head, but she was too worried about someone else popping out of the woods with a gun to get any words out of her mouth. She didn't know if Reid deliberately steered them away from where the other gunman had died, but she saw no sign of the body they'd left in the woods.

Two hours later, they were on the road. Shayla sat between the two men in the cab of the truck, feeling the tension emanating from both of them, but no one seemed willing to be the first to speak.

When they finally reached the main highway, Reid pulled out his phone. He punched in a number and said. "Kelton, I need a safe house." He listened for a moment. "Got it. Yeah, I found him, but not without some collateral damage. Two men, both looked ex-military." He paused again, then said, "We're two hours away."

"A safe house?" Shayla asked when he tossed the phone down.

"We need to figure out our next move, and this time I intend to do it in a high security building." He glanced past her to Robert. "Who's running the show at Abbott?"

"Hal Collins," Robert said.

"Lisa's new boyfriend. How nice."

"He's an evil man," Robert said. "I tried to warn Lisa about him, but she wouldn't hear me. All she could see was his money and what he could give her."

"Maybe she gets what she deserves," Shayla put in, thinking that Lisa had done enough damage on her own. Perhaps it was her turn to pay the piper. "There's something I'm curious about. When did you bury that information in the woods? And why did you put it there? Why not a safe deposit box?"

"Lisa knew where my safe deposit box was, and if I tried to open a new one, there would have been a paper trail. I needed to put the evidence somewhere safe, and I thought the mountains were the perfect place. If something happened to me, I needed someone who could find it. I was hoping Reid would remember the treasure hunts we used to go on with our grandfather. But just in case, I put the coordinates into the sketches so he could figure out the GPS."

"It was actually Shayla who figured it out," Reid said.

Robert smiled at her. "You've always been too smart for your own good."

"You can say that again," Reid muttered.

She frowned as the two men exchanged a look. "Hey, a thank you would be nice."

"Thank you," Robert said. "Seriously."

"You're welcome. I'm glad you're all right, even though I'm angry with you. I don't understand why you couldn't tell me what was going on. I might have been able to help you."

"I debated that option more than once. But I didn't think I could risk it. In fact, I tried to make sure there was distance between us. So no one would suspect you knew anything.

That made sense. In retrospect she realized that Robert had made a point of not spending much time alone with her. "I guess I should thank you for not putting me on the hit list."

"You don't owe him a thank you," Reid said, anger in his voice.

"Maybe you do," Robert said.

Reid gave his brother an incredulous look. "What would I possibly thank you for? You almost got us killed—three times."

"True, but today I did save your lives. Let's not forget that."

"You got lucky throwing that rock," Reid said.

"Luck was not involved at all. I computed the size and weight of the rock, the distance of the throw, and the trajectory. Oh, and I remembered what Grandpa always said, put your heart…"

"Into it," Reid finished. "It was a good throw," he admitted.

"Damn good, considering I couldn't throw a baseball to save my life."

"You did save our lives, Robert. I thought we were at the end," Shayla said, remembering that terrible moment when she'd thought for sure she was going to die.

"Don't think about it," Reid advised, putting his hand on her leg. "We're all safe now."

She looked into his eyes. "Are we? Or are we just getting ready for the next round?"

Reid shook his head. "There's not going to be another round, Shayla. Now that we have Robert and his evidence, we're going to take Abbott Pharmaceuticals down."

She liked that idea a lot, but she had a feeling that wasn't going to be as easy as he made it sound.

Chapter Twenty-Three

The safe house was a luxurious two-story mansion on the western edge of San Francisco in a neighborhood known as Seascape. There was only one way into the house, through a pair of iron gates. The back yard of the house extended to a steep bluff that made accessibility from the beach two hundred yards below an impossibility.

While Reid spoke to Matt Kelton and some other men, Shayla went out to the back deck and sat down on a beach chair. It was almost four o'clock in the afternoon, and the adrenaline high had turned into a heavy lethargy.

Robert sat down across from her and gave her a tentative smile. "How are you doing, Shayla?"

"I'm hanging in there. I'm trying to wrap my head around everything that's happened. I can't quite believe that Abbott Pharmaceuticals would do what they did. They're supposed to be in the business of saving lives not taking them. Is it everyone at the company? Or just Hal Collins?"

"It's not everyone but it's more than just Hal. They got greedy, Shayla. They saw a big payday coming with the drug we were working on. When results weren't what they wanted, they didn't want to see them."

"How long have you known that the drug wasn't working?"

He let out a sigh. "We've been working on variations of the drug for the past five years. Early results were good. That's what got everyone so excited. It got me excited, too. We started running clinical trials all over the world. The one I worked on in South Africa last year had mixed results, and it didn't compare with the trials run by others, so I thought it was an anomaly. I believed Colombia would be a better test based on the population and the cluster of Alzheimer cases. But six weeks in, I could see the same problems I saw in South Africa and more. The drug works some of the time, but with certain body chemistries it does more harm than good. I couldn't understand why my trial results were so different than the ones conducted by other researchers, so I started investigating. I pulled the raw data. That's when I began to see a pattern of deception."

"They were falsifying the results," she murmured.

He nodded. "Yeah. I couldn't believe it at first. That's when I talked to Karl Straitt. He told me I better have proof before I started making accusations, so that's what I did. When I first began, I really had no idea how many layers of deception I was going to have to go through. But it soon became clear that there was more going on besides the falsifying of reports. There were problems all over the place, and all of them were being covered up. Abbott wanted Branson to buy them, so they needed to look clean. And anyone who got in the way had to be taken out."

"The hit men they sent to the clinic were supposed to kill you."

"Yes, I think I was at least one of the targets."

"I'm glad you weren't there."

"I'm sorry you were. I really am. I should have sent you home from Colombia when I realized how bad things were going."

"I probably wouldn't have gone without asking you a

lot of questions."

"True. Your rotation was almost over and so was the trial. All I needed was a couple more weeks. But Abbott worried that I was going to blow it all up, tell the world what I knew, raise enough doubt to send Branson running."

She saw the strain in Robert's eyes and realized the pressure he'd been under. "You've been alone in this, but you're not anymore. We're going to help you take them down, Robert. We're going to make them pay."

"I really hope so. Abbott is going to smear me, Shayla. I doubt I'll have a medical career at the end of this."

"They may try, but once the world realizes what they've done, it will get worked out. And I'll do everything I can to help you."

He smiled. "I appreciate that. So…"

"So," she echoed.

"Did Reid fill you in on our history?"

"You mean Lisa? Yes. That was a shocker. Why didn't you ever tell me?"

"It's not something I'm proud of. I hurt my brother and my family. And while I'd like to blame it all on Lisa, I can't."

"Your brother's fiancée was off limits, Robert. I'm glad you're not trying to make an excuse, because there isn't one."

"You're right. I've regretted my actions every day since then. Reid and I weren't that close, but he was my brother, and I destroyed our relationship."

"Yet you still asked him for help. That took some nerve."

"I wasn't sure he would agree to meet me, but he was the only one who would be able to find my grandfather's cabin in the wilderness. And I knew I could trust him, if he was willing."

"I get it. And I think you knew that in the end Reid would help you, because that's the kind of man he is."

"My brother does like to be the hero," he said.

"You made him one in your graphic novel. Razor is so obviously Reid."

"You think so?"

"Yes, and I think Rocco was meant to be you, at least in the beginning."

He smiled. "You think I made myself the dog?"

She smiled back at him. "I absolutely think you did that. You wanted to be Reid's friend. Or Razor's friend. And you couldn't put yourself in the story, because you were up in your bedroom studying, so you gave Razor a dog that could be his best friend. What's interesting is that in the end, the dog is gone, and there's a second hero. I think you finally stopped watching life go by and put yourself into the action."

"Interesting theory."

"And it kind of parallels real life. You were always the brain, but you wanted to be more than that. Like Razor, you wanted to save the day, and isn't that what you're doing now? You're saving the world from the evil men at Abbott Pharmaceuticals. And you saved me and Reid, otherwise known as Razor," she added.

"I like your theory that in the end I'm the hero, but I don't think I was ever the dog, Shayla."

"Maybe it was in your subconscious. You can't tell me you haven't wanted to have a relationship with your brother, your twin brother, another fact you never mentioned to me."

"My relationship with Reid was not like the one you had with your brother."

"It was actually a lot more like it than you think. But instead of drawing what you want to have happen in your life, maybe you should ask for it."

"You think so?"

"Yes, I have it on very good authority, that the best way to get what you want is to tell someone what you want."

"That authority wouldn't be Reid, would it?"

"He's smarter than you think."

"I always knew he was smart. He was the one who had doubts." Robert paused. "You and Reid seem to have gotten close really fast."

"Well, that started when a car almost ran us down."

"What?"

"I'll tell you about that later. I'm all talked out right now."

"I need to speak to Matt anyway." He got up. "Are you and Reid going to be friends or more than friends?"

"We'll see. Your brother doesn't like to commit."

"That's because of Lisa. He gave her his heart, and she stomped on it. And when she was done, I did the same. I wish I could make it up to him."

"Start now. Be the man you want to be and the man your brother wants you to be. You've already started the process. You just have to finish."

* * *

"I guess you have to give your brother a little credit for trying to take down a powerful pharmaceutical company," Matt said as he finished going through the pile of evidence Reid had laid out before him. "I wish you'd told me where you were going. I could have provided you with some backup."

"I didn't know I was going to be dodging hit men.

Shayla and I are lucky to be alive."

"You should get your arm looked at."

"Shayla has already done that. I've got my own personal doctor."

Matt smiled. "Just how personal?"

"That's none of your business."

"It will be when you start working for me."

"I haven't agreed to that." Although the idea was more tempting now than it had been a few weeks ago.

"You will," Matt said confidently.

"We'll see. Right now I just want to get Robert's information to the right people and make sure that both he and Shayla are safe."

"My team is working on getting all the interested parties together without tipping off anyone at Abbott. And I've sent a team into the woods for cleanup."

"I suspect the second man is long gone by now," Reid said, wishing he'd been able to tie him up or put him out of commission, but he'd been more interested in getting Shayla and his brother to safety. And deep down he'd known that Shayla couldn't take seeing anyone else get hurt, even someone who had been about to kill her. She had an innate sense of kindness and compassion. He hated that she'd had to experience so much violence the past few weeks.

"It's not like you to leave a loose end," Matt said.

"I had other priorities."

"Yeah, I get that." Matt shoved back his chair. "I'm going to make some calls."

"Before I forget, thanks," Reid said, getting to his feet. "I really appreciate this, and I will pay for the time."

"Don't worry, I'm going to collect, but it won't be in cash."

As Reid walked out of the dining room, he ran into his

brother, and for the first time in almost eight years, it was just the two of them.

"What's happening?" Robert asked.

Reid was happy with the question. It was easier to focus on the problem at hand then delve into the past. "Matt's team is arranging for you to meet with the right people at the right agencies."

"And you trust him?"

"More than I trust you," he said dryly.

His words brought a gleam into his brother's eyes. "I guess I deserved that. But I did not deserve a fist in my face."

Reid studied his brother's swollen nose and the purple bruise under his eye and felt not even a bit of remorse. "That punch was a long time coming. Last time you ducked." He'd been so blinded with rage and betrayal after he'd found Robert and Lisa together that he hadn't even been able to throw a good punch.

"Last time I was expecting it," Robert returned. "But in retrospect, I did you a favor. Lisa was a nightmare of a wife."

"You know I actually believe that now. But I don't want to talk about her anymore. It was a long time ago, and I am truly over it."

"Good. Can we sit down for a minute? I want to talk to you away from Shayla."

"All right." They moved into the living room. Robert sat on the couch while Reid took a chair in front of the fireplace. "Say what you want to say."

"Thank you."

"You're welcome. But that isn't what you wanted to say."

Robert stared back at him. "I wish we'd been able to repair our relationship before now, and that it hadn't come down to a life or death situation to get us back in the same place at the same time."

"It was probably always going to take that. Both of us are stubborn."

Robert tipped his head. "Point taken." He drew in a weary breath. "I've made a lot of mistakes. I always thought the one thing I had that was better than anyone else was my brain. But I didn't use my brain. I didn't see what was right in front of me. I let myself be played, and in the process a lot of people got hurt. I think there's a chance I may end up in jail."

"Judging by the evidence you have, I'd say that's unlikely," Reid said, although he wasn't completely sure since he didn't have the whole story.

"I could have had more evidence if I'd started sooner, if I'd been a little more clever at getting it. I hope what I have is enough to destroy Abbott, even if it means I have to go down, too."

Reid had to admit he was both surprised and impressed by his brother's honesty and his acceptance of his mistakes. This wasn't the Robert he remembered, the one who'd tried to rationalize sleeping with his fiancée. This man was someone he could relate to.

"What?" Robert asked, giving him a quizzical look.

"Just thinking that you finally sound like my brother again."

"I'd like to be your brother if you're interested."

"Possibly. Let's see how the next few weeks ago."

"I'll take it." Robert paused. "So what's going on with you and Shayla?"

Reid gazed back at his brother. "That's our business."

"Fair enough. Just don't hurt her. She's very special."

"You're not in love with her, are you?" Reid asked, a little disturbed by that thought.

"No, not at all. She's like my little sister. I have absolutely no romantic feelings towards her. And she does not feel that way about me either."

"Yeah, that's what she said. But she does seem to like you. She was willing to risk her life for you."

"She's been a good friend. And she likes to save people, even if they don't always deserve it. She's kind of like you, Reid. In fact, the two of you make a good pair."

Reid stood up as Matt came into the room. He was actually grateful for the interruption. He didn't really want to talk about Shayla with Robert.

"We're ready," Matt said. "I'm going to take Robert to the meeting. Are you coming, Reid?"

Before Reid could answer, Robert jumped in. "No, he's staying here. He's going to protect Shayla until this is over."

Reid met his brother's gaze and nodded. "That's exactly what I'm going to do."

"I've got security outside and inside," Matt said. "You'll both be safe here." He paused. "There's food in the kitchen. Make yourself comfortable. It will probably be tomorrow before I can get back to you."

"Do what you have to do." Reid turned toward his brother, knowing that the next few days were going to be difficult. "Good luck Robert."

"Thanks. I think I'm going to need it."

* * *

After Matt and Robert left, Reid went looking for Shayla. She'd been on the deck earlier, but there was no sign of her now. He wandered up to the second floor of the beautiful home, thinking that this might be the nicest safe house he'd ever been in. Apparently, Matt's business was very lucrative.

At the top of the stairs, two double doors opened onto a luxurious master bedroom suite. He heard water running in the shower and realized he'd found Shayla. He was about to leave and give her some privacy when he heard what sounded like someone sobbing. Frowning, he inched closer to the door, torn between wanting to respect her desire to be alone and the fact that she was obviously upset and hurting.

He knew why. It was the come down after the rush. She'd been stoic and strong the last few days, but now she was falling, and he was going to catch her.

He knocked and then opened the door. "Shayla?"

She was standing naked in a steamy shower, her arms wrapped around her waist as she struggled with the sobs that continued to pour from her mouth. Her eyes widened in shock when she saw him, and he knew she wanted to hide her tears. But that's the last thing he wanted her to do.

"Go away," she said, the last word ending on a hiccup. "Please."

"It was the pleading blue eyes filled with pain that did him in." He kicked off his shoes and stripped off his clothes, then stepped into the shower and put his arms around her.

"You're crazy," she protested. "Your bandage is going to get wet."

"So you'll change it. Don't fight me, Shayla. I want to hold you."

"I—I don't want to fight you," she said, slipping her arms around his waist.

The warm water beat down on his shoulders as she put her head on his chest. He held on to her as tightly as he could, letting her cry her heart out. It was time to let it all go.

As the hot water began to turn lukewarm, Shayla's

sobs began to subside. She drew in a shaky breath, then another, and lifted her head, gazing into his eyes with a soulful smile that took his breath away.

She was so damned beautiful. How was he ever going to say goodbye to her?

"Sorry about that," she said. "Once I started crying, I couldn't stop."

"Do you feel better?"

She nodded. "Yes. Thanks for holding me. I don't know what you must think of me."

"You want to know what I think?"

"Do I?" she countered.

He smiled. "Always so mouthy, but I like your mouth, and I like the rest of you, too. Seriously, Shayla."

"Seriously? I thought you didn't like to be serious."

"I think you're the most intelligent, generous, courageous woman I've ever met. Wait, did I leave out beautiful?"

"I think you did," she said, her eyes welling with tears again.

"Hey, hey, no more crying."

"I can't help it. I love you, Reid. I know I shouldn't say that, because it will probably scare the crap out of you. But I want you to know how I feel."

His heart turned over in his chest, and he had a little trouble finding his next breath. He'd thought love wasn't for him. That he was over that messy, complicated emotion, but it turned out he wasn't done with love at all.

"You don't have to say anything," Shayla said. "You didn't make me any promises. I know you're going to go back to your life, and I'm going to go back to mine. And it's good. I don't regret what happened between us. My only regret is that we didn't have a little more time together."

"Who says we don't have more time?" he challenged.

"Well, I guess we have tonight, since it's probably a good idea for us both to stay here."

"And we have tomorrow," he said. "Next week, next month, next year."

Her eyes widened. "Really?"

"Yes, really, because I love you, too."

She shook her head. "Are you sure you're not just caught up in the moment?"

He laughed. "Only one way to find out."

"What's that?"

"We'll go on a date."

"A date?" she echoed, a smile blossoming across her face. "That sounds kind of nice."

"Oh, it will be better than nice." He cupped her face with his hands, then lowered his head and kissed her mouth. "I can promise you that."

"Well, I know you never make a promise you can't keep, so I'm going to hold you to that."

"There's something else I need to say."

"Okay," she said a little warily.

"I don't know what I'm going to do with my life. Maybe I'll work with Matt. Maybe I'll set up a wilderness camp in the mountains, I don't know, but what I do know is that I want to be with you. I don't know how much I have to offer, but—"

"But nothing," she interrupted. "I want to be with you, too."

"When you're not being a brilliant doctor."

"When I'm not being that," she said, meeting his gaze.

"Because you are going back into the hospital. You are going to do amazing things in your life, and I am going to cheer you on."

"Right back at you," she said, pulling his head back to

hers. "Why don't you start making good on that promise now?"

"Anything you want, Doc. I'm all yours."

Epilogue

Two weeks later

Shayla finished up her first shift back in the E.R. at seven o'clock a.m. It had been a long Saturday night of injuries and illness, but she handled each and every patient with calm competency, and she was damned proud of herself. After getting off work, she walked out to her car, surprised and happy to see a man waiting for her in the parking lot, a man with deep, penetrating green eyes and a sexy smile.

Reid greeted her with a bouquet of flowers and a kiss.

"What's this for?" she asked.

"You said no one ever gave you flowers."

"They're beautiful. What's the occasion?"

"First day back at work. How was it?"

"It was good," she said. "I didn't freeze once."

"I never thought you would."

"You've always had more confidence in me than I've had in myself."

He gave her a tender smile. "It goes both ways."

"It was nice of you to meet me, although we could

have done this at your place or mine."

"There's more to my surprise." He waved her toward his truck. "You can leave your car here. We'll get it later."

"Where are we going?"

"I'm taking you to breakfast."

"That sounds good. I'm starving."

"I figured you would be."

She got into the truck, sniffing the beautiful scent of flowers. "I love lavender."

"I know," he said as he started the engine. "Every time I smell it, I think of you. By the way, it does nothing to calm me. Gets me all worked up instead."

She smiled. "I like you all worked up. But if we're really going to have breakfast, we better table the hot talk until later."

"Good point."

"Where are we going to eat?"

"You'll see."

She could tell she was not going to get any more information out of him. "I've been so busy the last few days I haven't had a chance to ask you how things are going with Robert. Is the case still on track?"

Since Robert had met with the federal authorities, Hal Collins and two other executives at Abbott had been arrested and were currently in jail awaiting trial. There was also a thorough investigation being conducted by several agencies including the FBI and the FDA. Robert had been in seclusion while the authorities worked with him on their case, so Shayla hadn't seen him since the day they'd gotten back from the mountains.

"As far as I know, it's all going forward," he said. "Lisa called me last night."

"No way," she said, looking at him in surprise.

"She asked me if I'd consider helping her by telling

the authorities she couldn't possibly have known what her husband was up to."

"That sounds desperate. What did you say?"

"That she was a smart girl, and I had no doubt she knew exactly what kind of man she was involved with. She hung up on me."

"She had some nerve to call you."

"It actually made me laugh," he said. "To think I wasted any time at all trying to get over her."

"Well, I'm glad that you are over her. Because now you're with me."

He smiled. "Me, too."

"What about Robert? When did you last speak to him?"

"Yesterday. He's all right. He's doing what he needs to do."

She was happy to hear the pleased note in Reid's voice. The brothers had talked a few times in the past few weeks, and their truce seemed to be holding. "You're actually a little proud of him, aren't you?"

He tipped his head. "Let's just say I've seen him in a different light."

"I'm so glad."

"And because of that light, I've agreed to a family dinner when everything is over, which probably won't be for a few more weeks. So I still have time to get ready for that."

"That's great," she said. "Family is important."

"I hope you'll feel the same when you come with me to dinner."

She looked at him in surprise. "You want me to come, too?"

"Yes, of course."

"But it's *your* family."

"And someday, maybe it will be yours, too." He slammed on the brakes and pulled over to the side of the road. "I wasn't going to do this now, but I can't wait."

She stared at him with breathless anticipation. "Can't wait to do what?"

"Propose to you. I want to marry you, Shayla. I know it's fast. And a man should not propose to the woman he loves in a beat up pickup truck. I don't even have a ring. Thank God I got the flowers."

He was rambling in a way she'd never seen before. Reid was usually so self-assured, so in control, but not now.

"Here's the thing," he continued. "I know I don't have it all together. But I'm getting there. I have a job with Matt, and he pays really well, so I can provide for you."

"I can provide for myself."

"Okay, then we can take the extra money and get a real place to live."

"Reid, slow down."

"I can't. I want you to be my wife, Shayla. And to quote someone very smart and very close to me, if you say no, I'm just going to ask you again. And I'm going to keep asking you until I get the answer I want."

Her heart swelled with love at the deep and intense look in his eyes and the way he recanted her words. "Apparently, you do listen to me once in a while."

"Always. I know your career is important to you, and I won't get in the way of that. I won't put demands on you. We'll be engaged for a year or two or however long you want. But I want you to know that when you're ready, I'm waiting."

"I can't believe you're proposing. After what happened before with Lisa, I didn't know if you'd ever have the desire to walk down the aisle again."

"With you, I have absolutely no fear," he said. "I trust you completely, Shayla."

"I trust you, too."

"So you don't need to answer me now. I'm rushing you. You can think about it."

She saw the sudden nervousness in his eyes. "I don't need to think about it, Reid. I love you. I want to be your wife. I want to have your kids. You want kids, right?"

"With you, I want it all."

"Good, because I want it all, too, maybe not right away, but down the road." She licked her lips. "We should skip breakfast and celebrate our engagement."

He groaned. "I'd really like to do that, but we can't."

"Why not?" she asked as he started driving again. "You know this is kind of a crazy proposal, Reid. You didn't even kiss me. And now you're driving like a maniac."

"I know. I've messed it all up," he said, flinging her a smile. "Sorry. I'll make it up to you." He pulled the truck up in front of a diner with a sign that read Mabel's Pancake House.

Her heart melted. "Oh, my God, you remembered."

"The blueberry pancakes from Mabel's, the place where your family celebrates important milestones. I remembered. And today you get extra blueberries and whipped cream because you're back at work. You've conquered your fears. You've climbed the metaphorical mountain."

"And the actual one," she reminded him.

"That, too. So, can we postpone our celebration until after the pancakes?"

"Yes, absolutely." She got out of the truck and met him at the front. He put his arm around her shoulders as they walked together into the restaurant. And then she got another surprise when she stepped inside.

Everywhere she looked, she saw Callaways, her brothers, sisters, parents, even her grandparents. Eleanor gave her a little wave, a smile in her bright blue eyes.

"What is all this?" Shayla asked in amazement.

"I thought they might all want to celebrate your first day back on the job," Reid said.

"You did this? You called them."

"Yeah, because they love you, and they worry about you, and they needed to know you're all right. You couldn't convince them with words, so I thought we should show them."

She'd been trying to reassure her family that all was well after they'd found out about Robert and everything that had happened in Colombia, but she knew that they hadn't been entirely convinced she was okay.

"You've found a good man," her grandmother said, getting up to give Shayla a hug. "You hang on to him, all right?"

"I will. Thanks for coming, Grandma. I'm so glad you're here."

"I wouldn't have missed celebrating my brave girl."

Eleanor stepped back as Nicole and Emma came over to give her more hugs.

"How did it go last night?" Emma asked. "I actually thought about coming down to the hospital to see you, but I knew you would hate me checking up on you."

"I was fine. It went better than I could have hoped. I'm going to be okay."

Nicole gave her a smile. "We know you are. You're very strong, Shayla. You may be the baby of the family, but you might be the toughest of us all."

"I don't know about that. But thanks. Colton," she said, turning to her twin brother. "I know you weren't worried about me."

"Not a bit. But I've always liked Mabel's pancakes, so I figured I better come."

As Colton moved away, her other family members came forward one at a time. With every hug and kiss and complimentary word, Shayla's joy and happiness grew. She'd never felt so blessed, and it was all because of Reid. She'd always felt like the kid who didn't fit into the family, but she realized now that that wasn't true at all. She was as much a part of the Callaway clan as they were a part of her.

She looked over at the man, who was now sitting on a counter barstool next to her dad, and knew that the best decision she'd ever made was to go and find him.

She walked over to Reid and gave him a kiss. She thought about sharing the news of her engagement with her family but decided she'd keep it to herself for a little while longer.

Instead, she turned to the crowd, and said, "I think I'm the luckiest person in the world to have all of you in my life. Thanks for coming. And thanks to Reid for bringing you all together." She gave him a loving look, then turned back to her family. "Now, let's have pancakes."

The End

Dear Reader,

I hope you had a good time with Shayla and Reid's story. I loved their dynamics together. Two people who want to save the world but end up saving each other! I loved that they were both twins, too. Who knows—maybe one day they'll have twins! If you enjoyed the book, I hope you'll consider leaving a review and share your thoughts with other potential readers!

The next book in the Callaway series is book #7, WHEN SHADOWS FALL, and it will be released on September 18th. This story will feature Colton and will also unravel the grandparents' mystery for those of you who are interested in where that thread is going. I think you'll like all the twists and turns to come.

Burke's story will be told in SOMEWHERE ONLY WE KNOW, coming in January 2015.

If you'd like to stay up to date on my book releases and giveaways, visit my website www.barbarafreethy.com!

You can also follow me on Facebook
(www.facebook.com/barbarafreethybooks) and join me on
Twitter (www.twitter.com/barbarafreethy).

All the best,

Barbara

Book List

The Callaway Family Series
#1 On A Night Like This
#2 So This Is Love
#3 Falling For A Stranger
#4 Between Now And Forever
#5 All A Heart Needs
#6 That Summer Night

Nobody But You (A Callaway Wedding Novella)

The Wish Series
#1 A Secret Wish
#2 Just A Wish Away
#3 When Wishes Collide

Standalone Novels
Almost Home
All She Ever Wanted
Ask Mariah
Daniel's Gift
Don't Say A Word
Golden Lies
Just The Way You Are
Love Will Find A Way
One True Love
Ryan's Return
Some Kind of Wonderful
Summer Secrets
The Sweetest Thing

The Sanders Brothers Series
#1 Silent Run
#2 Silent Fall

The Deception Series
#1 Taken
#2 Played

About The Author

Barbara Freethy is a #1 New York Times Bestselling Author of 39 novels ranging from contemporary romance to romantic suspense and women's fiction. Traditionally published for many years, Barbara turned to Indie publishing in 2011 and has since sold over 4.4 million ebooks! Seventeen of her titles have appeared on the New York Times and USA Today Bestseller Lists.

Known for her emotional and compelling stories of love, family, mystery and romance, Barbara enjoys writing about ordinary people caught up in extraordinary adventures. She is currently writing a connected family series, The Callaways. The first six books in the series are currently available.

Barbara also recently released the WISH SERIES, a series of books connected by the theme of wishes including: A SECRET WISH (#1), JUST A WISH AWAY (#2) and WHEN WISHES COLLIDE (#3).

Other popular standalone titles include: DON'T SAY A WORD, SILENT RUN and RYAN'S RETURN.

Barbara's books have won numerous awards - she is a six-time finalist for the RITA for best contemporary romance from Romance Writers of America and a two-time winner for DANIEL'S GIFT and THE WAY BACK HOME.

Barbara has lived all over the state of California and currently resides in Northern California where she draws much of her inspiration from the beautiful bay area.

For a complete listing of books, as well as excerpts and contests, and to connect with Barbara:

Visit Barbara's Website: www.barbarafreethy.com
Join Barbara on Facebook: facebook.com/barbarafreethybooks
Follow Barbara on Twitter: twitter.com/barbarafreethy

Made in the USA
Lexington, KY
19 June 2014